Clarion Review: 4

Unyielding Destiny is a fascinating novel in which a mobster's story intersects with that of a district attorney's, resulting in questions about the nature of honor.

In Spiros Gratsias's novel *Unyielding Destiny*, a criminal and a lawyer try to lead their lives with honor.

In the 1960s, Frank is a mobster, a Korean War veteran, and a prisoner at Alcatraz. He plans on being the first person to escape the island. During a vaccination program at the prison, he meets Scott; Scott's father, Roy, died saving Frank during the war. Frank feels remorse over the fact that a good man lost his life saving him; he forms a connection with Scott.

Decades later, Frank, having escaped prison, is a hitman for the mob. When he learns that Scott is now an assistant district attorney who's probing organized crime, he worries that their paths will cross again—with potentially unpleasant results.

Though its pictures of mob life are familiar, the drama between Frank and Scott takes this thriller in new directions, including into a compelling and extended thematic focus on the nature of personal convictions. Frank, though his deeds are unsavory, abides by a certain code; he values principles, bravery, and honor. As such, even though he is a killer by trade, he expresses admiration for people like Roy and Scott; he regards them as natural leaders who fight hard to protect what it is that they believe in.

At his opposite, Scott begins the story as a boy who loves baseball and who mourns his father's death; these values mean that he's compelled to seek justice in his adulthood. And a menagerie of secondary characters are used to flesh out the men's worlds, including a wealthy smooth-talker, smart-mouthed fellow prisoners, hard-boiled prison guards, Scott's mother, and a former school friend with whom Scott reunites as an adult. Among this cast: each exchange is effectual and subtly expository.

The story is told from both men's perspectives; it moves at a steady pace, revealing information that would otherwise be hidden through each of them. Deviations to cover historical milestones, including the Kennedy assassination and the Moon landing, extend the novel's pages, which are otherwise devoted to generating suspense and tension around Scott and Frank's potential reunion. Meanwhile, Frank comes to understand that wars don't just occur on battlefields—they also occur in people's hearts and souls. This growing sensibility culminates in the novel's dramatic final act.

Unyielding Destiny is a fascinating novel in which a mobster's story intersects with that of a district attorney's, leading to questions about what it means to be a person of honor. –Katerie Prior *Clarion Reviews*

Unyielding Destiny is as much a book about Mafia hitman Frank Morris as it is a commentary on the inescapability of destiny. Gratsias opens by taking readers into the heart of New York City's tenements, introducing a young and untainted Frank. That innocence hardly lasts. In the blink of an eye, Frank's parents are dead, and he's being inducted into the Mafia's most powerful family. Cut to 30 years later: Frank is serving a 12-year sentence at Alcatraz. Destiny soon intervenes, paving the way for his escape and eventual return to a life of crime, kicking off a journey of revenge, power, and blood.

This fast-paced, grittily realistic novel hurtles forward in a series of action-packed scenes. Gratsias proves adept at capturing the tone and tenor of the criminal underworld, and some of his dialogue transports readers to society's underbelly, a place where jokes and threats go hand in hand. The plotting, though, can feel choppy, swinging from one time and place to another without clear direction, often interrupting the narrative flow. Gratsias relies heavily on newspaper reports and radio announcements to carry the story forward, with instances where a news report stretches almost four pages, diminishing the excitement of the events depicted.

Gratsias's feel for how these criminals talk and think: "Francesco, always remember that a man is defined by his honor," the don advises, not long after Frank's escape. That, combined with the cast's tendency to quote and discuss the likes of Dickens and Marcus Aurelias ("This guy Dickens would never have said that if he had gotten a good taste of Alcatraz") give *Unyielding Destiny* a distinctly philosophical bent. Throughout, Gratsias brings us back to his ultimate purpose in writing the book: to underscore the inevitability of destiny, and the need to accept it. Readers of mob stories and light philosophy will enjoy the story of Frank's rise, which is as fast-paced as it is philosophical.

Takeaway: A swift, thoughtful thriller for readers of mob stories and light philosophy.

Great for fans of: Leonardo Sciascia, Tod Goldberg's *Gangsterland.*
   –*BookLife* Review

This is one of the best books I have read over the last few years. I really warmed to Frank, although a part of the mafia, he seems different to your typical gangster. Anyway once the story picked up, I found myself checking how much was left as I did not want it to end. Something which I don't ever remember doing before. I would definitely recommend this book to anyone.

–Heather Temple, *NetGalley* Review

UNYIELDING DESTINY

UNYIELDING DESTINY

A NOVEL

SPIROS GRATSIAS

Hildebrand Books

NASHVILLE, TENNESSEE

Unyielding Destiny / Spiros Gratsias —2nd edition

Hildebrand Books an imprint of W. Brand Publishing

j.brand@wbrandpub.com

www.wbrandpub.com

Cover design by designchik.net

Available in Hardcover, Paperback, Kindle, and eBook

Hardcover ISBN: 978-1-950385-99-7

Paperback ISBN: 978-1-956906-02-8

eBook ISBN: 978-1-956906-01-1

Library of Congress Control Number: 2021922143

CONTENTS

Dedicated to the nymph

that made my dreams become reality.

Did a voice whisper in his ear that he had just passed the solemn hour of his destiny that there no longer remained a middle course for him; that if he were not henceforth the best of men, he would be the worst; that it behooved him now, so to speak, to mount higher than the Bishop, or fall lower than the convict; that if he wished to become good be must become an angel; that if he wished to remain evil, he must become a monster?

—*Les Miserables*, Victor Hugo

CHAPTER 1

1930, NEW YORK CITY, LOWER EAST SIDE

Frank Morris's memories began in a darkly lit, second-floor tenement, two-room apartment on 97 Orchard Street, in the Lower East Side of New York City. He was awakened by the diminutive light that filtered into the apartment from a single window overlooking the street below.

Frank's tenement was a cheaply built, dark brown brick building that stretched six floors in the direction of the sky. The façade was covered by the fire escape's clunky crisscrossing metal construction that began on the sidewalk and scaled all the way up to the roof. The combination of small and large metal beams and windows created a maze, as well as a choreography of moving shadows and reflections that entered the tenement, challenging its deep darkness.

The tenement smells filled the apartment, reaching him under his heavy woolen blanket. He would never forget that smell—the stench from the toilet in the hallway combined with the cooking odor of cabbage and onions. This year's freezing October weather forced the women to wash and wring their clothes indoors resulting in a constant presence of steam and soap filling the corridor and rooms.

The kitchen stove fire began to warm the two small rooms and Frank slipped out of bed, running and taking his usual morning position on the windowsill. Frank watched his mother prepare breakfast over the cast-iron stove, and the sounds of the awakening seventy souls living in the tenement's twelve apartments reached his ears as they echoed and collided through the shadowy building's corridor and staircase.

He looked below at the street; they were lucky to live in the front of the tenement, as most of the backside apartments did not have a window, and even if they did, it would look out at the dark brown brick wall of the next building over.

At least three times a day, his mother opened the door and walked into the dark corridor holding an empty water bucket, then headed down to the backyard to fill it. She returned balancing her body to keep straight, pulled by the weight of the full freezing water bucket. Carefully, she put it on the side of the stove and looked at him with a smile that lit up her face.

She walked over to him tenderly grabbing both sides of his face and giving him a heartfelt kiss on the forehead, whispering in Sicilian, *"L' amuri è come a tussi . . . nun si po ammucciari mio figlio"*—"Love is like a cough . . . impossible to hide." Then, she took him back to his bedroom and began to dress him with affection.

At four years old, Frank was a skinny child, having been sick since September with this fall's seasonal flu. He would cough almost every time he spoke and laughed, and the Sicilian quote fit him like a glove. Most of the other kids in the tenement and neighborhood were also sick, the sound of their coughing continuously present in the buildings and alleys where they played.

Frank's mother's name was Auclenzia. It was Sicilian and meant "one who dares and is fearless." Every time he looked into her dark olive eyes he saw and felt her strength. They both turned their heads toward the door, hearing and recognizing the heavy steps of his father coming up the dim wooden staircase, returning from one more night shift at the docks.

The door opened and his father, Arthur Morris, walked in and said with a low baritone voice and heavy Irish accent, "The king has returned with riches, my lady and prince!" He would bow to her and she would always rush into his giant embrace, kissing him with passion.

"Benvenuto nel tuo castello, amore mio!"—"Welcome to your castle, my love!" She would whisper in his ear and he would kiss her again, turning and picking up Frank with his giant arm around his waist. Holding them tightly, he would turn them in circles and they all laughed, Frank yelling joyfully, "Faster, faster!"

His father's deep blue eyes, square face, and strong jaw reflected his strength and resilience. Auclenzia helped him take off his heavy jacket and unbuttoned his cotton shirt, then she carefully removed and folded the newspaper pages that they had placed between his undershirt and his shirt before his shift.

The newspaper acted as a shield against the frozen wind that would whip him as he climbed up to the operator's cage of the massive dock crane. He called it his armor and would joke to Frank when he dressed. "Putting on my knight's armor, lad; all that I am missing is a giant black warhorse and a heavy lance! Beware black knight, for tonight you will meet your match!"

Frank smiled and yelled back, "Beware Black Knight!"

His mother would serve breakfast and they would all sit around the small wooden kitchen table. Frank loved the smell and taste of the hot bread covered with butter and the apricot marmalade that his mother had made.

"You won't believe what happened, Arturo," she said to her husband. His father always smiled hearing his name in Italian. "Signore Gerhard from the fourth floor has disappeared. His poor wife has looked all over since Monday, but he never came back from work and nobody has seen him. Poor woman with four kids. Mio Dio, how will they survive?" she asked with empathy.

His father nodded his head and replied with a hard tone, "Hard times make or break a man! Gerhard has shown weakness many times before. Remember last winter, we had the problems with the previous landlord. No matter, I will ask the lads at work if they have seen him anyplace."

She touched his giant hand tenderly and replied, "Thank you, *amore mio!*"

All the tenants knew each other well, and although they were of different nationalities—Italians, Germans, Irish—the moment they passed the gates of Ellis Island they found themselves in a strange and terrifying land with few friends and relatives, and this shared day-to-day existence under the same roof united them in a new brotherhood of painful toil. They all had the same dream but not the same destiny. Some survived, others perished; but they all had once existed in someone's memories.

When they finished eating, his mother put a dark shade over the window, and his father prepared for bed. The night shift had reversed their routine, turning day into night.

She readied Frank for their daily grocery visit, giving his father the opportunity for silence and sleep. Of course, silence in the tenement could never be found; it was alive twenty-four hours a day, and never slept. Those working in factories would enter and exit the building at least three times a day, and the children's and women's movements would be continuous at least from the early hours till nightfall.

She took his hand and they made their way down to the front door, where the street sounds invaded, rushing upward and filling the building with peddlers' shouts, police whistles, children's wails, and heavy hooves slamming on cobblestone.

Frank loved the excitement of the busy street and would run next to his mother, tightly grasping her hand as they crisscrossed between wedged pushcarts on the curb, passing numerous men and women selling everything from shoelaces to sour pickles. German, Yiddish, Italian, and heavily-accented English rang out in all directions, becoming an unrecognizable racket.

Delicious odors of steaming sweet potatoes and roasting chestnuts mingled with the smell of garbage and horse manure. One instance caused your mouth to water, and the next presented the urge to throw up. Auclenzia would slow down when crossing through the pleasant-smelling areas, and almost run when the smell of garbage became overbearing. She would buy only what they planned to eat on that day, like a quarter pound of parmesan cheese, half a pound of mincemeat for the meatballs and pasta dinner. Friday was special: Chocolate ice cream day for Frank, his reward for being a good boy.

Frank's tenement experience, where his memories were born, lasted only seven years, and then love was ripped forever from him by destiny. His father would be dead in three years—an unfortunate accident at the docks, they said. After that day, his mother slowly withered within deep mourning, draped in black, and Frank became her only reason for living. He felt her agony every morning the apartment door did not open announcing his father's return.

His father had worked for Don Cabineri as the dock crane operator, and after the crane accident, the Don paid special attention to the Morris family.

The Don had never visited them, but he would send them clothing, food, and supplies for the house.

By the time Frank was eight, his mother had passed as well, from a fierce fever and weak heart. "Poor boy, he's unlucky, marked by bad fortune," the remaining tenement souls whispered as he returned from the funeral with Mrs. Tenoreli from the third floor. She had volunteered to care of him until the social workers came to take him to an orphan house.

Mrs. Tenoreli took him to her apartment and silently gave him a glass of milk. Walking to and from the funeral she had held him by the hand but not spoken a word. Frank learned on that day that silence can be your best friend, because words are often painful whips of reality.

They sat and waited for what seemed like hours, but was actually just a few minutes, until he heard footsteps on the stairs, which finally stopped behind Mrs. Tenoreli's front door. He remembered the whispered knock, and the kind woman opening the door, slowly revealing a tall, meticulously dressed man. He entered holding his fedora hat, and Mrs. Tenoreli pointed for him to sit.

"Don Cabineri, it is an honor to have you in our house. Please forgive that my husband is not here to welcome you, but he is at work."

"Thank you, Signora, but of course you do not need to apologize. It is my honor to meet you and I would like to thank you very much for your help today." He bowed his head to her and turned unhurriedly to look at Frank.

"Please, Don Cabineri, have a seat. Would you like a glass of vino?" Signora Tenoreli pointed to one of the empty chairs around the small kitchen table. She did not wait for the Don's reply and moved quickly to grab a wine bottle and an empty glass. She put the glass in front of him and carefully poured the red wine.

"Thank you, Signora, you are very kind," he said. "Wine was given to us by the gods, it gives us strength for hard moments just like today." She nodded with agreement.

He picked up the glass, saluted her, and bowed with respect. "To you and your family's health and well-being, Signora."

She also bowed her head, placing her hand on her heart. "*Grazie mille*, Don Cabineri, you honor us!"

Frank studied every small detail and movement, and that whole day would be etched in his mind forever. He sat motionless watching them and wishing he could feel his mother's warmth next to him.

"Francesco," said the Don, giving his name an Italian scent. "Francesco my boy, I am Signore Joseph Cabineri and I knew both your father and mother very well. Your father worked for me at the docks, and you must always be very proud of who he was. He was a very honorable man, and your mother was one of the best women that Sicily has ever given birth to."

Cabineri ran his fingers through his heavy black moustache, cleared his throat, and continued.

"I am from Sicily, and very proud of your mother and who she was. Francesco, I know and understand how hard it is to lose your parents at your age. I feel your pain and I want you to know that your pain is my pain, my son! *Il tuo dolore è il mio dolore, figlio mio!*"

Frank listened and looked into the man's large dark-brown eyes. He saw and felt his generous disposition, but also his strength.

"Francesco, I have come to take you with me. You will come to my house and live under my roof. I cannot replace your father and mother, but I can honor their memory by having you enter and be part of my family," said the Don. "I am the father of my family and starting today you will be like a son to me."

Frank understood the words but could not understand why this strange man would take him into his home. He was confused, and his expression and questioning eyes spoke back to the Don in silence.

"Francesco, I know that you cannot understand why all of these things are happening or who I am," explained the Don. "But I am your family now, and in time you will understand and accept the hand of destiny."

Don Cabineri then stood over him, an air of command in his body movements. He was controlled, calculated. He looked straight into Frank's eyes and put his hands on the boy's shoulders. Frank felt that the Don's words and sentiment were both spontaneous and true.

"A very long time ago, a wise man said, *nothing happens to anybody which he is not fitted to bear,*" Cabineri continued. "This man's name was Marcus Aurelius, and I know that when you grow up, he will counsel you just like he counsels me. You, Francesco, can and will bear this destiny and survive these hard times. I can see in your eyes that you have the strength of your parents and I will make sure you grow up and honor their memory. But, more importantly, that you become a man of honor!"

He turned and nodded to Signora Tenoreli, who quickly opened the door for them. The Don took Frank by the hand and for the last time they descended the tenement stairs.

Below on the street, a black Cadillac sedan was waiting, and the driver jumped out the minute they exited the front door. Frank noticed that the stream of people passing by avoided coming close, passing to the opposite sidewalk before they reached the car. Meanwhile, the sidewalk in front of his tenement was empty.

The driver opened the back door of the sedan and the Don pointed to Frank to enter first, then followed right behind. The driver closed the heavy car door carefully, then quickly took his place in the driver's seat.

"Dino, this is Francesco. He is the new member of our family," the Don introduced him.

"*Benvenuto in famiglia,* Signor Frank," responded the driver respectfully.

"Take us straight home. I want Francesco to meet the rest of the family," said Don Cabineri. "Oh, yes, stop off at Andy's. Mama Cabineri wants me to pick up some tomatoes and oranges."

The Don looked at Frank and, leaning toward him, whispered in his ear, "If I don't do what Mrs. Cabineri asks, *Mio Dio!* My God! I will be in trouble." He smiled, but Frank's face remained expressionless. The Don patted him on the leg and looked straight ahead.

Dino started the engine, looked at the Don through the mirror, and responded while putting the car in motion: "*Si* Don, right away!"

Frank turned his head as they drove away and looked out the back window at his apartment window and the darkness beyond. *The lights were off,* he thought, *nobody was home.* He knew nothing would ever be the same for him. But even then, he knew that this was meant to be. It was the first time he recognized the hand of destiny, and at eight years old he left his childhood in that tenement apartment on 97 Orchard.

CHAPTER 2

1962, SAN FRANCISCO, PRESIDIO

The atmospheric compression high above the Gulf of Alaska pulsated downward, impregnating the low-pressure system with the seed of another winter storm. The storm center swiftly released its frozen, gusty winds and rain tentacles down the Pacific Coast. Finally, the storm reached the San Francisco Bay region just after midnight.

Scott Easten could hear, smell, and taste the heavy rain washing everything under its domain. The slow-moving lights of passing cars reflected off the raindrops that collided with each other, transmitting cycles of illuminations through his window. His eyes followed jumping shadows, passing and touching at some point everything inside his bedroom. The shadow's speed was regulated by the storm's intensity; more rain, more reflections.

He looked across his bedroom into his father's eyes. They had always looked back at him, every night and morning since he could remember. They seemed happier today. He probably enjoyed listening to the storm. His mother's stories and this family portrait on the wall was all he had of the first years of life, while his dad was alive.

The family portrait was taken one day before his father shipped out for Korea. His father had taken them to the Embarcadero for a long stroll and ice cream. Apparently, as they passed James Pictures and Portraits, Roy Easten insisted laughingly that a family portrait would be a great talking piece for the grandkids. Looking at his two-year-old excited expression, Scott knew that they must have had a hard time keeping him still and looking at the camera.

"Look over there, Scott, it's going to go bang!" he heard them both say while smiling at the photographer. His mother's eyes smiled but he could see them both counting the hours with sadness and fear until the next morning's good-bye. She was strong, but the eyes of the strong never lie. Scott imagined that just seconds before his father turned toward the camera, he was looking at them, etching their faces and smiles deep within the safety of his mind and soul. His eyes reflected the power they gave him, the strength to be strong, fight, and live.

"Sweetheart," his father said as he turned to her after the blinding camera flash. "Give it to Captain Johnston, he will send it with the first correspondence flight." He smiled and leaned to kiss her, neglecting the cameraman and waiting customers. They saw the uniform and respectfully understood this sacred moment. He lifted the baby high into the air and then pulled him into his hug, kissing the top of his head, transferring the love deep within his existence. Scott had reanimated that moment a thousand times.

Turning toward the alarm clock next to him, he saw it was only 12:15 a.m., and he still had six hours until the great adventure would begin. He turned his gaze once again to the family portrait, focusing through the room's diffused light and shadows targeting the framed certificate nailed right next to the portrait. He had read the words even before he learned how to read, and like a prayer, he read them once again without uttering a sound.

THE UNITED STATES OF AMERICA

TO ALL WHO SHALL SEE THESE
PRESENT GREETINGS:

THIS IS TO CERTIFY THAT
THE PRESIDENT
OF THE UNITED STATES OF AMERICA
AUTHORIZED BY CONGRESS
HAS AWARDED IN THE NAME
OF THE CONGRESS

THE MEDAL OF HONOR
TO
LIEUTENANT ROY F. EASTEN
UNITED STATES ARMY
FOR

CONSPICUOUS GALLANTRY AND
INTREPIDITY IN ACTION
AT THE RISK OF HIS OWN LIFE
ABOVE AND BEYOND THE CALL OF DUTY
ON 2 JUNE 1951

GIVEN UNDER MY HAND
IN THE CITY OF WASHINGTON
THIS TWENTY-SECOND DAY OF JUNE 1952

The intensifying power of the wind slammed lassoing fingers wildly on the windowpanes, giving the words more profound meaning. Being older, he understood their true importance, their eternity. Opening the bedside table drawer, he pulled out the yellowing letter, strangely sensing that this winter storm was more than just a natural phenomenon. Switching on a small lamp, he pulled his legs toward his body and read the words silently.

The War Department

Dear Mrs. Carolyn Easten,

We deeply regret to inform you that your husband Lieutenant Roy F. Easten United States Army Company C, 24th Infantry Regiment, 25th Infantry Division was killed in action on 2 June 1951 near Chipo-ri, Korea.

Citation: Lieutenant Roy F. Easten, a member of Company C, distinguished himself by conspicuous gallantry and intrepidity above and beyond the call of duty in action against the enemy. His platoon was attacking heavily defended hostile positions on commanding ground when the leader was wounded and evacuated. Lieutenant assumed command, rallied the men, and spearheaded the assault against the hill. Personally eliminating two hostile positions and killing six of the enemy with his rifle fire and grenades, he continued up the slope until the unit suffered heavy casualties and became pinned down. Regrouping the men, he led them forward under heavy fire, taking cover in a bomb crater with another three men. Pinned down by enemy machine nests, they received a shower of grenades one landing inside the crater. Lieutenant Easten courageously shielded his men, receiving a severe chest wound. The wounds received during his daring exploits resulted in his death, but his indomitable courage, superb leadership, and gallant self-sacrifice reflect the highest credit upon himself, the infantry, and the military service.

Every word transported Scott to his father's last few moments. He felt the burning pain of the shrapnel entering his body, his final fall, and eyes frantically searching for him and his mother in the sky.

He carefully folded the letter, placed it back in the envelope, and returned it to its place of rest. An unknown scary feeling overwhelmed him. He felt that this day would be different, and for some reason, he would never be the same again. He felt the fear of a child walking in a large crowd, holding hands with his mother, when suddenly their hands part and the child is left alone among all those strangers.

Reaching inside his t-shirt, he found and tightly closed his hand around his father's dog tag. Slowly pulling his hand out, he felt the edges of the thin corrosion-resistant metal digging into his palm, knowing its exact duplicate had remained with his father. Opening his hand, he read the inscription:

EASTEN, ROY F

US37068899

T-52　　　　A　　　　P

"Army Service Number US37068899, Tetanus Date T-52, Blood Type A, Religious Preference P," he whispered, closing his eyes, the whistling wind and rain helping him find the safety of sleep's darkness.

CHAPTER 3

1962, ALCATRAZ, CELL BLOCK B

The screams of the trapped men from the lower decks reverberated off the steel walls of the ship's smoke-filled, long, dark corridors. Streams of smoke continuously materialized through most of the air vents, wildly twirling upward, searching for freedom.

Frank Morris stared toward the top of the grand stairway at the eight-foot-high, one-thousand-pound bronze figural sculpture of a woman named "*La Normandie*," and wondered if the flames would melt her body, returning it back to its natural form.

In the stolen, bulky overalls belonging to one of the onboard workers, his 6'2" height and athletic torso seemed shorter and bulkier. He quickly found the closed, weathertight door and pushed outward, feeling heavy resistance from the outside gusts. His shoulder muscles tightened against the increasing force, and he exited slowly, gasping to fill his lungs with fresh air and the familiar smells of the New York dock.

Officer Lerving stopped in front of the darkened cell. Ten years on the job, and he was still amazed at the small size of these concrete domiciles—five feet wide, nine feet deep, seven feet high. Peering through the bars, he looked at the sleeping inmate's shadowed face. Frank Morris chose to lie opposite than most of the other inmates; head toward the steel cell bars and feet extending to the darkness.

Lerving wondered if he would sleep in the same manner if he was interned. Shaking the thought out of his mind, he stepped closer, right above the sleeping face. He looked at Frank's pupils moving vigorously, having recently read in *Reader's Digest* that when we are dreaming, rapid eye movement occurs, and that they called this the REM cycle of our sleep.

He stepped even closer, looking intently at Frank's facial expressions and the sweat beads slowly collecting on his forehead, some of them slowly rolling down toward thick eyebrows, then dripping down the right and left side of his face.

He turned and continued his midnight cell block check remembering what he read in the *Digest* article. *"While this rapid eye movement has long been associated with dreaming, the reason for the movement is still unclear."* While he loved a mystery, he was also disappointed that he would never know what Frank was dreaming of.

Standing with his head and back touching the cold exterior bulkhead wall, Frank oriented himself and realized he was right above the main deck. Taking another deep breath, he felt the clean oxygen combine with adrenaline, and a sudden dizziness instinctively made him push his body backward for support.

He closed his eyes and breathed slowly through his nostrils. His heart was pounding. His trained body immediately gained composure and he scanned the area preparing for his invisible escape.

The great ocean liner sensed that she was dying and moaned like a great whale when the final harpoon tears through its shimmery skin. The flames searched for openings that would satisfy their thirst for oxygen, engulfing everything in their wake.

He held his cap down, pushing his head farther inside its warmth. "*Dino will be very happy,*" he thought, "*the job had gone off perfectly.*" Like Dino repeatedly told him, "Frank, timing and execution are everything; hit them at the right time in the right way. That's the secret. It's like fucking. Timing and execution make the dames remember you forever."

Frank smiled, revealing a perfect set of white teeth that, in combination with his large, round black eyes produced a long list of dames wanting to feed his desires. Of course, being part of the Cabineri family also helped.

Exiting the darkness and smoke he turned right, running down the ship's long exterior staircase; the details of his deed played like a movie script, and he watched it carefully, checking for possible mistakes. Mistakes in this business were never forgiven; his orders had been explicit, "Must look like an accident, OK Francesco? No mistakes. This job is for the big boss, and Frank you know that Don Cabineri is doing this for Lucky Luciano. That means no fuckups!"

Timing and execution, he thought, while replaying the movie; sparks from a welding torch "*accidentally*" ignited a stack of life vests filled with flammable kapok in the storage area of the first-class lounge. The luxury liner's ongoing conversion to a troopship had not yet entailed the removal of tons of ornate woodwork, and the fire spread rapidly; the very efficient fire protection system "*unfortunately*" had been disconnected during the conversion, and its internal pumping system deactivated.

Reaching the bottom of the stairs, he jumped for the dock that suddenly disappeared into a bottomless dark pit. He fell headfirst screaming and grasping to hold on.

Frank jolted from his dream back to consciousness, drenched to the bone, shivering from the cold dampness of his cell. He tried some deep breaths to calm himself down, watching the shadows coming to life from the well-lit cell block aisle. He tuned in to the footsteps echoing through the corridor, realizing that it was midnight and the goons were making their checks. Wiping his brow, he turned the sweat-soaked pillow to its dry side and stared into his semidark cell.

Every night the same dream woke him and every night he came back to the present, continuing to live out his story, which picked up from the moment that he jumped toward the dock.

He harkened back to February 9, 1942, almost twenty years prior—7,287 days to be exact. His obsession with time had worsened since he arrived on the Rock. Every night before the "Lights out!" command, he would scribble and calculate the exact days between the two dates. This gave him a feeling of control over the endless empty hours.

The true definition of time did not exist in Alcatraz. The dictionary said time was "a nonspatial continuum that is measured in terms of events which succeed one another from past through present to future." In reality, Alcatraz simply defined and governed time as a twenty-four-hour repetition of the same events. One year or ten years were just a single, never-ending day. It was clear to the ones serving life sentences that the actual punishment was living daily the repetition of endlessness.

He took a deep breath, his mind clutching for that moment long past, freeing himself from the constraints of his cell, and smiled, knowing they could not stop this type of escape.

Reaching the bottom of the stairs, he jumped for the dock and ran toward the first group of crates, slipping quickly between their rows and disappearing. Pier 88 was his playground, and no one knew its secrets better than him. He turned and looked back at the great ship, now fully engulfed in black smoke and flames, and recalled her maiden voyage and magnificent entrance into New York harbor nearly seven years ago. It was May 29, 1935. He was ten years old and it was approximately one hundred yards from where he now stood when he first saw her. He smiled whenever his eidetic memory recalled images and information that he had been exposed to for only an instant or two.

In his dream state, the *New York Times* article flashed back, and he saw it as if reading it: Fifty thousand saw her off at Le Havre on what was hoped would be a record-breaking crossing. *Normandy* reached New York after four days, three hours and fourteen minutes, taking away the blue ribbon from the Italian liner, *REX*.

He noticed the firemen arriving at the scene, struggling in vain to fit the NYFD's hoses to the ship's nonstandard French inlets. The onboard crew was using manual means in a vain attempt to stop the blaze, but a strong northwesterly wind blowing over *Normandy*'s port quarter swept the flames forward, eventually destroying the three upper decks of the ship within an hour.

His flashback continued reading the newspaper article:

> The *SS Normandy* ocean liner was built in Saint-Nazaire, France, for the French Line Compagnie Générale Transatlantique. She entered service in 1935 as the largest and fastest passenger ship afloat; she is still the most powerful steam turboelectric-propelled passenger ship ever built. Her novel design and lavish interiors led many to consider her the greatest of ocean liners. Despite this, she was not a commercial success and relied partly on government subsidy to operate. Another of

the French liner's greatest triumphs was Normandy's slick and modern art deco interiors.

The loud orders of the fire chief turned his attention to the firefighters on shore and in the boats, pouring water on the blaze. Suddenly, the ship developed a dangerous list to port due to the weight of the water now filling the ship's seaward side. Frank had seen enough. Looking at his watch he saw it was 15:15, and Dino was waiting, so he slowly slipped behind the crates, discarded his overalls, and checked the periphery for anyone watching him as he entered Warehouse 13. He headed toward the longshoreman's union office. The yelling echoed toward the city and the twenty-minute walk granted enough time to continue memory reading.

The *Normandy* has twenty-four thousand pieces of crystal, adorning the massive Lalique torchières in the Dining Salon. The room's table silverware, chairs, and gold-plated bronze table bases, along with the custom-designed suites and cabin furniture as well as original artwork and statues that decorated the ship, were custom built for use by the French Line aboard *Normandy.*

What a fucking shame, he thought. All that cash going up in flames. But the boss had good reason, and that was good enough for him. He pushed his numbing chin down to his chest trying to grab his body's heat. February weather froze even the toughest into submission.

Frank increased his strides, moving faster toward the union office anticipating the hot woodstove's warmth and a couple shots of the best whiskey on the east coast. The boss always kept a crate of Danzante from each of the shipments that went through their care and management. Smirking to himself, he said aloud, with a heavy New York Italian-American accent, "Fuggedaboutit! Our job is to CARE and MANAGE our product and of course satisfy our customers." Dino's favorite quote.

Fucking Dino, he thought, *nobody he knew could say so much with so few words.* His lungs filled with the motley whiffs of the dock, fresh rotting fish and human waste.

With one last glance back, he saw a huge, rising, thick fire cloud; a multi-projection of dark orange flashes of light coming from the great inferno below reached and lit the continuously transforming dense body of black smoke. "Now that's what I call a blaze," he whispered between clenching teeth.

The swirling shapes of smoke reminded him of his childhood cloud-gazing fantasy game. With his best friend Marcello, he would exit his second-floor bedroom window and, lying flat on their backs on the hot black tar roof tiles, the game would begin. They watched the clouds moving across the sky, shaping themselves into swirling forms that filled their thirsty fantasy. Impressive dinosaurs battled each other while an assortment of animals fled in fear. They yelled and counted the number of images their minds and eyes materialized.

"Number 5! Look Marcello, it's a snake's head opening his mouth and, whoa, look at those fangs!" he could still hear himself yelling with excitement, and Marcello yelling back with yet another—and better forming—shape.

Tonight's clouds were not nature's doing but his. Focusing on the dematerialized remains of the once magnificent ship, suddenly the serpentine body of a giant dragon materialized, quickly rising from the burning ship.

Orange scales armored the dragon's long, slender limbs. It had three weathered fingers on each foot that ended in sharp, glowing claws. The dragon's mouth was composed of a pronounced jaw, and irregularly shaped teeth made up most of its face. Its small round nostrils exhaled hot fumes rising and sometimes hiding snakelike, slanted, red-lit eyes. Its legs seemed to rise out of the billowing smoke and flames, ready to push upward in unison with its giant wings. It turned a fiery gaze on Frank, thanking him for starting the fire that gave it life.

The flapping of giant wings ushered him back to reality. His eyes returned to the cell—he needed to feel the strangling of its confinement; this feeling strengthened his desire to escape.

He heard the 2 a.m. alarm and knew that he had to get some sleep. Turning toward the chilled wall touching his cot, he remembered Steinbeck's quote, "*Death was a friend, and sleep was Death's brother.*"

CHAPTER 4

1962, SAN FRANCISCO, PRESIDIO

S cott jumped out of bed and rushed toward the tin box on the bookcase holding his baseball card collection. Taking position in the middle of the room and sitting cross-legged, he began the narration with confidence.

"Welcome back live, from Forbes Field in Pittsburgh. It's Game 7, bottom of the ninth of the 1960 World Series and this epic battle between the Pittsburgh Pirates and the New York Yankees continues."

He beamed himself to Thursday, October 13, 1960, 1:00 p.m. at Forbes Field in Pittsburgh, Pennsylvania. The Pittsburgh Pirates and the New York Yankees had battled for seven games and these were the final moments that would write their names in baseball history. It was the day after Nikita Khrushchev infamously pounded his shoe on his desk during the U.N. General Assembly. It was the day after Richard Nixon and John Kennedy engaged in their third presidential debate.

Taking a deep breath and tightening his throat, he continued imitating the high-pitched tone and speed of the imaginary radio announcer. Practice makes perfect and his morning ritual of repeating the last game of the Series had been going for nearly two years, making the reenactment surreally perfect.

"And Ralph Kerry, of course on the mound, will be facing Mazeroski, and to go over that Yogi Berra play once again, it was a hard-hit drive down the first base line, but Rocky Nelson fielded on the first half and tagged the bag on first, and that eliminated Berra—he was out. And then Mantle could have been in the run down but it was not the case—he dove back safely to first base." Another breath and he continued.

"Here's ball one, too high now to Mazeroski. And the Yankees have tied the game in the top of the ninth inning." He imitated the exciting roar of the crowd and, taking a big breath, continued with an even higher pitch for enthusiasm.

"Kerry throws, and the hit is a high fly-ball going deep to left field. This may do it. Back to the wall goes Berra . . . it is . . . over the fence! Home run, the Pirates win! Aaaaaaaaaaaaaaaaaaaaaaaaa!!!!"

Falling backward with his hands waving like crazy, the roar of the crowd covered the roar of the storm outside. Scott continued bringing radio listeners more valuable information.

"Listen to this crowd going crazy, the Pittsburgh Pirates are the 1960 World Series champions. An exhilarating climactic Game 7 that had the lead change hands four times, and of course not a single strikeout. The only time this has happened in World Series history."

Deep breath, and his finale—he must satisfy his listeners.

"It was a mammoth blast to left field: 365 feet down the line and 435 feet to the flagpole in deep left-center field. As Berra turned around to chase the ball, you could see it fly over the 406-marker carved out of the ivy. Considering the eighteen-foot wall it flew over, Mazeroski's home run must have traveled 430 feet or so."

"Let's go, Scott. Game over, sweetie! The taxi will be here soon, and the Rock awaits!" Mother's voice reached his bedroom as Scott was raising his hands triumphantly into the air. His daily unbroken ritual was always interrupted by her voice calling down for breakfast. He darted toward the hallway and immediately ran down the stairs two steps at a time.

"Scott!" she yelled. "I've told you a thousand times not to do that."

Lieutenant Carolyn Easten stood in front of the house's main door wearing her crisp army nurse uniform, her arms tightly crossed over her chest and her face painted with a stern motherly look that, combined with the uniform, was even more authoritative.

"Yes, ma'am," he replied, knowing he would repeat the same acrobatics the next time.

He could hear the rain and wind pounding at the door, violently trying to enter the warmth of their house. "Ready for our grand adventure, Scott?" she asked with excitement, erasing any sign of her previous strictness, knowing their trip today was more than an adventure for him.

For as long as he could remember, an obsession with Alcatraz fed his imagination with daydreaming adventures. One moment he was a prisoner and the next a guard, planning escapes and captures. The bad guys were unceasingly changing roles: villain then hero, bad to good, escapee or captured criminal. She understood his imagination, and shared his excitement, making it even more real for him. The taxi signaled its arrival with a quick sharp honk.

Carolyn opened the door and taking his hand, she pulled him under the protective perimeter of the large black umbrella.

"And we're off!" she laughingly yelled, as they dashed toward the waiting cab, trying to avoid gathering pools of water. She released his hand, guiding him into the backseat while trying to hold the umbrella over their bodies as long as possible, then entered only after she carefully placed the drenched umbrella in front of their feet.

He looked at her illuminated white skin, and her almond-shaped, light-blue eyes that sparkled as she exhaled. She looked back at him and smiled, opening her naturally red, full lips ever so slightly, revealing the whiteness of her straight teeth.

"Where to, ma'am?" asked the round taxi driver as he investigated the rearview mirror. Scott observed his tiny eyes, deeply embedded in his swollen face, and imagined the driver was fused to his seat, a living part of the vehicle.

"Good morning. To begin with, please take us to the Letterman Army Medical Center. I need to pick up a parcel. Afterward, we will go to Pier 33," Carolyn answered, while pulling the fitted skirt of her nursing uniform around her knees. Scott loved every detail of her nursing uniform: the sleek sleeves, short apron with patch pocket, and modest neckline adorned with a rounded collar secured with a single button. He always thought his mom was born to be a nurse, that the uniform was created for her, and believed that it would not exist if she did not exist.

"Yes, ma'am. Quite a storm today, and not the best day to visit the Embarcadero," the cabdriver responded while he pulled the gear stick into drive. "Did you know, ma'am, that the Embarcadero means *a place to embark*?" He continued without waiting for any acknowledgment. "Embarcadero is derived from the Spanish verb *embarcar* meaning to embark." He proudly nodded his head while taking the first right at the end of their street.

"Very interesting, thank you," she politely answered, a sincere tone highlighting the *you* of thank *you*.

"You are most welcome, ma'am! You know, with the number of tourists coming and going all year long, I try to make their rides as pleasant as possible, and trivial information about our city always gets them excited," boasted the man, his eyes alternating between the road and mirror. "I remember one time I was taking a couple to Fisherman's Wharf and was telling them about the Fish King, Achille Paladine, the late 1800s Italian immigrant who founded the Paladine Fish Company."

He drew a large gulp of air and continued.

"Well, ma'am, you won't believe it, but they both screamed in amazement and delight. They started to speak in Italian and the woman pointed toward the man and began repeating "Signore Paladine! Signore Paladine! Si, Si, Signore Paladine." Well, it took me a couple of minutes to understand that her husband's name was Lorenzo Paladine. They were from Italy, visiting San Francisco for the first time and did not know that another Paladine had ever come to America. Well go figure, they thought they were the first! A little strange, don't you think?" He laughed and nodded in agreement with his own assessment.

"Yes, quite an amazing coincidence, sir, amazing," she answered with feigned enthusiasm. She looked at Scott and opened her eyes warningly, knowing if he started to laugh her composure would be lost, and they would probably not stop laughing until the end of the ride, unless the driver kicked them out before that.

"Yes, ma'am, amazing," answered the driver with a self-congratulatory tone, convinced he had again astounded a fare with his storytelling abilities. He pulled closer to the car wheel in hope of improving his visibility against the intensifying sheets of rain pelting the windshield. Gusty winds hammered the vehicle, which resisted and rocked as a giant might when trying to find his balance by pivoting his huge feet.

Reaching the main entrance of the medical center, they came to a stop under the protective canopy designated Visitors Only. She opened the door and waved her hand toward the main entrance, shouting above the gales.

"Nancy, Nancy!" She stepped out and ran toward a woman who was headed toward us, holding a small parcel. "Thank you, dear. Tell Doctor Mattis I prepared the medical files he wanted, and Lieutenant Percy has them," she said. "Thank you, Nancy, see you in two days, sweetie!"

She ran back and entered the cab holding the box with both hands. The taxi driver backed up and slowly turned on to Letterman Drive toward Lombard Street.

"With this weather, it's going to take us a good forty minutes, ma'am," reported the driver in a professional tone. Apparently, he had time to think about his earlier narration and decided to be silent for the rest of the ride.

"Thank you! It's ok, our appointment is at twelve-hundred hours," Carolyn said. Her military tone confirmed further the need for his disciplined silence.

"Yes, ma'am," he responded, digging his large buttocks farther into the driver's seat.

The commuter traffic came to a crawl when they turned on Lombard Street and the usual amazing view of the bay and Alcatraz was hidden by the heavy rain. Scott disappointedly tried to see through the weather and as his gaze stubbornly persisted, he thought and wished for Superman's powerful x-ray vision.

"Don't worry, Scott, you will see it from the pier, honey," she whispered in his ear, once again understanding his intentions and needs.

The car windows continuously fogged up and the driver nervously wiped the inside of the windshield and murmured his frustration. They stopped and moved a yard at a time for what seemed hours, but in reality, forty minutes later, the taxi came to a final stop and the driver rotated his torso, requesting his hard-earned remuneration.

"That comes to $4.75, ma'am," he said.

The request had a joyfully playful tone, but as he turned his head to look back at them, the pain from his stiff neck muscles made his eyes roll upward. She smiled with politeness, trying to avoid his weird expressions and uncontrolled facial tics.

"Here we go and keep the change!" Carolyn said, handing him $6.00 and reaching for the umbrella lying at their feet.

"Thank you very much, ma'am, thank you very much indeed, and have a great day, enjoy the Embarcadero," responded the driver, his head revolving back to its locking position.

They stepped out of the taxi and, under the opened umbrella, faced the grandness and power of San Francisco Bay. The heavy precipitation had changed to a sturdy drizzle, and the clouds moved quickly over the wind-stirred swells. Scott squinted toward Alcatraz and the powdered white high peaks on the other side of the bay.

CHAPTER 5

1962, ALCATRAZ

The trembling lump of lemon Jell-O liquefied in his mouth while his gaze drifted between the seated inmates of the prison dining room. Morris, Sam West, Dave, and Tim Anglin shared the same table since Warden Blackwell had recently replaced the long tables with smaller, colored table sets that seated four.

Two months had passed since he had noticed the green mold building up around the air vent on the right side and below the washbowl in his cell. Using his nail clipper, he picked at the mold-infested concrete at the edge of the metal grill and a few grains fell to the floor. The concrete's age, combined with the bay's humidity, had caused it to soften, igniting in Morris the first real hope of escaping.

"Storm's on the way," said Dave.

"It's going to snow tonight," replied Sam with a full mouth of macaroni and cheese.

It was ironic, but the food in America's most no-torious prison was great; so good in fact, that the guards and prison staff ate the same exact meals as the prisoners.

The warden believed, and told every new guard and government inspector, "Most trouble in prison is caused by bad food. Yes, sir, bad food incites violence."

The day would begin with a breakfast of cereal, eggs, fruit, and toast, and dinner would follow with chili dogs, butter-drenched potatoes, fried pork chops, biscuits and gravy, and banana pudding.

"Definitely going to fucking snow," Tim added with the confidence of a weatherman.

Morris hated chitchat. He investigated his empty bowl, refraining from telling them both to go fuck themselves. Keeping his face down he whispered be-tween his teeth, "How's the book going, guys?"

"It was the best of times, it was the worst of times," recited Sam with what he thought sounded like an English accent.

"This guy Dickens would never have said that if he had gotten a good taste of Alcatraz; he would prob-ably write, 'It was and is the worst of fucking times,'" quipped Sam, grinning with satisfaction.

Morris had asked permission to form a read-ing club with the other three, so they could justify talking together about "the book." They noiseless-ly shared the actions and progress of their escape plan. When they spoke about "the book" they really meant "the escape plan"; and progress of chapters was their timeline to freedom.

"I'm very close to finishing chapter three," re-sponded Dave.

"Me too," added Sam, and continued with his makeshift old English accent, "something of the awfulness." He repeated his memorized book quote, and grinned once again with satisfaction.

"Stop grinning, asshole, the last thing we want is for the fucking bulls to wonder why you are so happy," barked Morris in a hushed voice. His tone was always intended to remind them that he was running the shots. It was his plan and he knew there was no room for the slightest mistake.

Morris sensed that Moloney, one of the overseeing bulls, had noticed Sam's excitement and grinning, and began walking slowly toward their table.

Moloney was born to bully, so being an Alcatraz guard was the best job he had ever had, a government license to fuck with minds and bodies. It filled his need for power. His oversized crew-cut oval head sat on top of a short, round body. He came closer to them switching the black baton from hand to hand.

"That's a lovely grin, Sammy, it's making me hard just looking at it."

Moloney's voice was directed to Sam, but he wanted everyone to hear its authority.

"It reminds me of a whore I used to fuck up the ass, she always grinned when she was taking it."

"Let me ask you, Sammy, do you also have something up your ass? Mm? Is that why you're grinning, boy?"

He slightly cleared the hoarseness from his throat and continued.

"Talking to you, Sammy boy, and when I talk to you, what do you need to do, mm?" said Moloney. He reached out the baton and touched Sam on the shoulder, slightly pulsing the hard tip into his bicep.

"It was just a joke, sir," responded Sam, looking straight ahead.

"Just a joke, mm?" Moloney chided. "Well I love jokes. Why don't you share it with us, Sammy boy! I'm sure everyone wants to hear it. Right, guys, don't you want to hear it?"

The silence from the surrounding tables was that of an audience watching a thriller, waiting for the "what's behind the door" scene; at least their boredom would be broken and that would be better than the Jell-O.

Morris dug his nails deep into his left thigh underneath the table; two months of planning and preparation was about to be blown if Sam didn't keep his cool. All of this because of a fucking grin. He held his breath and looked straight ahead, sensing the sweat beads rolling down his back.

"Yes, sir!" answered Sam, face frozen as he continued with a sweet tone. "It's an old joke about a judge."

Morris did not like Sam's sweetness. He had heard it before and it usually meant trouble.

"Let's hear it, Sammy boy!" replied Moloney, pushing the baton deeper into Sam's shoulder.

Sam smiled, still looking straight ahead, and began narrating with a slow, determined tone.

"There was a judge, you see, a judge that grew tired of seeing the same town drunk almost every other week in court. The judge, you see, looked down at the wino who was still drunk and yelled, 'It is the sentence of this court that you be taken from here to a place of execution and there be hanged by the neck until DEAD!'" Sam took a deep breath and continued.

"The wino fainted, falling like a sack of potatoes, you see. The shocked bailiff looked up at the judge and the judge said . . ." Sam stopped and slowly turned, looking Moloney straight in the eyes. Grinningly he said the punch line, "'I've always wanted to do that.'"

The silence was deafening, as Moloney's white freckled face filled with the redness of rising blood pressure. His baton hand was trembling, and everyone knew he was going to lose it.

A few weeks prior, Tim Larsen woke up in the hospital ward with a broken jaw and serious concussion. Tim, while mopping the mess hall, had knocked over the water bucket and Moloney's shoes were splashed. The bulls on duty all testified that Moloney was defending himself.

"Moloney!" yelled Harrison, the head bull. "Time for your break, officer!" Harrison approached Moloney from the back of the mess hall. He had been watching all along and did not want another incident on his watch.

Harrison reached out and tapped Moloney's shoulder, saying with clarity, "Break it off, time for a smoke, like I said."

Harrison hated Moloney and would have loved to fire him, but Moloney was the warden's wife's nephew. He also looked like the bitch, thought Harrison, so he just tried to keep him on a long leash. Last time he had spoken to the warden about his conduct he just replied, "The boy is young and will learn from his mistakes."

Moloney lowered his baton and growled a "Yes, sir!"

He looked at Sam and leaned down, close to his ear, and whispered, "If I had my way, fuckups like you would never get out of here. A deep hole is waiting for you and guess who's going to drop you in it?"

Sam continued to stare into his eyes, smelling and tasting Moloney's sweat and Old Spice. Sam's grin had turned into a frozen stare, the look as Morris called it. It was the look of promise: a promise of pain.

Harrison tapped Moloney's shoulder harder than before and said, "Moloney, let's go."

They walked away, and Sam turned and stared into the empty Jell-O bowl.

"I'm going to fuck his asshole until he bleeds to death," he growled between his teeth.

Morris spooned another lump of Jell-O. His face was staring at the back of the mess hall, but his eyes turned toward Sam and he said quietly, "Remember Sam, if you fuck things up, Moloney will be the least of your worries. We need to keep our fucking heads down, make the bulls believe that we are just doing our time. We need to focus on finishing the fucking book. You understand, goddamn it!? Only the book!"

Morris felt the hollowness of fear deep in his stomach. They had a long way to go and keeping the other three guys in line was becoming harder than the escape plan itself.

"File up!" yelled Harrison. "Back to your caves, gentlemen!"

They all stood and filed in the center dining room aisle with the guards on the front, sides, and back.

Slowly they walked out and toward their designated cell block areas.

Morris entered his cell and checked his watch. It was 4:45 p.m. It was always 4:45 p.m. when they marched back from the mess hall.

"Doors closing!" yelled one of the bulls, and the cell doors began to roll shut, sending chaotic banging and cracking sounds through the block.

The cell doors did not have individual locks. Instead, the entire row of twenty was operated by a device with various levers that could open or close one door at a time or all the doors at once.

Frank tried to study every small detail of the building, cell block, and locking mechanisms. He knew he would never escape if he did not know what the functional and psychological intent of his surroundings was.

He was convinced that everything had been designed and built not only to make escape impossible, but more importantly, to destroy the spirit and will to escape. The heavy line of doors closed behind him and the guards began individual confirmation. "Number eight, closed and secure!"

The sound of a steel cell door was special, almost unique. It seemed to yell and scream to every living soul across the entire cell block the word "imprisonment." Frank let the vibration pass through his body, and used its energy to satiate his desire for escape. He extended his arms and touched the right and left walls of his cell. It was a ritual that he did at least once a day. He imagined the five-by-nine-foot slab like a box rather than a room. It made sense to him that the builders of this institutional hell considered the inmates vermin, as vermin are placed in boxes.

They designed everything with the intent to punish and erode freedom from the mind of the incarcerated men—the sinners of society who had to pay their dues. The cells had no windows, the small sink only cold running water, the toilet was exposed, and privacy was nonexistent.

Frank repeated these thoughts daily; they gave him strength and, more importantly, a "sense of purpose." The war in Korea had taught him that it was critical to survival. Without purpose, you died.

He turned toward the bars of his cage and smiled, imagining a conversation with his buddy back home.

"Hey Vinnie, how do you make a door disappear?"

"Don't know, Frank, how do you make a door disappear?" the imaginary Vinnie replied. "Don't put no lock on it, Vinnie. No lock and the door becomes a fucking wall," he answered laughingly.

Facing the corridor, he stood waiting for 4:50 p.m. The standing count in the cells by both shifts of lieutenants and cell guards. He had memorized the daily schedule and every day at 4:45 he would recite it in his mind, word by word, another ritual he had established like a prayer:

8:00 p.m.: Count in the cells.
9:30 p.m.: Lights-out count.
12:01 a.m.: Count by lieutenants and the cell house guards of both shifts.
3:00 a.m.: Count in the cells.
5:00 a.m.: Count in the cells.
6:30 a.m.: Morning whistle.

Prisoners arise, make beds, place all articles in pre-scribed order on shelf, clean wash basin and toilet bowl, wipe off bars, sweep cell floor, fold table and seat against the wall, wash themselves, and dress.

He remained standing as the left side bull passed and recorded that prisoner #AZ1441 was safely be-hind bars. Every day, when the bull recorded and called out his number, Frank remembered meeting the warden on his first day; it was his way of count-ing the days. He remembered sitting in front of the large mahogany desk and looking straight into the bitty eyes of Warden Blackwell for the first time.

"I don't know what you did in your life before you embarked on your criminal career, Mr. Morris, but here on Alcatraz everything is simple," the warden said, eyeing Frank above his reading glasses. "Yes, Mr. Morris, and you know why everything is simple? Because everyone on Alcatraz follows the rules," he continued with a hollow voice.

He looked into Frank's eyes trying to determine if his words had the desired effect. Then he brought the fat cigar to his lips and took a long inhale before continuing his rhetoric, the words exiting his fat lips along with puffs of smoke.

"Isn't this right, Captain Jones?" he asked the tall captain towering over the sitting inmate. "Yes, sir!" replied the captain with authority.

Welcome to the asshole hour, thought Frank. He had met and lived with these types all his life, es-pecially in the army. But assholes like these did not exist for long back home. *No, sir, someone would shut their mouth fast if they dared to play the big shot.* He would have smiled or rather smirked at them but held his composure with an ice-cold poker face.

"We are a small community," continued the warden. "Yes indeed, a very small community, with a very large jail. This institution has a long history of disinfecting society, by holding in its grasp some of the worst criminals of the United States. Public enemies, every one of them, or rather all of you, Mr. Morris."

He stopped and took another deep but slow inhale, then smacked his lips together and continued. "The convicts that we receive come to us with long records of successful previous escapes or attempted escapes. But, of course this ends when they arrive to Alcatraz."

Taking another breath, he intentionally paused to make his words more memorable. "Of course, as you know, Mr. Morris, we have made certain there will never be a successful escape from Alcatraz. But I don't fool myself and I know that all of you convicts brought to Alcatraz are the very best at what you do. I know that you have twenty-four hours a day, seven days a week to figure out how to get out of here."

He concluded by lowering his glasses to the tip of his nose, and added quietly with his cigar pointing toward Frank's face, "But I also know that you will fail."

Frank smiled from behind iron bars and knew that he would not fail.

CHAPTER 6

1962, SAN FRANCISCO, PIER 33

H and in hand they walked toward Pier 33, which extended into the bay, just one of many piers along the three-mile man-made seawall. To their left, they could see the crawling commuter traffic on the Oakland Bay Bridge; the storm had clogged the main arteries of the city and thousands would be late this morning.

A boat bounced against the dock's landing, rising and falling by the force of the swells, and it took several rises for Scott to read its name. The Warden Johnson, named after James Aloysius Johnson, the first warden of Alcatraz Federal Penitentiary.

They headed straight for the boat and the two armed prison guards standing in front of the bobbling rope bridge linking the dock with the ship.

"I promised you an amazing day, Scott. Well? What do you think of where we are? Eh?" she asked, showing her own excitement.

"It's swell, Mom, just amazing. I can't believe we're here, so close to the Rock!" he yelled back, trying to be louder than the wind and swell hammering the pier. Finally reaching the guards, his mother let go of his hand and presented herself to the men.

"Good morning, I am Lieutenant Carolyn Easten from the Letterman Army Medical Center and I have a medical parcel for Doctor Erwing." Without waiting for a response, she continued with a commanding tone, "Doctor Erwing is expecting us."

Scott looked beyond the guards toward the boat's bridge and distinguished moving shadows behind steamed windows. The side door of the bridge opened, and the skipper glanced toward them, yelling, "Eh, Ed! Hope they get here on time. We're going to cast off late again, and you know what happens when we are late. A goddamn fucking shit storm."

He turned and glanced at the fermenting whitecaps on the bay, then quickly back toward them, and finally at the gateway to the pier. "Goddamn it!" the captain cursed while slamming shut the bridge door, disappearing into its warmth.

The guard apologetically looked at Lieutenant Easten and, clearing his throat, responded, "Yes, ma'am, let me get Sergeant Johnston. He is leading our guard detail today, one moment please."

He turned and began a wobbled journey over the hanging ladder, finally reaching and entering the main cabin door. The remaining guard smiled and anxiously looked toward the pier's gateway.

"We're waiting for an extra passenger from Virginia, but it looks like the storm must have delayed the overnight train arrivals from Los Angeles," he stated. "Sorry for the captain's cursing, ma'am, but all hell breaks loose when we arrive late. The warden, you see, doesn't like the day's schedule to be changed, not even by God's weather."

The younger guard seemed inclined to explain the captain's reaction and his own nervousness. She smiled and reverted in kind.

"No need to apologize, I am quite used to army officers expressing their concern in the same manner. Army nurses hear a handful of Shakespearian rhetoric every hour of every day." She smiled and continued with a sturdy English accent, "There is nothing either good or bad but thinking makes it so."

She ended the Shakespeare quote with a smile while the young guard's face mirrored his brain's struggle to understand the meaning of the words. She realized his confusion and, feeling bad for having caused it, immediately turned the conversation to a simpler subject.

"This is quite a storm; I wonder when it will let up?"

The officer quickly grasped the opportunity to express his knowledge of the latest weather alerts and responded with confidence, "The storm will begin to let up tonight, and tomorrow they say it will be much better, ma'am!"

Scott caught him looking at her in a different way. He couldn't understand the difference but felt its unspoken message.

He quickly looked at his mother's eyes, suddenly defensive, or rather deflective. Her increasing facial and neck redness reminded him of the other times he saw it, always the same, always instigated by the gaze of men.

"Thank you for the information, officer!" she answered, looking away quickly and turning back to Scott. She smiled and pulled his scarf closer together, protecting him from the cold.

The honking of the black limousine hurtling through the pier's gate grabbed everyone's attention and they all followed its path toward them. It braked violently just a few feet away and the driver's door swung open, revealing a huge black-uniformed driver, who exited and hurriedly reached for the passenger door handle.

He ceremoniously opened the door and stood at attention, statue-like. A man of medium height and build wobbled out and, without a single hesitation, darted between them, disappearing into the bridge. He momentarily stopped, looking left and right before the door magically opened for him to enter. Almost immediately, the door opened once again, hot air exiting the overheated bridge, surrounding and twisting around the returning guard. He was followed by a much older prison guard who headed toward them.

"Good morning, Lieutenant, I am Sergeant Underwood. I've been asked by Warden Blackwell to welcome you aboard. I hope the bumpy ride isn't going to be too rough for you and the boy."

Sergeant Underwood's welcoming words spilled from his mouth with a mixed expression of urgency.

"Good morning, Sergeant," started the lieutenant. "Major Anderson sends his best wishes to Warden Blackwell and hopes the flu shots will help this year's winter season." Carolyn's professionalism was always highlighted by the firm tone of her voice and her higher rank was clearly transmitted to the sergeant.

"Thank you, Lieutenant. Eh, the flu, yes, it's bad news, but prison flu is a breed of its own," explained Underwood. Drops of sweat streamed down his forehead, past thick eyebrows, to his cheeks, firm chin, and marbled jaw. Scott enjoyed following the paths of his dripping sweat. The sergeant smiled at them and nervously wiped his face with a dirty white handkerchief. "The cold weather precautions for the ship have the heaters running full blast, and the bridge is hot as hell. Please follow me, Lieutenant," he said almost apologetically.

They crossed the small hanging bridge and stepped on the rocking boat deck. Scott adjusted his stance for balance, and his imagination transformed him into Blackbeard looking toward the horizon at the warship heading their way.

"Get ready, mates! Get ready the canons and let's give the queen a taste of our powder," he imagined the pirate captain roughly commanding.

"Scott, Scott, the captain is talking to you!" His mother's voice snapped him back to reality and he turned toward the now-opened bridge door and the towering form of Captain James.

"Welcome aboard!" he shouted above the winds and the sea's cries. He then looked at Scott with his joyful, deep blue eyes and shouted once again. "Here we go," said the captain, while handing them two bright yellow nautical jackets.

"You are most welcomed to stay inside, but I assumed that a first-time ride to the Rock would be better enjoyed on the deck," advised Captain James with a twinkle in his eye. "Am I right, matey? I've been waiting all morning for you to arrive."

Scott looked at his mother's approving nod and immediately answered the Captain. "Aye, Aye, Captain!" The experience of playing pirates with the guys was paying off, and Scott proudly assumed the first mate's role.

Scott and his mom put their jackets on and in unison pulled the hoods over their heads. Looking at each other they laughed, realizing that they were two sizes bigger than needed. Carolyn reached out and rolled his sleeves twice so his hands could peek out.

"Now, Scott, you look like a real first mate," she said.

"Yes!" continued the captain. "He really does. OK, mister, let us get under way."

He turned toward the bridge and yelled at the top of his voice, "All-ahead full!" Then he stared over the ship's popping bow, spreading his legs apart to hold himself upright.

The ship began to move, the vibrations of the engine humming through their bodies. Scott turned to his mother, and his visible excitement made her smile and laugh. The ship cut through the madness of the waves, speeding across the bay toward Alcatraz.

"It's a one-and-a-quarter-mile distance, matey; hope we don't meet any pirate ships on the way!" yelled the captain. Scott nodded and continued to look ahead as their destination slowly grew in size through the rain and mist.

"This crossing usually is full of fog and mist so thick you can hardly see your nose!" yelled the captain, and Scott imagined him in a pirate's uniform. He was perfect for the role.

Back toward San Francisco, several sailboats breached the waters and then disappeared behind the tips of rollercoasting, darkening waves. Returning his gaze to the island, he saw screaming storm-panicked seagulls rushing toward Alcatraz's safety.

"Here, matey, take the binoculars for a closer look at everything. As my first mate, you are my lookout for the duration of the trip."

The captain's order was given with starkness and Scott responded with respectful obedience. He grabbed the navy-issued binoculars and tightened his fingers around the cold metal, quickly steadying them with a second hand to support the surprising weight.

"Yes, sir!" Scott responded as professionally as he could.

Scott moved to the center of the mid-deck directly under the boat's bridge, holding and pushing himself upright against the galling wind and rain. Raising the binoculars, he turned the focusing knob until he could see clearly.

Scott began to inspect the surrounding landmarks, beginning at Angel Island, Treasure Island, Oakland Bridge, and finally the Golden Gate Bridge. The rolling of the boat under his feet moved the targets, and he tried to keep his hands steady. Finally, turning toward Alcatraz, he focused on the bright familiar beam coming from the lighthouse. It was operating this morning due to the low visibility created by the storm. As long as he could remember, every night he had watched its piercing path from his bedroom window, thinking about the notorious place that it protected.

As the boat began its turn toward the southeast corner of the island, he saw Alcatraz's first welcoming message to visitors. Scott read the words excitedly, his anticipated adventure becoming more real by the minute. "WARNING: PERSONS PROCURING OR CONCEALING ESCAPE OF PRISONERS ARE SUBJECT TO PROSECUTION."

The captain instinctively realized he was focused on the message and helped with an explanation. "The sign tells boaters to stay out of the three-hundred-yard Alcatraz shoreline limit. The other day some hothead kids came as close as one hundred yards and they will never forget the sound of the guard's warning shots. *Ha!* You should have seen the way they turned their boat. Almost capsized it, they did!"

Scott looked over at his mother, who was nervously smiling at the captain's comments. Alcatraz was viewed by everyone as a notorious place, built to hold "the worst of the worst." As they came closer to the island, the boat's speed fell, and the power of the waves gave them a strong taste of rocking and bobbing.

"Get ready for docking!" yelled the captain. As they approached, he fixed his binoculars on an old ramp that consisted of an angle iron covered by wood. The ramp was being lowered by a winch that would control its level depending on the level of the tide.

"Look over here, matey!" said the captain, pointing toward the barracks building. "The cannon battery over there is part of the original fortress built in 1852. They built the barracks above the structure in 1909, and that's where U.S. army prisoners were kept. The barracks were converted into apartments for U.S. federal prison personnel and their families in 1934 when Alcatraz switched from a military prison to a maximum-security penitentiary." He took a deep breath and continued.

"The doc is waiting for you on the dock," he said with a wink. "And I am sure he will give you a detailed tour of the site. Alcatraz has a great history and we are all very proud to be part of it."

"We appreciate the details, Captain," his mother answered.

The ramp greeted the edge of the vessel, and both shore and boat personnel scrambled to fight the bobbing, lashing, heavy ropes that would keep the Warden Johnson safely docked.

With gymnastic agility the sailors jumped from boat to ramp and back again until they secured the lines, adeptly employing navy knots that had been used for hundreds of years.

"It was a pleasure, matey; hope you have a great time on the Rock!" offered the captain, as he retrieved the binoculars from Scott's hand and tousled his hair with a giant hand. "Thank you, Captain," Scott answered excitedly.

"Thank you very much, Captain, I appreciate your attention," complimented Carolyn, adding emphasis and appreciation for the captain's special treatment of her son.

"My pleasure, Lieutenant, and please be gentle when you give me the flu shot," answered the captain, smiling at Scott.

She moved behind Scott as they lined up behind the other passengers to exit the bridge's main door. Given the weather and other distractions, they hadn't realized there were so many other passengers aboard.

Two women hugging large, brown, paper grocery bags gossiped unabashedly as they moved toward the ramp. Right behind them was a short man of medium height and build, who stared at them through wet, matted hair. He seemed oblivious to the discomfort of the nasty weather, and held a dark brown leather suitcase below his armpit, with the air of a man about to deliver something of importance to someone of importance. Scott imagined he was a lawyer delivering the final verdict to a prisoner's request for early parole.

They moved slowly down the unwieldy ramp, and finally stepped onto the wet wooden boards of the gangway toward the landing area. Scott's eyes absorbed everything like a sponge and he was transported into his own imaginary world, transforming the scene into another reality.

His wrists were gripped by handcuffs, clamped to a padlock chain around his waist, continuing down to bare feet chained to leg irons. Heavily armed guards yelled orders and pushed him forward. He was a dangerous convict, public enemy number one, and after three prison breaks, they had finally delivered him to the world's most secure maximum-security penitentiary. Nobody had ever escaped from the Rock, but he knew nothing could keep him locked up. He would escape or die trying!

The moment they stepped off the gangway, a bolt of lightning struck the lighthouse, followed by a crack of thunder, as if Alcatraz was welcoming their arrival.

"Scott! Scott! This way, sweetie!" His mother's voice transported Scott back to reality and he quickly followed behind her toward the edge of the dock.

Doctor Wealton smiled, revealing two gold teeth on the left side of his mouth. His completely round face, red cheeks, large ears, and button-sized black eyes reminded Scott of a Disney character sketch.

"Welcome to Alcatraz, Lieutenant, young man! I am sure over the next three days you will make many friends here," said the doctor with a semi-high-pitched voice, complementing the Disney characterization.

"I am Doctor Wealton the chief physician, and in charge of the Alcatraz prison hospital," he joyfully added, extending his hand first to Carolyn and then to Scott.

"Thank you very much, Doctor Wealton, for having us; it is a great pleasure to be part of your flu vaccination program," said the lieutenant. "Major Danaine sends many regards and extends his invitation for you to visit the Letterman Army Medical Center."

Doctor Wealton nodded and smiled and continued courteously.

"Thank you and please extend my thanks and appreciation. It will be both an honor and pleasure to visit. I have heard about the great work that you have been doing for our boys in arms. Congratulations!"

Scott saw that his courteous and respectful tone was pleasing to his mother, and he immediately placed Doctor Wealton on the nice guy list.

"Thank you again for your kind words, Doctor Wealton," she replied. The doctor nodded again and pointed toward a concrete paved path.

"Well, I hope you had a good boat ride and it was not too bumpy," he said while starting to walk ahead.

"We were too excited to notice the rocking," answered his mother, following behind and making sure Scott was along.

"That is good to hear, Lieutenant. Let us begin your personal tour," began Doctor Wealton. "There are three hundred civilians living on Alcatraz, and that includes both women and children. Building 64 is the primary living quarters and we have prepared a room for you. There are also three apartment buildings and a large duplex on the other side, plus four large wooden houses for our senior officers."

He took a deep breath, cleared his throat, and went on with pride.

"We have a bowling alley, a small convenience store, and a soda fountain shop for our younger residents." He smiled, winking at Scott. "I think you will enjoy that, what do you say, young man?"

"Yes, sir!" Scott responded without hesitation, imitating his mother's military tone.

"I am sure he will, Doctor!" added his mother.

The doctor continued.

"Our families do most of their shopping on the mainland since the prison boat makes twelve runs to Van Street Pier each day. The warden lives in that large house adjacent to the cell house, and the inmates with good conduct are used for cleaning and cooking. So, don't be alarmed if you see any convicts roaming around."

Doctor Wealton laughed with himself and they both smiled nervously. Inmates, convicts, both words jolted Scott to the reality that he was at a prison.

They all looked toward the house and saw three inmates weeding the garden and the grassy yard.

Scott thought how surreal it looked. If you removed the surrounding buildings, it looked like a normal high-class suburban family home. If someone saw a picture of only the house, they would never imagine it was situated twelve-hundred-feet from one of the most notorious prisons in America.

"Throughout the mid-to-late 1800s, Alcatraz was the biggest U.S. military installation west of the Mississippi. During the gold rush of the mid-1800s, the installation protected U.S. Civil War soldiers from Confederate sympathizers."

Doctor Wealton lowered the tone of his voice as much as possible, conscious of its high pitch.

Scott gazed at his mother with exuberant eyes. He loved history and this live lesson was a great present to him. Carolyn joyfully shared in the excitement.

"We really appreciate this tour, Doctor Wealton," she said. "Scott is a real history buff and your narration is wonderful."

"Thank you, Lieutenant, it is my pleasure and I am very happy you are enjoying it. I am also a history buff and it is very rare that I get the chance to guide someone through the past and present of the island. We don't get many tourists. But in your case, Lieutenant, the warden instructed me to make your stay as memorable as possible. Now please follow me."

With quick, short steps he took the lead toward the back side of the large apartment buildings. "This area is called Chinatown because of its similarity to the narrow alleyways of that section of San Francisco."

He continued to the south end of Chinatown taking them up a flight of stairs toward a wooden door marked 108.

"Lieutenant, we have prepared this one-bedroom apartment as your quarters; it is usually reserved for couples without children or single officers. I hope you will be comfortable," said Dr. Wealton.

Doctor Wealton unlocked the door and they entered a small living room furnished with a couch, small coffee table, and an old TV set that stared back at them hoping someone would turn it on. The adjacent kitchen had one wall full of recently painted cupboards and cleanly scrubbed appliances. Another wall was decorated with wallpaper full of fruits, and in the middle sat a small kitchen table and three chairs.

"This is just fine, Doctor, we will be very comfortable," replied the lieutenant.

The doctor nodded and waved them toward the bedroom door, wanting to show them everything—as if they were going to rent the place or something.

Scott ducked inside the bathroom for a look, then headed toward the living room balcony door, side-stepping a built-in ironing board that had been left open, waiting for the next pair of pants to be pressed.

The balcony ran the length of the building and was a good twenty-five feet above the ground, even though it was on the first floor. His mother and Doctor Wealton joined him, and the doctor pointed toward the sea.

"From this position, you have a commanding view of the dock area, guard tower, and the surrounding East Bay," he boasted. "It's quite a view, right, son?"

"Yes, sir!" Scott responded.

"Lieutenant, here are your keys. Let us continue your tour, if you don't mind. I have an appointment in an hour, but I would like to show you some more of our facilities."

"Of course, Doctor," she responded. "Come on, Scott, more to see."

They exited the apartment. His mother locked the door and they worked their way across the first floor, passing a large storefront window with Post Office written on it.

"I do not think that you will have enough time to either write or receive a letter, but if you did, here is our own post office." The doctor pointed toward it.

Peering through the window, Scott stared at the 1930s hanging light fixture beaming yellowish on the surrounding shelves filled with parcels and envelopes. The image of a convict slowly opening one of these letters flashed across his eyes, and a strange feeling of confinement filled him for the first time since they had arrived.

"And here we have our small but miraculous grocery store. If you need something, you always can find it, anything," explained the doctor. "Kevin Regan is the owner. He is an ex-guard who decided that, after twenty-three years of service, Alcatraz was home. So, he bought the grocery store and stayed."

Kevin opened the door and greeted them with a happy grin. His red, round cheeks and large smiling eyes could have been the face of Santa Claus. Scott looked at Kevin and he thought that he would have never guessed that this good-natured-looking old man could have ever been a hard-knuckled guard. Kevin invited them in for a chocolate bar, but the doctor explained they had limited time.

"OK, Doc, please feel free to drop in anytime, and if you need something special, just ask, and I'm sure that I will find it."

"I am positive you will," replied the doctor, followed by snorting and heavy laughter as he waved them along.

They followed him into the main hallway of the building, revealing a shadowy staircase that led upward and, strangely, stopped at the ceiling of the second floor. The doctor looked down at Scott and continued his narrative.

"Weird staircase, eh, Scott? Another Alcatraz mystery." He shrugged. "Actually, Building 64 was originally built as an army barracks. When it was converted to apartments, the stairway was not needed, but rather than remove it they decided to keep it, even though it ascends to nowhere."

His voice took on a deeper, more mysterious tone, and he continued, "Rumor has it that they left the staircase to trick and trap escapees who might think it was a way out."

The doctor laughed again, clearly showing his enjoyment of storytelling, then led them through the main exterior door, and all three exited Building 64. They strolled across Chinatown and down some stairs onto a parade ground, like the one back home at the Presidio.

"This was mainly used for military drills and parade formations up to 1934, when the prison was given to the Federal Government," Wealton went on. "Since then, it functions as a playground and gathering place for families living here. We also have, as you can see, gardens surrounding the area, facilities for handball and weight lifting."

A group of kids playing handball waved toward them and yelled in unison, "Good morning, Doctor Wealton!"

"Hi, kids, I got a new player for you!" said the doc by way of introduction. "This is Scott. You'll get to know him, but for now I need to show him around."

The tallest of the group waved and called back, "Hi, Scott, I'm Sam, and we can always use a new kid on the block. Come and find us whenever you want."

"Hi, guys, I will!" Scott shouted back.

"The game must go on!" said the doctor cheerfully. "No matter how bad the weather, this bunch will always meet and play."

Passing a giant water tower, the breeze transported a strong scent of seagull guano and salt water. "As you can smell, the island's true inhabitants are the gulls and of course the sandstone," he joked.

As he laughed, a group of seagulls went screaming upward and veered quickly toward the safety of the breaking waves. The clanging of a small buoy reached them, and the doctor continued his narration.

"During World War II, a submarine net was stretched from the edge of Fort Point under the Golden Gate Bridge, connected to the headlands a mile to the north. Now let us head toward our Industries Building; there, the inmates work their shifts cleaning laundry, sewing work gloves, and repairing small machinery, etc. The warden believes that a hard day's work gives them a sense of purpose; incarceration is a living hell for the toughest man."

Doctor Wealton looked at his wrist watch and suddenly stopped walking. "I'm sorry, Lieutenant, I must run off to my appointment. I'm very sorry for the abrupt tour stop, but, duty calls."

"Of course, Doctor, don't worry, we greatly appreciate the time and fantastic tour. It will be a memorable event for both of us," answered Scott's mother.

"I'm glad to hear that, Lieutenant. Please let me guide you back to your apartment; it's on my way," said the doctor.

CHAPTER 7

1962, ALCATRAZ, BUILDING B

Alcatraz welcomed the familiar thick fog rippling in from the Pacific Ocean. It mingled with the darkness, carrying the refraction of the guard tower lights as it searched and refocused to fill the hollowness of night.

From his bedroom window, Scott overlooked the progressive onslaught. His nightly unbroken ritual found him sitting with folded legs on the thick wooden windowsill. Scott's breath condensed on the windowpane and he imagined that its misty white diminishing form might summon the fog, fooling it into believing that it was an ingress into the house.

His imagination was broken by a muted voice from the small transistor radio next to him. *"From midnight to six in the morning, this is the Charlie Dune show on KHIP, the station with music power. K-H-I-P. And now a brief newsbreak, and we will be back with your musical entertainment."*

Scott exhaled with all his strength onto the windowpane while moving his mouth from top to bottom and from left to right, trying to mist up the entirety of the glass.

"*From KHIP, this is the morning news with Tom Brookes. Good morning. San Francisco is waking up to a strange and surprising sight, the heaviest snowfall since 1887. The weatherman is reporting that snow has begun to cover the sunset district, Westlake, and varying depths of the Peninsula. He is also forecasting that the freezing and near-freezing temperatures will keep the snow unmelted for the duration of the day despite the forecasted bright sunshine.*"

Scott looked toward the radio, then looked upward toward the sky, pressing his nose against the glass. His eyes tried to peer through the thinner patches of fog. Trying to improve his vision, he wiped with his jean shirtsleeve on the window glass and looked with intensity toward the sky.

A moving stream of light passed between the dark and light fog patches, but seconds of anticipation were lost when he realized that the source was the lights of San Francisco. He realized he was on Alcatraz looking back for the first time!

The silence was once again broken by the small radio. "*Good morning, lovers, I'm back. This is KHIP and the Charlie Dune show, featuring the best and newest top chart songs. Now sit back and enjoy "Soldier Boy" by The Shirelles. Dedicated to all the sleepless Presidion GIs and their sweethearts.*"

Scott swung his legs around while remaining seated on the windowsill. He heard and smelled breakfast being prepared, and his mouth watered when the familiar smell of bacon reached his nose.

"Scott! Breakfast is ready, sweetheart, come before the eggs get cold," called his mother.

Jumping from the windowsill he ran out of the room, sliding on the wooden floor and pretending he was on skates. Swinging an imaginary hockey stick he yelled, "He shoots, he scores!" and followed with the loud roar of the crowd.

"Come on, champion, I'm going to be late for my appointment with the doctor," ordered his mother. She walked over to the table, emptying the contents of a frying pan onto a large plate.

"I can't believe we are here! Alcatraz! My God, imagine that. All my life I've looked at this island from across the bay and never would have imagined that I would be on it," he said with excitement.

"Now Scott, I will be with the doctor until late this evening and I need for you to be on your best behavior, OK, sweetie?" she reminded him, not expecting more than a nod. Scott's mouth was already full of bacon, and his fork held a large piece of fried egg over his mouth. She leaned over and kissed him on the head while taking her apron off, and then hurried out the door.

Scott heard the front door closing and picked up his baseball glove and hat, then put on his coat and ran straight out of the house. Turning left toward the direction of the baseball field, the first thing he saw was the guard tower looming over the south jailhouse wall. With a quick stride, he started down the winding road, mostly looking at the jailhouse windows, wondering if any of the inmates were looking at him. Halfway down, he stepped to the side of the road for a passing truck. Suddenly, the truck came to a squeaky halt and the driver's window began to crank down.

"Good morning, son, where you heading?" said the gray-uniformed guard behind the wheel.

"To the baseball field, sir," responded Scott.

The guard's eyes scanned Scott from top to bottom and, satisfied with his short investigation, he replied with a stern and commanding voice, "Straight to the field, young man, no wandering about, OK? Off you go now."

Without waiting for a response, he rolled up the window and the brakes squealed as the truck inched down the steep road. Scott stood looking at the slow-moving truck wondering what that was all about. Then he considered that it was routine for guards to be curious and on alert for anything out of the ordinary. He continued toward the baseball field, now stepping into the shadow of the looming tower. Everything was dead quiet except for the sound of gulls squawking overhead and the wind rattling a window somewhere.

Laughter from the baseball field reached him before he passed the small shed that obstructed his view. He saw the assembled boys and approached them with confidence. The tallest boy looked over at him and greeted him with a friendly tone.

"Hi, bud! Great timing, we were just about to start a game. I'm Sam, and these guys are the Alcatraz 12, the best civilian baseball team of the United States penal system," said the boy with assurance. "Let me introduce you to the guys," he added, and started calling out their names one by one.

"Hi, I'm Scott. Scott Easten," replied Scott, his voice sounding surprisingly like a girl's. These days, he never knew whether he was going to sound like Minnie Mouse or Ray Charles.

The boys laughed, and Sam immediately interrupted the heckling.

"Welcome to the club of changing voices, Scott," said Sam with an apologetic note. "I'm sixteen and only recently stopped the ups and downs. Jerry over here gets so high-pitched that the guards think the fire alarm has sounded."

They all started to laugh and wail in soprano, "Jerryyyyyyy, aaaawwwww, Jerryyyyyyy."

"You can say that again," said a short, fat boy between bites of cinnamon nut cake that flew out of his mouth as he spoke.

"Eh, Bolder! Stop spitting, you going to make the field slippery," replied Sam, clearly the leader of the pack. Sam threw the baseball he was holding into a gloved left hand and yelled at the top of his voice, "Stan and I will be captains!"

They started picking players and Scott figured he would be the last pick because no one knew how he played, but to his surprise Sam picked him third for his side.

Stan and Sam counted off hands up the bat to see which team would hit first, and Sam won. They headed for the dugout and Sam pulled Scott aside.

"Hey, Scott, can you hit?" he whispered.

Scott shrugged. "I'm no Babe Ruth, but I'm not bad. I'm better on the field, though."

"But you can hit, right?" repeated Sam, pushing for Scott's confirmation.

"Yeah, I can hit," answered Scott with confidence.

Sam smiled and started giving his team instructions.

"OK, Scott, you're leadoff. John, you're second up. I'm third, and Mason you're cleanup. After that we'll see where we are. OK, boys! Play ball!"

For emphasis, he threw an easy ball with a high arc to a kid in the infield, who waited a beat and returned a stinger. Sam caught the ball easily, but his eyes revealed the sting felt by his hand through his glove.

"Good one, Jerry, you've just been nominated pitcher of the day," he complimented.

"OK, Stan, take the field and let's move, guys, go go go! Good to have you on the team, Scott," he turned and said smilingly as they walked toward home plate.

Scott picked up one of the bats lying in the grass and gave it a swing. It felt a little light, but he decided to use it. He stepped up to home, anxious to do well and impress his new friends, and most importantly, his captain, Sam.

He got into his stance and looked toward the pitcher, and now there was nothing but him and the ball. The pitch came in slowly, and he waited to swing. He heard the bat whistle through the air as the ball sailed past.

"Strike one!" the catcher yelled.

Scott shouldered the bat and the pitcher launched a fastball toward him. The pitch was exactly where he liked it, and he made solid contact this time.

He felt the impact and heard the crack of the bat, which to Scott had always been one of the most exciting aspects of the game. The crack reverberated across the field and everyone looked up, trying to track the ball's trajectory. Even the two inmates on garden duty outside of the warden's house instinctively turned toward the noise and searched the sky in anticipation.

It was a perfect swing, and Scott silently wished his coach was here to see it. The ball kept climbing, fighting gravity's pull, then reached its apex, and stopped for a millisecond, looking down at them.

Then it let itself go and started to fall, gaining speed as it came closer to earth. Scott estimated how far it would go and deemed it a certain home run. The outfielders' heads looked like the radar tracking antennae back at the base and moved slowly and perfectly in sync with the falling object.

"It's out of here!" yelled one of the kids.

"It's a HOME RUN!" roared another.

"It's falling in the warden's yard, boys!" screamed Sam from behind the dugout.

"Yeah!!! Right in the middle, boys, it's heading to the warden's house!" added the right fielder.

They all sprinted toward the house, and Scott, realizing that it was a home run as he rounded first, followed the others as fast as he could.

Scott looked straight toward the warden's house and saw two men with rakes in their hands, dressed in the standard prison uniform, looking at the sky for the incoming ball. A guard overlooked the yard, holding his rifle in readiness.

The boys screamed at the top of their voice as they neared, "Heads up! Heads up!"

The ball struck exactly in the center of the living room window sash, frame and grilles vibrating violently. The ball bounced toward the inmates with broken glass flying in all directions. The inmates instinctively brought their hands up to protect their faces. Frank Morris quickly jumped upward and grabbed the moving object, turning his body toward the incoming glass that bounced off his back and into the yard's grass.

The kids had reached the edge of the house's yard at the same moment the prisoner's hand closed on the baseball. They all stood silently looking at each other, and Frank slowly walked toward them holding out the baseball. For some reason he looked straight at Scott, who was panting for air after the long run, his dark green eyes revealing intelligence and determination. His bold, controlled gaze, coupled with his good looks and the faintest hint of a smile at the corners of his mouth, reflected experience and strength that matched his distinct walking style.

"Is this yours, son?" He directed his question to him as if he knew the answer.

"Yes, sir," Scott responded.

"That was quite a hit, kid, too bad you don't play for the Yankees. Mantle would have a run for his money," he continued with a distinct New York accent.

"Easy, Frank," signaled the guard, holding the rifle with both hands across his chest.

"Take it easy, Trevor, just giving the ball back to the kid," replied Frank in a controlled manner. He continued to approach Scott.

"Here you go, kid, the home run ball returns to the champ," Frank said in a low voice.

Frank was now almost arm's length from Scott when his eyes squinted eagle-like, reading the name on the dog tag hanging on Scott's chest. It had come free from inside Scott's shirt during the hard dash from the field to the warden's house.

Frank's natural trained poker face did not reveal his surprise.

"Let's go, Frank, snap it up!" yelled the guard who was slowly moving toward them.

"You know the rules, no talking to the civilians."

Frank looked at Scott with dead blue eyes and said coolly, "Here you go, kid," his arm outstretched and holding the baseball. At that moment, the guard reached them and quickly interrupted the handoff.

"Morris, give me the ball and start cleaning the glass up right now or so help me you will sleep in the fucking hole tonight," barked the guard harshly, grabbing the baseball from Frank's hand.

He turned toward the boys and made an underhanded toss to Sam, who snagged it with a bare right hand.

"Everything OK, Trevor?" yelled a guard from the nearby tower who had been watching the encounter with his rifle ready.

"Yea! Everything under control, no problem," replied Trevor at the top of his voice, raising and waving his hand toward the guard tower.

Frank pushed a hand through his thick, dark hair, flicking it out of his eyes as he bent over, carefully picking up pieces of broken glass from between the wet, half-frozen blades of grass.

The guard looked over at the kids and spoke with a commanding voice.

"OK, boys, off you go now, enough excitement for today. Let's see what the warden will say when he sees his broken window. I'm pretty sure your old man will give you a long talking-to tonight, Sammy boy." He directed his orders and comments more to Sam than to the other boys.

"OK, Mr. Trevor, no problem, sir! Game over, boys! Time for a soda!" ordered Sam with his team captain tone, while he nervously hammered the retrieved baseball into his glove. They all moved quickly away from the warden's house, heading toward Building B.

Scott turned around and saw the inmates cleaning up. He felt bad that his home run had caused so much trouble and wondered if he would get in trouble if his mother found out about the warden's broken window.

A short, fat boy ran up to him and whispered, breathing hard in Scott's ear, "That was a great hit, Scott. You broke Sam's record. First day on the Rock and you broke his record!"

Scott smiled, not knowing how to respond; he brushed his sweaty hair out of his eyes and followed the boys, synchronizing his stride with theirs.

His first day at Alcatraz was more exciting than he could have ever imagined: a home run, a broken window, and a live encounter with hard-core inmates of the Rock! *The guys back home would never believe him,* he thought, while trying to keep up with the others.

CHAPTER 8

1962, ALCATRAZ

They reached the Soda Shop and Sam took the order from everyone.

"What'll it be, guys? Show of hands: Cokes? Dr. Peppers?" He counted the raised hands and yelled to Pop, the Soda Shop owner. "OK, Pops, eight Cokes and four Dr. Peppers please!"

"Acht plus vier ok, Sammy. Vat's the celebration, boys?" Pop replied back in a heavy German-sounding accent.

"Well, Pop, Mr. Scott over here broke my home run record and also broke the warden's window, and all that on his first day here!" said Sam, pointing to Scott.

"Well done, my boy! But to be honest, the good news for me is the warden's broken window! I would love to see his face when he gets home. That son of a bitch needs more than a broken window, I tell you,"

Pop said with an angry tone that showed his opinion of the warden.

Everyone laughed, and Pop dived into the large red Coke freezer, reaching for the cold soda bottles. Sam approached Scott and sat next to him, pushing a little with his shoulder.

"Hey bud, what's up?" he started. "That was one hell of a hit; nobody ever got close to breaking my record before you, you know."

"Sorry about that, Sam, just a lucky hit!" answered Scott.

"Lucky hit my ass, you can really swing a bat, mister," complimented Sam as he nudged Scott again with his shoulder.

Pop handed out the bottles and Sam paid him on the way back behind the wooden bar.

"Eh, Scott, how about taking a walk down to the dock and I show you around the place? It's not every day you get to be on Alcatraz, right?" asked Sam, his voice insisting and assuring at the same time. Scott liked the idea of going down to the ocean. The sea always gave him a sense of freedom and security. He turned to his newfound friend and nodded in agreement. They got up and Sam yelled to the other boys.

"See you later, guys, we're going to take a walk. Stay out of trouble and no more broken windows today, ok?"

Scott also waved to them as they walked out, and pulled the door shut behind them. They said nothing, just moved one step after another, Scott following Sam who knew the island like the back of his hand. Sam broke the silence.

"This way is faster and usually not too many people use it; they go the long way because the pavement is in better condition. The island roads and buildings, as you may have noticed, are falling apart. No money coming to Alcatraz, my old man says."

Sam took a sudden left turn, leaving the path and heading down to a beach between several large boulders that stood as if they were ancient gates.

"Follow me and careful of the wet stones; they slip like soap. As a matter of fact, John broke his ankle right at this very spot not too long ago," cautioned Sam.

Scott looked down and stepped carefully around the round and shiny rocks, polished by winds and water for centuries. They exited from behind a column of boulders and landed on a small, hidden stretch of sandy beach that could only be seen from the sea.

"Here we go, Scott, welcome to my office," Sam said laughingly. "Not even the guards know about this place."

Scott looked around and realized that nature had built a totally private twenty-meter-long beachfront with protective giant boulders guarding visitors from the cold wind.

"Now the surprise," Sam whispered and moved toward the end of the beach. "Welcome to Captain Sam's own private cave," he said and pointed between two giant boulders. Scott looked and saw a small opening and darkness beyond. Sam put his right hand behind the left side boulder, searching, and finally pulled out an old leather handbag. He opened it and revealed from inside a couple of Cokes, a large flat bottle opener, and a flashlight.

"Follow me, Scotty," he said, switching on the flashlight and heading into the crevice. Scott followed, and a few feet inside the flashlight illuminated a small cave.

"Welcome to my pirate cave, mate!" Sam said, waving the flashlight around. Scott grinned widely and nodded in amazement.

"Wow, now this is really cool!" he said excitedly.

Sam pointed at the floor and said, "Take a seat, mate, and have a smoke," as he produced a pack of Lucky Strikes and offered one to Scott.

"Thanks, but I don't smoke," Scott shyly responded, not wanting to turn down his friend's offer.

"It's ok, bud. I only started this year," Sam said.

Sam lit the cigarette, and took a long, deep drag followed by a loud swallow of Coke. "My old man says sixteen is the first year a man has no more excuses."

He finished by letting out a deafening burp and yelling at the top of his voice.

"Fuck you, Santa!" They both broke out in laughter, almost falling from their sitting positions.

"Fuck you, Santa?" repeated Scott. "What's that about?" he asked.

"It's an Alcatraz saying the inmates yell at Christmastime, I guess they mean that they don't give a fuck if Santa doesn't bring them any gifts. It's like a big fuck-you to the world beyond this place, you know what I mean?" asked Sam.

Scott nodded in amusement and looked at the mesmerizing waves.

"So, how many days are you staying, bud?" asked Sam.

"Two more," Scott responded, a bit sadly.

Sam looked at the dog tags still hanging outside his shirt and asked, "Where did you get those?"

"These were my father's. He died in the Korean War when I was three," he explained, showing Sam the tags.

"Sorry to hear that, buddy," replied Sam. "My old man didn't go, he became a prison guard instead, and now he's a captain here on Alcatraz." There was a tone of pride in his voice.

Not to be outdone, Scott piped up, "My father died in battle and received the Medal of Honor for conspicuous gallantry and intrepidity in action at the risk of his own life above and beyond the call of duty on June 2, 1951."

Scott recited the Medal of Honor citation almost robotically, his eyes emptying their gaze toward the horizon. Sam felt embarrassed having admitted that his father chose the prison over Korea, even more so after seeing Scott's demeanor in speaking of his father's death.

"I'm sorry, Scott, but you must be so proud of him. I mean, the Medal of Honor, that's amazing," said Sam with respect and thoughtfulness.

Scott turned to his new friend and replied sullenly, "If you ask my mother and me, a medal can never replace a husband and a father, no matter how well they write the epitaph."

The maturity of Scott's words caught Sam by surprise and he realized that Scott was no ordinary boy.

"I'm sorry for bringing all this up, Scott," Sam apologized. "Didn't want to make you feel bad, but it's not every day someone sees the real dog tags from the Korean War."

"It's OK, Sam, I'm OK. It's just that ever since I found out we were coming to Alcatraz, I've been thinking about my father nonstop," Scott offered, sounding a bit overwhelmed. "Can't figure out why. I mean I think about him a lot but not like this."

"I don't know, buddy, maybe deep down you wish he was with you and your mom. I mean, it's not that common someone gets to come to Alcatraz, especially as a civilian," Sam said sympathetically.

"Yeah, my mother mentioned that if my father was around he would've come with us, but the feeling I have is much more than that. I can't explain it," answered Scott, staring at the light coming through the cave's opening.

Sam stood and, kicking the sand off his running shoes, tried to change the subject. "So, Scott, I heard my mom say that your mom is an army nurse at the Presidio. You live on the base? That must be fun."

Scott appreciated Sam's empathy and attempt to brighten the mood.

"Yessir! We live on the base and my mother is a lieutenant army nurse! As a matter of fact, if we had binoculars I could show you my bedroom window from here," he said and pointed his index finger toward the Presidio.

"No way!" Sam yelled. "I'll get my father's binoculars tomorrow and you can show me the house."

"Great idea, Sam," replied Scott, adding with enthusiasm, "and guess what, when I get back, we can signal each other on a clear night with our flashlights. I look at the searchlights on Alcatraz almost every night."

"Don't be stupid, it's too far for a flashlight," Sam replied with a pat on Scott's back. Then he looked at his watch and said, "Let's head back, I need to do some chores for my old man."

They started the hike back accompanied by silence and thoughts of their new friendship. Both boys felt like they knew each other for a long time.

When they reached Building D they waved goodbye. "See you later, alligator!" yelled Sam, and they both started singing the popular 1961 Bobby Charles refrain as they simultaneously laughed and ran to their apartments.

CHAPTER 9

1962, ALCATRAZ

Frank watched the boys walking away and focused on the back of Scott's head. His face revealed no emotion, but he was drenched with a cold sweat that, combined with the chilly wind, produced a continuous uncontrolled shiver. He quickened his pace, hoping the physical activity would warm him, but the more he moved the colder he felt. He remembered having the same feeling in Korea and he recognized its source: fear.

The dog tags and Roy's name had reached deep into his mind, opening the darkness of the past. A special type of fear was the master of men during war, and hidden memories were unlocked by the tags on that kid.

Roy Easten. Lieutenant Roy Easten, how was it possible? Ten years later on this godforsaken rock, and he read his name on dog tags worn by a kid. "What the fuck is that all about?" he asked himself, knowing there was no answer to the impossible coincidence.

"Come on, guys, let's finish up," barked Trevor, bringing him back to reality. They quickly picked up the overflowing garbage bags and rakes and headed back for the main prison building. After dumping the garbage in a large green barrel, they entered the tool shed and hung their rakes on the wall.

"Let's go!" snapped Trevor once again. He always felt the need to show he was in command, the perfect cliché of a powerless man doing what he needed to live with himself.

The two cons and Trevor entered the dim cell block and headed directly for the middle of the left cell block row. Frank felt even colder as he entered his cell and rushed to wash his hands and face, with the frozen tap water sending shivers up his spine. He heard his cell door close, and, for the first time since he arrived, felt safe and secure from the outside world.

He climbed into his bunk and covered himself with the brown, standard prison-issued blanket. He tried to control the shivering that pulsated through his body.

Shoving his head into the pillow, he began rubbing his arms, chest, and legs in an effort to get warm. A few minutes passed, and he felt slightly better and under control. The dog tags returned to his mind and he realized that facing them was the only way to gain back his control.

He closed his eyes and Roy Easten's face materialized. Lieutenant Roy Easten was a pure warrior leader. He had instincts and inspirational traits that anyone would desire in a leader during a time of war.

They met in boot camp and reached Korea in 1951, and fought side-by-side for almost eight months. In battle, most people take cover and wait to see what everyone else is doing. Not Roy—he knew what to do and when to do it. That is what a natural warrior does. Everyone in the squad followed him because Roy always found the time to show them what had to be done.

They recognized Roy's ability to remain alert, a quality more remarkable than it sounds. All war veterans remember that the most difficult part of war is not combat, but the waiting. Most of their time was spent shuffling here and there, and the actual fighting was just a small percentage.

Frank felt the warmth of the blanket reach his core and his shivering come to a stop. He continued his recollection of the tedious lulls during war; how the quiet gives birth to gloomy thoughts, stress, and fear. These deathly quiet moments make war indeed a living hell. As a result, everyone complains, grumbles, bitches, and in the end just wants to go to sleep.

Sleep is the best defense a man has against his fears.

But the natural warrior does not allow the quiet moments to control his thoughts and Roy was that sort of man. He would be off in the corner oiling his rifle, arranging his gear, always preparing for battle. And although everyone wanted to ask him what the fuck he was doing, they all knew he was right and, somehow, he gave them the strength to follow his actions.

Frank recognized in Roy the same traits as his leader back home. Don Cabineri was also a natural leader of men. He protected the honor of the family and always performed the essential duty of a leader before battle; he gave everyone the conviction that they were right, and the enemy was wrong.

Men cannot go to war believing they are wrong. And this conviction of righteousness can only be given by a natural leader, a true warrior. Roy could have led any group of men, gangsters or soldiers alike, and they would have followed him because he truly believed that winning the war was his personal responsibility.

Most soldiers try to be inconspicuous when the captain asks for night patrol volunteers. But Roy would already have camouflaged his face and been ready to fight, kill, or die. That was Roy Easten, and he had saved Frank's life, and this, Frank could and would never forget.

Frank shook his head once again, thinking of the dog tags. Maybe it was a dream and he had not seen them? But then the image came back, and Roy's face materialized in his mind. "Who was that kid?" he asked himself.

He searched his memory for any clues that Roy may have given to him about his family back home. He concentrated, and like an unveiling fog he remembered walking up to Roy's bunk while he was lying down reading a letter from back home. On his chest lay a photo, a photo that he picked up and proudly showed him as Frank sat on the bunk next to his.

"Hey, Frank, let me introduce you to my son Scott," he recalled Roy saying with pride. "Be careful, Franky, if you have any daughters, my friend, this boy will be a heartbreaker when he grows up." Frank remembered the family portrait with Roy in his uniform, his wife, and a round-faced blond baby in between them smiling toward the camera.

"Fine-looking boy, Lieutenant, but I'm sorry to disappoint you, my daughters will be boys and they will both be known as the heartbreak brothers of New York!" Frank remembered answering and hearing the laughter from the rest of the guys in the barracks.

"Frank's daughters will be boys! Hell, Frank, is that because of their beards?" yelled someone from the nearby bunks.

"Fuck you, Dennis! At least my kids' names won't be mistake number one and mistake number two," Frank replied, laughing even louder.

"Enough horseplay, boys!" yelled Roy with a commanding voice. "Lights out, children, we have a picnic starting tomorrow at five hundred hours." He concluded by carefully folding his letter and sliding it and the picture back into the envelope.

"Picnic" was what Roy would call a forty-mile hike finishing with a three-mile double-time dash back to the camp.

Frank opened his eyes, returning to reality, and repeated Roy's words, "Hey, Frank, let me introduce you to my son Scott." *Could that boy today be Roy's son?* Frank wondered.

Eleven years had passed, and Roy's son would be approximately the same age as the boy with the dog tags, plus Roy was from San Francisco.

The puzzle began to take form in Frank's mind except for one thing: What was Roy's son doing on the Rock? Had his wife remarried to one of the guards or civilian personnel? *That could be it,* Frank thought. *Yes, so she was also here.* He felt exhausted, drained, and needed sleep to bring him peace. His eyes closed, and he drifted into darkness. In the darkness of sleep, he dreamed of his last moments with Roy.

The enemy was pounding our defenses near Chipo-ri under a sunless sky. Our orders were to guard the rear of the 2nd Infantry Division as it retreated in the face of overwhelming odds, under attack from five Chinese divisions.

"Listen up, men," yelled Captain Simpson, with Roy at his side as second in command. "We need to give everything we have today. The gooks are throwing everything they have on us and the 2nd Infantry Division is the only thing holding our front lines from breaking apart."

Captain Simpson looked at our faces and continued with confidence. "I know that you will hold the fort as always. Lieutenant Easten will give you your individual orders. Godspeed, men!" the captain concluded and headed toward the HQ tent.

"OK, guys, you heard the man," called Roy. "Johnson take four men and man the left side machine nest defenses."

Roy's voice had a certain ability to be both commanding and reassuring. Frank remembered its vivid tone deep in his dream. "Everyone else follow me; the gooks are waiting for us to kick their asses." Roy waved his arm and we followed him up the hill.

Even in his dream, Frank's unique ability to remember details filled his subconscious. Close to the small ridge the ground became slippery with sludge and we were met with sounds of screaming and screeching soldiers. They walked between fallen men, titian-red blood spurting from their wounds. A gash of radiant yellow light broke through cauldron-dark clouds, revealing the destroyed burning vehicles, smashed trees, and fallen bodies of the surrounding battlefield.

The ground became softer and the sludge thicker, the steps and boots of the men sticking deeper and getting harder with every step forward. Movement slowed just like in a nightmare when you're frozen by fear and unable to run away. Frank looked at Roy waving the platoon onward and urged his legs forward with greater determination.

He had brought his men through many dangerous moments in the past and they trusted he would find a way for them to survive once again. Johnson, the radio operator, came quickly up to Roy and whispered in his ear, and Roy's face froze with a combined expression of anger and sadness. He turned and flatly gave the news.

"Captain Simpson is dead. The HQ tent was hit by battery fire, no survivors. I have been ordered to relieve him immediately. OK, guys, let's go make the captain proud by killing as many gooks as possible. Keep your heads down after the ridge."

We silently followed over the top of the ridge, almost in unison. Frank looked around and noticed that the surrounding sludge was burnished with human tissue, and a sickly odor rose up from it. Suddenly the sound of machine gun fire was concentrated on our position and Roy commanded at the top of his voice.

"Take cover! Rogers, Thomson, give me cover fire!"

Frank felt a gust of warm air and a fountain of blood soaked his face. It tasted vinegary. He turned and saw Thomson's body falling, half of his head and face missing. He jumped forward, following directly behind Roy, who jumped into the safety of a bomb crater littered with bodies.

"Keep your heads down, men, we need to kill those goddamn machine gun nests," Roy shouted, then turned to see it was only me with him in the crater. He looked back at our previous position and saw the others were either pinned down or dead.

"Fucking bastards!" he screamed, and taking aim, he raised his body out of the crater and emptied his M2 toward the enemy positions down the ridge. Frank could hear the hissing of the bullets passing overhead and pushed his back into the sludge, while watching Roy attempt to cheat death, firing back with his body half out of the crater.

Abruptly Roy's body jerked backward, his shoulder rising toward his ear. He fell on his knees, his left hand reaching for his right arm. Frank saw a red circle of blood seeping through his jacket, staining his sleeve and finally dripping down his fingers, and his spine tingled with fear. Roy defiantly reloaded his M2 carbine and looked straight into Frank's frozen eyes.

"Don't worry, Franky, help is on the way," he told him with confidence, trying to give him hope. *Immortal Achilles was wounded,* Frank thought, remembering the Don reading to him from *The Iliad* when he was young.

Thick smoke passed over the crater in intervals, providing a game of hide-and-seek between them and their enemy. Roy once again raised his body and emptied his M2 blindly in the direction of the incoming rounds, red-hot bullet casings flying through the air and sizzling as they contacted cold slush.

He ducked below sight and reloaded again, grimacing from the pain of using his wounded shoulder. He looked at Frank; it was the first time he saw Roy's eyes blank of expression. They seemed to be looking at something else, like they were searching another place, another time. He was looking straight at Frank, but Frank knew that Roy could not see him.

The enemy's battle cries and screaming brought them both back to reality, and then the grenade fell, right between them. They watched it land simultaneously, and sink, half buried in the sludge waiting to spread death.

Roy reacted without hesitation. He flung himself on top of it and stared straight into Frank's eyes for the last time. A diffused explosion pushed his body upward and violently slammed him back to the ground. The blast covered Frank's body with sludge and blood, and he stopped breathing, thinking that death felt a lot like living.

Frank heard and felt the enemy jump into the crater and one of them stepped hard on his left arm, pushing him even deeper into the sludge. Their screaming commands froze his blood, aiding his ability to play dead. He knew the slightest movement would be his last.

The tip of a bayonet pricked his left thigh, prying for life, and he didn't know why but the blade entering his body felt mesmerizing, even magical. He felt its cold but not its pain. Numbness was saving his life. The deeper it entered, the more it convinced the gook he was dead. It pushed farther inside, stopping only at the resistance of bone, then, satisfied that it found death, it slowly withdrew.

More yelling followed, and suddenly the crater was empty. Frank allowed himself to breathe, and slipped into unconsciousness.

Hours later he was awakened by strong arms pulling him out of the sludge and onto a medical stretcher. "This one's alive, Sergeant!" yelled one of the medics.

"Send him with the second wave back to the M.A.S.H, Corporal!" replied the deep-voiced sergeant.

They pulled the stretcher almost vertically out of the crater, and Frank looked down at Roy's body as they turned it face up. His eyes were still open, still searching. The medic grabbed and snapped his dog tags. He separated the tags and pushed one inside Roy's mouth, hanging its twin with a stack of others, dangling off his belt. Then the stretcher flopped back to the ground, and Frank could only see dark clouds.

A few minutes later, two medics carefully wheeled him up the muddy road to a waiting transport truck. As they pulled him on the truck, he looked back and realized that Roy was staying there forever. He died to save Frank's life. A life that, compared to Roy's, was not worth saving. Roy Easten was an honorable man, a true hero and leader of men. Frank was a low-life criminal. "Why should he die, and I live?" Frank pondered. "Why this sacrifice?"

After the battle it was reported that more than five thousand American soldiers were killed, wounded, or captured, and many of those taken prisoner did not survive the harsh conditions of North Korea's POW camps. Only one officer from the 2nd Engineering Battalion evaded both capture and death.

All this in mind, the painful question woke Frank up. His eyes opened, and he was once again in his prison cell, far from the nightmare of the battlefront. He knew this question would haunt him for the rest of his life or at least until God revealed the answer. "Was I saved for a reason? Or was it just chance, pure chance, an event without meaning?"

Up to today he had believed the latter, but now the dog tags had found him. Roy had found him.

CHAPTER 10

1962, NEW YORK CITY, BROOKLYN HEIGHTS

The stench of the sealed apartment engulfed him as he walked into the living room awakening the old wooden floorboards, which screamed in high-pitched creaks under every heavy step of his perfectly shined black shoes. As he closed the door behind him, the doorknob tongue resisted, wanting to retain its freedom. Finally, inertia snapped it into its waiting tomb, signifying its entrapment with a loud clunk. The dull metallic sound reverberated throughout the dusky three-bedroom apartment, and slowly faded to silence.

He stood perfectly still, looking at the reflection of his six-foot, four-inch heavy build in the full-sized mirror; he admired himself in his new black wool and Vicuña overcoat. Turning sideways, he studied his form while pushing his right hand under the coat's lapel, toward its interior pocket. He loved the feel of the satin lining and caressed it habitually, checking for his wallet.

Drawing his hand out, he remembered the coat salesman's descriptive pitch. *"Made with the finest and softest wool in existence, this rare Peruvian Vicuña was woven in Scotland; the coat is lined in satin and has an interior pocket and two exterior ones."*

He smiled, revealing a perfect set of white teeth that, combined with large, round, olive-black eyes and almost perfectly symmetrical cheeks, nose, and jaw, were good reason for the long list of dames wanting to nourish his undying hunger.

His lips had a fullness usually associated with a good-natured character, but when looking closer at the corners of his mouth, not the faintest hint of a smile line existed.

He focused on his eyes' reflection and silently whispered, "Mr. Adams, why did you take the coat?"

His smile grew even larger remembering Sherman Adams, President Dwight Eisenhower's 1958 powerful chief of staff, and one of Washington's most influential men. His career had ended abruptly after he accepted a $21,000 Vicuña overcoat from a textile magnate under federal investigation. Despite his protestations of innocence, he resigned in a scandal that was dubbed the Vicuña Coat Affair.

The smile disappeared as quickly as it had appeared, and his eyes began scrutinizing the apartment's high ceilings, yellowing walls, and plaster ornamentation. He listened intensely for any noise out of the ordinary, whether from the interior or the exterior of the residence. Satisfied with his going-over, he turned and walked toward the living room's rectangular windows and hid behind drawn, heavy, dark brown curtains.

He stood sideways and slightly drew open the curtain, still hiding from view. His facial expression showed disgust, as the humid smell of cigarettes, deep-fried burned oil, and age poured out of the curtain at his touch.

Looking downward he scanned Hicks Street from left to right and back again, then focused on the side wall and backyard of Grace Church. He smirked remembering the Don's reaction when he told him that the new safe house he bought was in Brooklyn Heights, right across the street from a church.

"Antonio my boy, now that's what I call *safe!*" he had exclaimed. "*Sicuro, mio rapido angelo.* Bravo Antonio, it makes sense that my swift angel finds such a safe house for the family."

Antonio Ganvelosi was born in the city of Palermo, Sicily, in 1923 and had entered the United States on December 23, 1936, at Norfolk, Virginia, aboard the ship *SS Vincenzo Florio*. He had been sent by his uncle Santo Ganvelosi after his parents' fatal car accident. Antonio was thirteen and could not survive alone the hardships of Palermo, especially as an orphan.

His uncle arranged the voyage and provided enough money to endure the month-long transatlantic trip. He finally joined his cousins and began his American rebirth in New York City.

Three years later, he joined a crime family headed by Joseph Cabineri, one of the larger crime families in the city. Antonio became involved in robbery, thefts, and illegal gambling.

By twenty-one, he was a made man and inducted into the Mafia or Cosa Nostra, Italian for either "This thing of ours" or "Our thing," depending on who's translating.

The old prewar, three-story apartment house on Hicks Street was known only to himself and Vinnie Tangliazo; they had bought the place in '61 for any emergencies the future may bring. He smiled remembering the boss giving them the order.

"Antonio, go with Vinnie and buy something in Brooklyn Heights. Preparing for the future is what made the Roman Empire great," ordered the Don.

Less than a year later, it seemed that the future was now. It was the first time that it would be used as a safe house for the family, and looking at the church right across the street gave him a strange sense of security.

The ringing phone broke the stale-smelling room's silence like glass.

He picked up the receiver but waited to first hear the caller.

"Hello, hello, boss, it's Vinnie," came a voice.

"Yeah," he acknowledged.

"We just passed the bridge and should be there in an hour. Fucking traffic is crazy coming into the city," reported Vinnie.

"OK," he responded and gently put the receiver back.

Antonio walked toward a stocked bar opposite him, while looking at himself in the mirror behind the booze. He opened a bottle of Canadian Club and sniffed the contents as he always did, before pouring himself half a glass. He savored the first swallow and the burning sensation deep in his throat.

From his pocket, he pulled a gold cigarette case lined with Lucky Strikes, then put one to his lips and lit it with a gold-plated lighter. As he inhaled deeply, the smoke combined satisfyingly with the whiskey's aftertaste.

Pulling the folded *New York Times* from inside a deep coat pocket, he opened it, reading once again the front-page headline: "Three Alcatraz Convicts Cut Their Way Out with Spoons." 13 June 1962. *Ten days have already passed*, he thought.

Antonio removed his coat and carefully laid it over a living room chair. He sat deep inside a brown leather chair and put the glass on the coffee table. He aligned the newspaper and began to read the article once again, possibly for the twentieth time. No matter, each time he relished every word even more.

"SAN FRANCISCO: Three Alcatraz convicts, serving long terms for robbery, used spoons to dig and cut their way out of the island penitentiary in San Francisco Bay early today. Whether they escaped to the mainland, drowned, or found hiding places along the island's waterline was still undetermined, at nightfall."

He filled his mouth once again with whiskey and brought the cigarette to its end, then pulled out another and lit up before continuing.

"Helicopters, patrol boats, and roadblocks were used in the search, which covered the Golden Gate, bay islands, and hilly, deep, indented Marin County shoreline north of Alcatraz. The missing convicts are Frank L. Morris, 35 years old, and John Anglin, 32, and Clarence

Continued on page 28, column 2"

He turned to page 28, then half-folded the page to column two.

". . . Anglin, 31, brothers. The break was believed to have been masterminded by Morris, who has an intelligence quotient of 133. Average IQ is considered to range between 90 and 110."

The loud rattling of a passing truck turned his gaze toward the window and he waited until the sound dissipated. Taking another puff, he returned to his reading.

"The three men combined extraordinary patience with considerable ingenuity. Using spoons, they dug through the four-inch concrete wall of their cell block over a period of many months. Within easy visual range of guards in the gun galleries around the federal prison, they loosened rivets in a five-foot section of ventilator to prepare for their flight. They postponed discovery of their escape by the use of dummies in their beds. The dummies had plaster heads made lifelike with painted faces and hair contrived from the bristles of paintbrushes."

Antonio stopped and smiled, shaking his head in disbelief. He loved this part; *it was better than fucking sex,* he thought. "Well that makes sense when you consider that these guys fucked the system," he joked to himself.

"Officials of the penitentiary said evidence indicated the fugitives may have used an improvised raft or driftwood to get away from the island. The nearest shore is Marina Green on San Francisco's northern edge, one and one-quarter miles to the south.

Yesterday, Morris and the Anglin brothers were locked in their cells, along with the 264 other inmates, at 5:30 p.m., the usual lock-up time. They were seen by a guard on the 9:30 p.m. inspection tour. Thereafter, on two checks, guards reported the three convicts sound asleep in their cots.

At 7:15 this morning, the guards, making a routine head count, discovered the dummies and sounded the alarm."

Antonio imagined the guard yelling at the sleeping convicts to wake up, and the fright and wonder of pulling their blankets back and revealing dummy heads and pillows for a body. He imagined the painted dummy eyes looking back at the guards, laughingly saying, "Fuck you, motherfuckers." He would bet a thousand clams that they had painted a smile on every one of those dummies just to smirk at the guards when they were found. He smirked himself and reached for another Lucky Strike.

"The other convicts were kept in their cells so that custodial officers could be free for a search of the twelve-acre land. In the vacated cells, guards found the worn stubs of spoons, stolen from the mess hall. The convicts had used the spoons to chip at a mesh-covered air vent at the base of each cell. They had camouflaged this work with cardboard painted to resemble mesh. How they obtained and hid the cardboard and paint and plaster for the dummies was a mystery. Sometime during the night, they squeezed through the widened apertures they had cut in the wall, emerging into a utility alleyway between the cell blocks. They climbed drain pipes to the top of the block and made their way through a ventilator to the roof."

The screeching of car brakes broke Antonio's attention, and he hustled back to the window. A car had stopped in the front of the next house and an elderly couple exited and headed for the staircase. The old woman waved good-bye and the driver yelled, "See you next week, Mom!"

He had instinctively put his hand on the gun below his left armpit—this instinct had saved his life on several occasions. Clear of threats, he pulled his hand out of his jacket and returned to the chair, picking up the glass and emptying it with a hungry swallow. He half-filled the glass again and sat in the warm leather with the newspaper opened as before.

"In clear view of a gun tower, they moved across the roof and then descended a wall by sliding down a kitchen vent pipe, about fifty feet to the ground. The wall was brightly illuminated by a searchlight.

The search was joined by agents of the Federal Bureau of Investigation, the Coast Guard, the California highway patrol, Sheriff's deputies, and policemen of various cities in the area.

No trace of the fugitives was found.

Warden Olin G. Blackwell, who abandoned a fishing trip to return to the prison, was asked if the men might still be on the island. 'I don't know—I just don't know,' he said."

"That's right, fucking asshole, you definitely DON'T know!" Antonio said out loud, followed with a final "Fuck" that exited with contempt and disgust.

He looked at his watch. Half an hour had passed since Vinnie's phone call. He shifted deeper into the chair and continued reading.

"The most spectacular escape attempt in the twenty-five-year history of the prison occurred in May 1946, when thirteen convicts seized a cell block and held off even the Marines for two days. Two guards and three prisoners were slain. Two other convicts were later executed for their role in the attempt.

Morris is under a fourteen-year sentence for the burglary in 1955 of a bank in Slidell, LA. The burglary was carried out after Morris escaped from the Louisiana State Prison at Angola, where he was serving a ten-year term for armed robbery."

He placed the paper on the coffee table and closed his eyes, listening to the silence.

He must have dozed off, because the doorbell shook him back to reality and his hand once again searched for the security of his .45.

Irritated, he pushed the downstairs buzzer. He hated waking up like this. Footsteps came up the main staircase, and Antonio unholstered his gun and unlocked the apartment door. Opening it slightly with his back to the wall, he held the gun extended, and ready for any strange head that might appear.

Vinnie's distasteful laugh came just before his large, bald head. Antonio pushed on the door with all his weight, catching Vinnie's top torso in between the door and the casing, and he heard him growl in pain.

"What the fuck!?" called out Vinnie.

The gun barrel touched his temple and pushed inward just enough to make him once again call out in pain.

"*Bang* you're dead, stupid idiot. What's a matter with you, no checking what's behind the door?" barked Antonio. "I'm telling you, Vinnie, the fucking peace is making you soft and *BANG*! One day you'll wake up in hell not knowing how you got there."

Antonio was yelling and spitting on Vinnie's vised face, hoping this time his message would get through that thick skull.

"I'm sorry, boss, but no one knows about this place and I thought," Vinnie caught himself midsentence. ". . . don't worry, it won't happen again."

"I'm not worried, Vinnie, because we are protected by the enormity of your stupidity."

Antonio loved quoting movies, and Alfred Hitchcock's *Notorious* was one of his favorite flicks. Whenever he could, he would use this line to get a laugh from the guys.

Stepping back, Antonio released Vinnie from the grip of the door and his friend entered, rainwater dripping from his thick black hair. But he seemed oblivious to any discomfort.

"You got me, boss!" he said, followed by whistling laughter that came through his mouth and nose.

"Well did you get him?" asked Antonio.

"Yeah, boss, he's still in the trunk, wanted to make sure everything is ok," answered Vinnie.

"OK, great! Make sure the street is empty and bring him up," said Antonio.

"Sure thing, boss, right away," said Vinnie as he turned to leave the apartment.

Antonio refilled his glass and anxiously waited. A few minutes later, he heard the knock on the door and, as he opened it, Frank Morris walked in wearing a dark blue sailor's coat and cap. A broad grin filled his face and eyes and he shouted, *"Andiamo e ritorniamo paisan*! Let's go and let's return, brother!"

Morris recited the old Sicilian war quote perfectly. Being part of the Cabineri family since he was eight years old, he spoke and understood enough Italian to communicate effectively.

"The Don told me to tell you *benvenuto a casa*, welcome home, brother," Antonio said, and they kissed once on both cheeks, shaking hands with their right hand while placing their left hand on the other's shoulder. Antonio was like a brother to him but the Don was truly his father, and he suddenly remembered his words.

"Francesco, always remember that a man is defined by his honor. And honor is defined by the rules by which you choose to live," the Don said. "The first step to being an honorable man is your personal sense of justice. If you are wronged, it is up to you to redress the wrong. We do not run to the state to do our bidding. We redress this wrong personally.

"Of course, for this to work, every family member must clearly understand what is wrong and what is right. This common sense of justice and the rules that apply is what we call Cosa Nostra. When you return from war you will be ready, you will have proven your honor, and then you will belong to the family forever."

Don Cabineri had told him this after Frank volunteered for Korea. He was saddened that Frank had enlisted, but also very proud that he was willing to fight for what he believed was right. It was an act of honor, and Don Cabineri told everyone proudly that Francesco was "like the Christian knights going off to fight the infidels."

"Francesco *sta combattendo per la Cristianità*! Francesco is fighting for Christendom!"

Don Cabineri kept his promise, and Frank became the first half-Sicilian to be fully initiated in the family. He personally sponsored Frank to be a made man, and stood proudly next to him when he took the oath of Omertà, the mafia code of silence.

After the induction ceremony, Frank officially held the rank of *soldato* (soldier) in the family hierarchy. Don Cabineri kissed Frank on both cheeks and introduced him to the gathering.

"I would like everyone to welcome Francesco a *uomo d'onore* (man of honor) into our family, and forever he is to be *one of us*!"

Frank stood next to Don Cabineri, and he understood that to be recognized as a made man in the Cabineri family entailed not only privileges but also duties.

CHAPTER 11

1934, NEW YORK CITY, LITTLE ITALY

Frank never forgot the first time he entered the Don's second-floor, three-bedroom apartment on 146 Mulberry Street in Little Italy. He did not know that houses could have more than two rooms. He was greeted by Mama Cabineri, the Don's wife, and his two daughters.

Mama Cabineri was an elegant-looking, lean-framed, average-height woman with dark, sun-bronzed skin that shined brightly in the light. She had a slender neck and her beautiful face was complemented by the fullness of her natural red lips and perfectly straight Grecian nose. The brightness of her olive-green eyes was enhanced when she smiled. Her glossy thick black hair was pulled back tightly into a large bun.

"Welcome to your new home, Francesco," Mama Cabineri said with a sweet voice. She pointed to her daughters standing next to her and added, "These are your sisters Addolorata and Serafina." She paused. "I say prayers for the souls of your parents every day, Francesco."

She looked up toward heaven, crossing herself.

The Don gently tapped Frank's back and directed him to enter the large living room. He turned to him and said, "Francesco, from this day you have a new family."

He took him into his arms for a quick embrace, and without further words or discussion Don Cabineri completed Frank's induction into his family. From that moment, Don Cabineri always treated Frank like a true son.

Mama Cabineri took Frank by the hand and into the kitchen where she served him a hot dish of spaghetti with oily, rich tomato sauce. He had never forgotten that taste.

Addolorata and Serafina quietly sat at the kitchen table looking at Frank eat. They were both the spitting image of their beautiful mother and could easily be mistaken as twins. Addolorata was two years older than Frank, and Serafina was born a few days after him.

After Frank's arrival in the family, every September Mama Cabineri arranged a common birthday party for both Frank and Serafina with two giant birthday cakes. Both girls treated him like a brother, and Frank immediately accepted the responsibility and emotional attachment that goes with it.

Don Cabineri enrolled Frank in the same Catholic school his daughters were attending, Our Lady of Pompeii School located in the heart of Greenwich Village. Every day, Dino Laventi the Don's driver would drive them to and pick them up from school.

Dino was the Don's most trusted bodyguard and an enormously powerful man. It was Dino who tracked down and wiped out single-handedly the contracted Irish gunmen that had tried to assassinate the Don a few years ago. Dino always operated alone and became the protector, *il protettore* of the Cabineri family. Although he was sheer terror to the Don's enemies, he was Uncle Dino to Frank and the girls, always laughing and joyfully playing with them.

"If you get good grades today, I'll bring you a box of cannolis," he promised them as they drove to school.

"Cannolis is good for the heart, the more you eat the more you want," he sang, laughing with all his heart. "And Signor Frank, don't try to bribe the teacher with a cannoli; I will find out. Uncle Dino always finds out." Dino mentioned this because Frank had already tried to bribe a teacher not to tell his parents he'd been caught fighting.

In the years that followed, the Don continuously showed Frank affection while teaching him discipline, just like he was his own son. He personally took him to the doctor, and Frank especially remembered when he was ten years old and the Don took him to a specialist that cured his painful chronic ear infection. "This *dottore* will make the pain go away, I promise you, Francesco," he told Frank on their way to the doctor's office.

Frank nodded. He did not really know the extent of the Don's power, and the powerful meaning behind his words "I promise you!"

Don Cabineri never made empty promises, nor weak excuses. He did not even request repayment for his help. The only thing he demanded was the voluntary and true declaration of your friendship. After that it did not matter how poor or powerless the applicant was, Don Cabineri would make the man's troubles his own. And he would always promise to find a solution. In this way the Don had been rewarded with many strong friendships and respect.

The Cabineri household would endlessly receive parcels of homemade wine or specially baked sweets as gifts of friendship.

Right after high school, Frank had no desire to go to college, so he told the Don that he wanted to work for him. The Don accepted his decision, and cautiously began to involve Frank in the family business.

By that time, Don Cabineri had grown the family into one of the strongest in New York City. The other families recognized Don Cabineri's unique ability to effectively manage and balance their needs without conflict. The other families were all content with peace; it was more profitable than war and all that they wanted was the means to make more money and have more power.

Of course there were always the ones that could not satisfy their greed, and they were willing to do anything necessary to feed their hunger. Dino started taking Frank with him to explain and re-solve the many conflicts these greedy men created.

In 1950, Frank Morris was twenty-two years old and very happy with his life. He enjoyed the contin-uous action of the Cabineri family business and the personal hustling and schemes on the side. Frank had moved out of the Cabineri house the previous year, when the Don bought and moved to an estate on Long Island. Preferring Little Italy, he found a two-room apartment on the corner of Grand and Baxter.

Frank hung around with Antonio Ganvelosi, who was seven years older and well-versed in the night-life and crazy gaming of New York City. They would also take Vinnie Tangliazo with them. Vinnie was a soldier and sometimes slow to understand, but they liked him as a sidekick. He would always find a way to make them laugh with something he said or did. Also, Vinnie was reporting to Antonio in the family structure and they were glued at the hip most of the time.

The Don told Frank when he moved out of the house that he must be responsible for his financial situation, and that a man's financial situation and savings was proof of his abilities.

"You have a job in the family business and you get paid for that job. You are now a man and very soon will begin your own family," he cautioned. "You ask for independence, but you need to fight for it by proving that you can survive."

Frank understood but never took the Don's advice to save. The amount of money he would spend with his friends was dazzling. The bars and nightclubs were delighted to welcome them and their giant cash tips. Frank spent his money, then would borrow from his friends until the next payday or side score. Borrowing money from friends was seen as a dishonor by the Italian community, but Frank trusted his friends not to tell anyone—they were his brothers. There were always a couple of dirty side deals waiting to be collected. They were known as the Cabineri wolfpack and burned the candle from both ends, going from one club to another, finally waking up with their clothes and shoes still on, either in a free room of the airport or midtown motel managed by the family.

And finally, there were the girls who always cost money. A night around the clubs, expensive motels, and gifts.

Suddenly, on the morning of June 25, 1950, destiny knocked on Frank's life. Waking up next to a beautiful, tall blond called Alison, he heard the loud radio in the next room through the paper-thin motel walls announcing that North Korean troops, in their Soviet-made tanks, had smashed across the 38th Parallel. He dressed and dashed down to the hotel lobby to get more news. A group of men and women huddled over a large Marconi radio set that was loudly and dramatically repeating the news.

"North Korean leader Kim Il-sung sought Chinese and Soviet backing for the invasion; Stalin had agreed on the provision that Soviet troops would not take part, for fear of inflaming a war with America. The invasion began at 4 a.m. local time at eleven different points along the border. President Syngman Rhee of South Korea, who had attempted brutally to suppress communism in the South since the establishment of its government in 1948,

informed the United Nations Commission in Korea that North Korean tanks and armored cars were on their way to Seoul.

North Korean radio justified the invasion by saying it was retaliation for several South Korean border incursions in the early hours of the morning. By noon, it was announcing a state of war between the two sides. The United Nations Security Council immediately denounced the invasion and called for a cease-fire. On hearing by secret communique that Soviet troops would not be deployed, President Harry Truman is determined to prevent the loss of South Korea to communism, and mobilized US forces."

Frank could not explain the feeling that overwhelmed him, listening and looking at the fear on the people's faces around him. All he knew was that he was compelled and obligated to join this fight. He knew that everyone would try to stop him, especially Don Cabineri, but without a second thought he walked out of the motel and headed for the nearest army recruitment office. When destiny commands, nothing can change its course.

CHAPTER 12

1962, NEW YORK CITY, BROOKLYN HEIGHTS

Antonio repeated Frank's words, "Let's go and let's return, brother! That is fucking exactly what you did, Franky my man!" yelled Antonio, grabbing and pulling Frank into his arms. He kissed him in the Sicilian manner and gently smacked his cheek a couple of times before stepping back.

"Let me see you, Frank, lost a couple of pounds, *paisan*! Well I guess the lasagna wasn't too good on the Rock, Franky. We will fix that right away here in New York. Isn't that right, Vinnie?" yelled Antonio with excitement.

"Yeah, that's right, boss, we'll fix that up right away!" answered Vinnie, also excited by the reunion.

"OK, enough bullshit! Get the man a cold beer! Come on, Frank, let's take a sit-down, my man. We have lots of catch-up to do, *paisan*."

Antonio grabbed Frank by the arm and pulled him toward the large living room couch.

"Yes we do, my friend, it's been a long time," answered Frank.

They both sat down, and Vinnie handed them two cold bottles of beer.

"*Cento di questi giorni*," said Antonio, and Frank hit the two bottles together, repeating in English, "One hundred of these days."

He was still dizzy from the long trunk ride, and the cold beer felt like medicine.

"So, Frank, I was reading about the escape. You guys really fucked them over, man! The word is that they think you all bought it in the bay," said Antonio in a more serious tone.

Frank nodded his head with a gloomy expression.

"The other two guys didn't make it; the fucking current took them. I don't think they're alive; the last I saw of them they went under the water heading toward Angel Island. I was lucky and the current split and took me straight to shore," Frank said, sounding tired.

"Here, Frank, maybe this will help; it's yesterday's *Times*," said Antonio, handing him the newspaper.

"Read it to me, Antonio, my eyes are still fucked-up from the salt water. They are burning and blurry," replied Frank.

"Sure thing, Franky," answered Antonio, opening up the paper and taking a serious tone. He deepened his voice more than usual and read slowly, sounding like a radio announcer. Frank closed his eyes and listened and eventually Antonio found his way back to where he had been prior to Vinnie's arrival.

". . . The finding of a plastic bag containing personal effects has strengthened the belief that the three convicts who fled Alcatraz Prison last Monday night drowned in San Francisco Bay."

"That's right, assholes, a drowned man is sitting right next to me right now!" said Vinnie, who was still standing next to the couch.

"Eh, Vinnie, shut the fuck up and sit down over there!" yelled Antonio forcefully.

"Sorry, Frank, you know Vinnie and his big fucking mouth, always blah this, and blah that," Antonio continued loudly.

"Hey, guys, take it easy with the yelling. My head is pounding; give me a break, OK?" pleaded Frank, rubbing his temples and eyes. "Go on, Antonio, finish the article and please don't yell."

"OK, Frank, sorry about that," answered Antonio, staring down Vinnie, who looked back at him with open hands like, *what did I do*?

Antonio repositioned the newspaper on his lap and continued reading more quietly.

"James V. Bennett, director of the Federal Bureau of Prisons, said the contents of the bag had been traced to the three escapees. The bag was encased in a larger one, also of plastic.

"Frederick T. Wilkonson, assistant director of the Bureau of Prisons, who was sent here to investigate the escape, said he leaned to the belief that the three felons had drowned in the bay's swirling currents.

"The escapees are Frank Morris, thirty-five years old and a member of the New York Cabineri crime family, who was convicted of murder conspiracy and other racketeering offenses; and convicted bank robbers, John W. Anglin, thirty-two, and his brother Clarence, thirty-one, both from Florida.

"Officials said the bags had been picked up Thursday afternoon off Angel Island, about a mile northeast of Alcatraz, by a boat of the Army Corps of Engineers, the Coyote. The boat is equipped with a sweep underneath that is used to clean debris from the bay.

"'We were following the riptide containing debris,' the skipper, Captain Edward Thompson recounted. 'Among the stuff we picked up, one of my crewmen pulled out this double bag.'"

"That's right, we hit a riptide—it's like two water faucets running together," explained Frank. "Two different currents met, and the water became very rough, and we split into two different directions. I was on the smaller raft and the guys were on the bigger one, but they had forgotten the second oar and it was hard to navigate. I was already in the water and saw them carry their raft to the surf, climb on, and push off into the dark.

"I could hear them nearby; they were heading toward Angel Island when suddenly I felt the water push me toward the harbor. I got a look at their shadow, and Clarence waved and yelled something, but I couldn't hear him. I was fighting to hold on, and when I looked their direction again, I couldn't see anything but waves."

Frank spoke as if he was talking to the reporter.

Antonio could see that his friend felt bad, and he understood the comradery Frank must have felt for the two men. They had worked together for more than six months to break out, and that kind of experience builds brotherhoods.

"Frank, I don't think you could have done anything to help. Thank God you didn't drown also. And you never know, maybe the guys made it just like you." Antonio comforted him as best as he could.

"I don't think they did, Antonio, the fucking current and waves were really bad, that's why nobody has ever made it from the island to the shore," Frank explained gravely. "Either the currents or the sharks will finish you. I was very lucky, that's for sure. Lucky in Korea and now lucky in Alcatraz."

Frank's face became darker with the mention of Korea and his eyes clouded.

"Go ahead, Antonio, continue the story," he asked quietly.

"Yeah, eh, where was I?" replied Antonio, searching for his place. "Here we go . . . 'my crewman pulled out this double bag.

"'He said it held a receipt for a ten-dollar money order made out to Clarence Anglin and cashed by the mail teller at Alcatraz. It also contained, he said, fifty to sixty photographs of children and adults. There were also several names and addresses. The skipper said he turned his find over to the FBI.'

"One result of the break has been to renew the Justice Department's interest in closing the Federal prison on 'The Rock,' as the tiny island north of San Francisco is sometimes called. This is a political as much as an administrative question for Attorney General Robert F. Kennedy and Mr. Bermett. However, the attorney general said, 'I think we'd be inclined to want to close it.'"

"How about that, Frank, you are responsible for closing down the great Alcatraz! You took down the Rock," announced Antonio. "Now that, my friend, is a hell of an accomplishment. All the other greats who did time there did not do what you have done, even Al Capone. Fuck me, Frank! What a fucking story, man!" yelled Antonio again, his voice filling the apartment.

"Take it easy, Antonio, the windows of the building next door are going to break," Frank said, pointing at the wall.

"Oh, yeah, and this guy Robert Kennedy is one tough son of a bitch." Vinnie changed the subject. "Don Cabineri was saying the other day that the boys in Chicago are really pissed off with him and his brother. It looks like Giancana helped Kennedy win the elections and remember, Frank, it was fucking close, right?"

Frank stopped him, raising his hand, listening to approaching police sirens. They got closer, passed the house, and headed up the street screaming.

"Don't worry, Frank, this place is as safe as it gets," Antonio said confidently. "Nobody knows about it except for me, Vinnie, and the Don."

"That's right, Frank," added Vinnie with vigor, and he continued. "And Frank, regarding the presidential election of 1960, it was one of the closest in American history. J.F.K. won the popular vote by a margin of approximately one hundred thousand votes!"

Frank and Antonio looked at each other and busted out in laughter, almost falling off the couch.

Vinnie had a talent for remembering in detail the strangest things.

Vinnie joined in the laughter and they all fell back on their seats with tears in their eyes. After they regained their composure, Antonio turned to Frank and with a serious tone said, "Frank, Don Cabineri told me to tell you it would be too dangerous for you two to meet at this time, but he wanted me to give you this letter. I'm supposed to take back your answer today."

Antonio pulled a sealed envelope from his pocket and handed it over. Frank took it and without answering, tore it open and began to read silently.

Francesco,

I am so happy and proud of your accomplishment, my son! I am sorry we cannot meet in person, but they are watching my every move and it would be too dangerous for you. Not even the phone is safe for us to use. The bastards are hounding me continuously, but I am a fox they cannot catch. The important thing is that you are safe, and we will make sure that you are even safer. I will share with you my thoughts and you will give your answer to Antonio to bring back to me.

First it is important that everyone believes you are dead; this gives you the power of anonymity and stealth. But in order for you to remain anonymous you will have to make a very serious decision. You must become unrecognizable, and this my boy will be the hardest thing you have ever done in your life.

You need a new face and a new identity; this I can arrange if you decide that you want it. Your other choice would be to run and hide from the hounds for the rest of your life.

If you decide to proceed with this new identity, you will be a secret weapon for the family. A weapon like they have never seen. The dagger of honor, *il pugnale d'onore*. But this new life, Francesco, will be a life lived in the safety of darkness.

If you say yes to this, my son, go to the mirror and look at your incredible face, because as of tomorrow night Francesco Morris will have a new face and a new identity.

I have made all the arrangements and if Antonio returns with your positive answer, your new life begins. A doctor will be brought to you tomorrow morning and everything will happen in the safe house. It is too dangerous to move you. If your answer is no, you can remain at the safe house for as long as you want, and I will arrange for safe passage out of the country. This is the best I can give to you under the circumstances.

Francesco, no matter what your decision is, you have made me very proud, my son, and brought great honor to our family.

I thank you, my *soldato*!

Don Cabineri, your Father!

Frank lowered the Don's letter and looked into space. He knew the Don was right regarding his choices. He could either run and hide forever, or decide to bury Frank Morris, and be reborn into darkness. He also understood the meaning of his new life as the *secret dagger of honor* for the family. He would be the invisible assassin. The execution- er. The ultimate weapon. The ultimate power for a criminal is to have no identity. Then they could never find you or link you to anyone.

He recalled Don Cabineri's word to him: "Fran- cesco, always remember that a man is determined by his honor. And honor is defined by the rules by which you choose to live; the first step to be an hon- orable man is your personal sense of justice."

Twelve years later, he understood and felt deep in his soul that this was his destiny.

He was going to be the dagger of honor, *il pugnale d'onore*!

He looked at Antonio and said, "Tell Don Cabin- eri, YES!"

Antonio understood; taking Frank's hand he kneeled and kissed it, saying, "*Andiamo e ritorniamo paisan*! Let's go and let's return, brother!"

Antonio stood and reached for his coat. "I need to go to the Don's house right away with your answer."

Frank nodded understanding Antonio's urgency.

Antonio fixed his coat lapel and continued. "Vin- nie will drive me, the fridge is full, keep out of sight *paisan*." He opened the apartment door and carefully peered left and right into the empty corridor before exiting and closing the door behind him.

Frank slowly walked up to the door and turned the main lock nob than he secured the chain lock in place. He then walked over to the window over- looking Hicks Street and carefully slightly pulled the curtain open peering down. He saw Antonio getting in the passenger side of the black sedan. The car slowly drove off passing Grace Church picking up speed down the empty street.

Frank's eyes climbed up the churches green molded walls and steeple stopping at the giant cast iron cross. Dark clouds gathered in the horizon and an occasional lightning flash heralded the arrival of another New York summer rainstorm.

The reiterating lightning flashes illuminated the profile of the cross transforming it into a beacon signaling lost souls. Frank looked past the cross into the looming clouds finally excepting that nobody could struggle against their fate, and that everyman has only one destiny. Today he had chosen his destiny without any regret or fear.

The twenty-minute drive from Brooklyn Heights to Little Italy gave Antonio a chance to reflect in silence, he had told Vinnie to keep his mouth shut and just drive when he got into the car. Their many years together had taught Vinnie to know when Antonio really meant what he was saying, so he focused on driving and headed towards Little Italy.

The Black sedan arrived and parked directly outside the main entrance of the Don's building on Mulberry Street. The outside staircase was manned by three security guards 24/7 and one of them ran and opened the sedan's heavy door for Antonio to exit. Antonio looked right and left down Mulberry Street and quickly climbed the staircase, the main door was being held open for him by one of the other guards. The Don did not want to move out of Little Italy and had purchased the three-story apartment building expanding his old three-bedroom apartment into a two floor eight room suite. The first floor was transformed into a reception and office space for his real estate business. The Don felt that his family would be more secure and safe in this location and did not like the seclusion of the mansions the other heads of the family's had chosen to live in. "The neighborhood is our true home, our village; this is where we first came, and this is where we should grow old and die." The Don would say on many occasions.

He reached the second floor and knocked on the door, Silvia the maid opened it wide and waited for him to enter. "The Don is waiting for you in his office Senior Antonio," she whispered to him. He noticed that the house was dark, the curtains drawn and only a few small table lamps were lit. "How is Mama Cabineri?" he asked Silvia. Her eyes filled with tears, she looked down and whispered back. "The Seniora will never be the same, Senior Francesco's loss has taken part of her soul. The girls are trying to comfort her, but she has not left her bedroom three days now." Silvia looked into Antonio's eyes and continued, "Senior Francesco was the son she never had, the son that would have inherited her husband's legacy."

Antonio gently squeezed her arm and started to slowly walk towards the large mahogany office door. He knocked softly and waited for a reply.

"*Entrano*," replied the Don in his usual tone of voice.

Antonio entered the room closing the door behind him, he looked at the Don sitting on his huge leather armchair behind his desk. The Don looked into Antonio's eyes searching to read Frank's decision.

Antonio's eyes sternly spoke back to him and with a single nod revealed Frank's decision to stay.

The Don nodded back accepting his son's decision without any emotions except for a minute of silence. He waved for Antonio to come closer and sit in a chair that was on the side of the desk near him. This chair had been used many times as a place where only the most trusted could sit. Antonio sat and the Don came closer to him whispering almost into his ear. "Antonio, from this moment Francesco is alive only to the two of us." He stopped and allowed the words to embed themselves. "Francesco is dead to everyone that loved and hated him. He drowned in the San Francisco Bay his body taken by the Pacific never to be found." Again, he stopped and listened to the silence of the room. "This very moment his mother and sister's mourn him upstairs. Their tears are real and therefore his death must also be real." The Don's eyes teared, Antonio had never seen the Don like this, and he felt numb by the power of the Don's words.

The Don took another deep breath and his face beamed with a renewed force and strength, looking straight into Antonio's eyes he continued. "Antonio listen very carefully, when Francesco goes for his surgery, you must convince Vinnie that he has left for another country that not even you know where he is. Vinnie must believe this, and he must understand that if he ever reveals to anyone that Francesco is alive, it will be Francesco's death. The long friendship between the three of you is the only reason Vinnie continuous to live, so, I hold you responsible to convince him and make sure he never speaks of Francesco again." The Don's expression now changed into the one that Antonio had seen many times when he spoke and ordered with conviction.

"Antonio, do you understand?" Antonio nodded and bowed his head.

The Don put his hand on Antonio's hand and continued.

"Francesco's new identity must remain our secret until my death. Tomorrow you will begin planning Francesco's funeral, exactly as we would have done if he died. We will bury him and weep at his funeral, comforting his mother and sisters."

Don Cabineri got up and Antonio automatically stood up at the same time. The Don put his hand on Antonio's cheek than embracing him said in Italian, "*Sei sempre stato un buon soldato, e, un vero amico per mio figlio.*"

"You have always been a good soldier, and, a true friend to my son. Now, you will be my only connection to him. Although he lives, for us he will be a ghost. We must learn to live with this pain, and, Francesco must learn to be a dead man among the living, our invincible dagger of honor." He slowly started to walk toward the door and repeated in Italian, "*un invincibile pugnale d'onore.*"

He opened the door and silently went up to his bedroom to comfort his wife and daughters.

Antonio sat back into the side chair for a few minutes in silence and than reaching for the phone began to make arrangements for the funeral of his best friend.

CHAPTER 13

1962, SAN FRANCISCO, PRESIDIO

The sound of a fast-moving helicopter passing above his house returned Scott from his dream, waking him up. He heard his mother bustling in the kitchen below. He stretched his body, and throwing his blanket on the side, sat on the edge of his bed. He looked out the window and could see it would be another sunny day.

"Breakfast is ready, Scotty!" yelled his mother.

He quickly dressed and flew out his room down the staircase, jumping from the fourth step, landing and sliding on the carpet as he did every morning when he came down for breakfast. He ran into the kitchen, following the smell of the bacon like a bloodhound.

"Take a seat, young man, and eat fast, or you're going to be late for school again," said his mother while filling his plate with scrambled eggs and bacon.

"I have some news for you, Scotty, look at the headlines," she continued. "It looks like some of our 'friends' from Alcatraz escaped!"

Scott's eyes widened. He turned the *San Francisco Examiner* right side up on the table and quickly read the bold headline across the top of the front page: "Big Bay Manhunt on for Three Alcatraz Escapees: Bloodhounds on the Rock."

He looked at the three mug pictures of the escapees, and froze on the second picture, immediately recognizing the man's face. It was the guy that caught his baseball, the guy that was cleaning the warden's yard! He read out loud the name under the photo and his eyes widened with excitement even more than before.

"Frank Lee Morris. Ma, I know this guy! This is the guy that gave us the baseball back after I broke the window!" he said excitedly. "He was cleaning the warden's yard and then he caught the ball and then . . ." He spoke as fast as he could, trying to explain to his mother and swallow at the same time.

"Slow down, sweetheart, what are you talking about?!" she replied with an anxious tone.

Scott put his index finger on the picture and repeated, slightly slower this time, "This guy is the guy that caught the baseball after it broke the warden's window. Look right here. This guy."

He tapped the paper with his finger repeatedly and continued.

"Frank Morris. Look, that's his name! Whoa, I don't believe it, wait till I tell the guys at school. That's really cool, I know an escaped convict!" he yelled in his excitement. "Look, they passed right behind our building. It shows their escape route: A) up the roof; B) down pipe; C) over fence; D) into bay. This is so cool! Can I take the paper to school, Ma? Eh, can I?"

His mother turned the newspaper toward her side of the table and started to read the details. A sensation of trepidation filled her. It was scary enough to have escaped convicts in the area, but the news that Scott had met one of them scared her even more.

"I think that you are going to stay home today, young man," cautioned Carolyn Easten. "I don't think it's safe for anyone to be out and about with three convicts roaming around. As a matter of fact, I believe that the mayor will order the school to close today, and for the base to be put on alert." Her voice was steady, but Scott sensed her fear.

"Let me call HQ and see what the orders are," she said, getting up and reaching for the telephone on the kitchen wall. She dialed a number and waited.

"Hi, Sergeant, it's Lieutenant Easten. Any special orders today? Yes, a-ha, OK, clear. Thank you and please call me if there are any developments." She hung up the phone and returned to her seat.

"I knew it—the major ordered general alert, all Presidio base civilians will stay indoors, and that means the school will be closed today," she said, sounding calmer than before.

Scott frowned at the thought of staying home all day. He looked down at his feet and said nothing.

"Come on, Scotty, we're going to have fun together, a whole day relaxing," she tried, but he did not respond. "OK, well let's see what the paper writes about this great escape, and in particular your friend Frank Lee Morris!"

She placed her index finger under the mug picture of Frank and began to read.

"Age 35; height, 5' 71/2"; hazel eyes; black hair; regular build; tattoos: Italian phrase on lower right arm, *Morte prima del disonore*, meaning 'death before dishonor.'"

She stopped and looked at Scott, squinting her eyes inquisitively. "That's strange. His name, Morris, sounds English or Irish. Why would he have a tattoo written in Italian?" she asked out loud, and moved the newspaper closer.

"Three Alcatraz convicts who made their way out, digging through concrete cell walls with teaspoons, were gone without a trace yesterday. Officials of the grim island prison said they were virtually sure they were off the Rock. But whether they had drowned or reached some shore haven was not known. The only clue was provided by a bloodhound which led searchers to a cave where the trio might have prepared for the flight to freedom."

Frank jumped out of his seat yelling, "The pirate cave, I don't believe it! Sam's pirate cave!"

"What are you talking about, Scott?" asked his mother.

He turned red, remembering that he had not told her about his Alcatraz discovery walk with Sam. "Errr, well Sam . . . you remember Sam, right? Well, he took me to the cave down the beach after the baseball game that day. I forgot to tell you!"

Carolyn shook her head, not believing a word, especially after his red face could not hide that he was lying.

"We will speak about this later, young man; your face is redder than Rudolph's nose," she said sharply, then refocused on the article.

"It was learned reliably that the FBI is questioning a fourth Alcatraz inmate, who claims he was supposed to go along, and that the plan had been to make for Angel Island. What credibility authorities place in this story is unknown. If they are in the clear and alive, the convicts are the first to make a successful escape since the Bay-rimmed crag became a federal prison in 1934. At least seven have died trying. Subjects of one of the greatest manhunts in California history are: John William Anglin, 32; his brother, Clarence, 31; and Frank Lee Morris, 35. The brothers were doing ten to thirteen years for deep south bank robberies, and Morris was doing fifteen years for armed assault in a New York crime family assassination attempt."

"Whoa, Scotty! Your friend is quite a character!" exclaimed Carolyn. "New York. A-ha, that explains the Italian tattoo."

"Morris, a convict with a 133 IQ, considered superior, is believed to be the instigator of the ingenious escape."

"Double whoa! Crime family member, plus a 133 IQ. Now that is what I call a top-rated criminal," she commented. "You should have asked him to autograph your baseball! He is quite a celebrity."

She smiled once again at Scott, but her face was full of worry. This man was dangerous, smart, and free. She took a sip of coffee and found where she left off.

"The three vanished completely unnoticed, sometime Monday night or yesterday morning, through an ingenious escape avenue never attempted by their predecessors. Artful dummies in their beds helped the vanishing act. Reports of raft-like objects on nearby Angel Island brought a swarm of investigators there. San Francisco's Marina Green became a popular gawking spot—it is the closest part of the mainland, only a mile and a quarter from Alcatraz.

A special military force was ordered to Angel Island last night, and three families on the island were ordered to evacuate for their own protection."

"You see how dangerous it is?" she reflected to Scott with a meaningful tone.

"At least twenty-five army men were brought into the search."

"These are Presidio soldiers for sure," added Scott with pride. She nodded and continued.

"'A speeding car with three men in it forced a motorist off Highway 108 near Modesto and started a subsidiary manhunt there. But all that was known was that the prisoners were gone, and, in sketchy fashion, how they did it,' said Warden Olin D. Blackwell."

Scott repeated with a high-pitched voice, "Warden Olin Blackwell! He's very black and in a deep well! Olin's in the well!" and burst into uncontrollable laughter that shook his body. He intentionally slipped from his chair onto the wooden floor, slamming his hands and repeating Olin Blackwell.

His mom joined his laughter and they filled the house with the sound. Scott loved it when they laughed together like that. Her face reddened, and her eyes filled with tears that washed away the silent sadness he could see. He knew she missed his father even more than he did.

They slowly recovered, and she fixed her hair and said with a smile, "Let me finish the article and don't make me laugh, OK, Scotty?"

He nodded, and she found the place she had left off, avoiding reading the warden's name again.

His mother continued to read the details of the escape, silently shaking her head with disbelief. "What an amazing story. I bet you they'll make a movie out of it, for sure, Scotty," she added.

"At 5 p.m. Monday, as usual, all Alcatraz inmates were locked in their cells for the night. Lights-out was at 9:30 p.m., and at least one of the escapers was warned to shut off his light by a guard. During the hourly checks at night, the dummy heads—'They sure looked lifelike,' the warden reported, 'the faces were painted flesh color'—reposed convincingly above bodies fashioned of pillow and blanket. Not until 7:15 a.m. head count for breakfast was the escape discovered."

"Wow, this guy Morris is amazing; imagine how long this took them to prepare," added Scott, his imagination visualizing every detail she read.

"During the night, the three scuttled through the small burrows, covering them with cardboard, painted to look like metal vents. Once in the service alley, they went thirty feet up a pipe, dismantled a five-foot stretch of an air-conditioning vent, and somehow pried or wrenched some bars off it. That got them to the roof. By scuttling a hundred feet over the mess hall to the northern end of the prison compound, they were able to clamber forty or fifty feet down an outside drainpipe that was dangerously illuminated by a searchlight. That left them about 100 to 150 yards from the water's edge, between the power plant and the employees' recreation hall at the northeast end of the island. Their choices were few: to crouch in one or more of the numerous small caves that dot the rocky shore, particularly at the nineteen-acre island's north rim, as so many of their predecessors tried with no luck. Or to make a swim for it to Marina Green a mile and a quarter away, or Angel Island nearly two miles to the north. Or to find or fashion a raft from flotsam and go with the tide.

The warden sounded convinced that they were no longer on the Rock. He also explained that for most of the night a moderate 2.7-knot current was flowing past the island toward the ocean, a death trap for all but the most magnificent swimmers. No escape craft was found during a land, sea, and air search. Units of the army, coast guard, FBI, and various sheriff's offices joined in the hunt."

"I heard the helicopters flying this morning," added Scott with excitement.

"The warden was away fishing at Lake Berryessa and sped back upon the news of the escape, arriving about noon to take charge. He said the escapees hadn't taken anything along with them, so far as an inventory could show, and if they were armed it probably was with something they had fashioned themselves."

"What a story," Carolyn repeated and looked at Scott with worried eyes. Then she looked at the clock and said, "I have to go to the hospital for a couple of hours. Promise me you will not step out this door. I'm going to call you every hour to make sure, ok, mister?"

She kissed the top of his head and picked up her bag, heading for the front door.

"Lock up, and, like I said, no leaving the house," she cautioned, and blew him an extra kiss as she left.

CHAPTER 14

1962, NEW YORK CITY

F rank woke up remembering the doctor's voice asking him to count to ten. It felt like just a minute ago. He tried to open his eyes, but flashing jabs of pain filled his head and a deep animalistic groan left his closed mouth.

"Mr. Morris, please don't move your head," he heard a woman say, and felt her hand on his. "I am Nurse Lanfee and will be assisting your recovery. Doctor Jennings has instructed me to explain your rehabilitation program."

Frank tried to speak again, and another flash of pain drove nails into his face. The groan was louder this time, and the nurse squeezed his hand even harder with empathy.

"Please, Mr. Morris," the nurse went on. "Do not try to speak or open your eyes. If you understand what I am saying, please squeeze my hand once for yes and two times for no."

She waited for a response, then asked again, "Mr. Morris, do you understand me?" Frank squeezed her hand once.

"That is excellent," she replied, and continued. "Mr. Morris, your operation went perfectly, and your face has been bandaged for you to heal properly. Rest is absolutely mandatory, and I have elevated your head with several pillows. Please be careful and do not sleep on the side of your face but always sleep with the back of your head on the pillow.

"There are tubes on both sides of your face to catch any drainage. This will prevent fluid buildup and pressure and provide relief from the swelling. Your dressing should be left undisturbed until the doctor removes it in approximately seven days for a first examination. There will be a small amount of bleeding from the incisions for the first twenty-four to forty-eight hours."

At this point, she stopped, adjusted one of the draining tubes and asked in a sweet tone, "Mr. Morris, was that all clear?"

He gently squeezed her hand once and she squeezed back.

"For the first week your face and neck will feel very tight, but don't worry, this is normal. It will also be difficult to open your mouth for several days. Please avoid opening your mouth and turning your head. Understand?"

Frank squeezed.

"That's great, Mr. Morris. Thank you for your co-operation. I know how hard it is, but trust me, in a few days you will feel much better.

"Finally, you should know that numbness is very common and will go away naturally over the coming weeks. Dr. Jennings will visit you tomorrow, and again in seven days. His next visit will be one week later, when the rest of your stitches will be taken out. Dr. Jennings will then schedule a follow-up for two to three weeks later, or as needed."

Frank listened between jabs of pain and found Nurse Lanfee's voice calming. He envisioned her as pretty, a picture driven by desire, as it had been almost three years since he had touched a woman. Though he knew better than to laugh, he found it funny that even with this horrific pain, his hormones drove his top priority.

"The doctor will give you further instructions tomorrow. I am leaving for a few moments, but if you need anything please ring this bell," she added, and he felt her put a small metallic bell in his hand. He listened for her footsteps and heard the door squeak open and close behind her.

Anesthesia aftereffects took command of Frank's consciousness, and he surrendered to the darkness of sleep. It felt as though he woke a thousand times through the night, his mind drifting in a fog of pain and the unending days since his escape. He had traded a cell for the three tiny rooms of the safe house.

After he accepted the Don's offer, his successful transformation was the only priority on his mind. The Don had sent Dr. Jennings to explain what would transpire. Every step was planned to the last detail; Antonio and Vinnie were the only contacts he had. Letters from the Don gave him the strength to honor his pledge.

"Good afternoon, Frank, how are we doing today?" Dr. Jennings' voice woke him, and he instinctively tried to open his eyes, but the imaginary needles shot through his face again and he clenched his fists and moaned.

"Sorry for waking you, but it's time for my first examination. I hope Nurse Lanfee explained in detail the program of the next few weeks."

Frank felt the doctor's hands on the left and right side of his face, his trained fingers very slowly starting to peel back the dressings.

"Let's see what we have done, Frank, me with the scalpel and you with your willpower. A man's willpower is the most important ally to any surgeon," Dr. Jennings said encouragingly. He began to carefully peel back the side dressings and visually inspect the primary stitching.

"Good, very good," said the doctor, and he continued his examination.

"There should be no strenuous activity this first week, as this may increase facial swelling and compromise the result. And absolutely no exercises that require severe turning of the head, for at least the next four weeks after your surgery. After four to six weeks, the areas will be fully healed, and normal activity can be resumed.

"Now remember what I explained before. It will look worse before it looks good. In other words, your scars will go through multiple stages of healing and at times look better or worse. OK, Frank, I will remove the bandages from your eyes but please keep them closed; the light will hurt even with your eyes closed, OK?" He held his hand for Frank's response. Frank squeezed once, and the doctor responded.

"OK, Frank, let's do this," he added, and proceeded to pull back the bandages covering Frank's eyes. The light passed his eyelids, and he once again felt ice picks.

"Just a few more seconds, Frank, and we will finish," Dr. Jennings stated with certainty. Frank squeezed his fists and waited.

"OK, Frank, the examination is over, and everything is good. The initial healing has begun, and the swelling is normal. I will re-dress you and you can rest."

The doctor performed the re-dressing with care, being sure not to touch Frank's sensitive skin.

"I planned and placed your incisions in the most hidden areas, and I am confident they will heal adequately by themselves, but as I explained, if needed I will perform minor revisions to improve their appearance," concluded the doctor, giving Frank a pat on the shoulder.

Frank knew Dr. Jennings was under incredible pressure. This was no typical patient. The Don had made sure to explain that mistakes were not allowed, and if any mistakes did happen, the doctor would need a doctor.

"Frank, I just need you to be patient for a couple more days," the doctor continued. "Nurse Lanfee will be with you continuously, and in two days you will be able to speak again, a little. I will be back in three days, and until then get plenty of rest; sleep helps mend both the body and the mind." And with that, he was out the door.

Frank remembered going to the mirror for the last time before the operation. He wanted to see his face one last time before it disappeared forever, along with Frank Morris. He had looked closely, remembering the description the doctor had given him regarding facial reconstruction.

"We have forty-three mimetic muscles to express emotion and articulate speech. We have four major muscles on each side of the face that move the jaws, and complex lingual muscles that assist in swallowing and speech. The face is also made up of layers of blood vessels, sensory and motor nerves, cartilage, bone, and fat."

He looked deep into his own eyes, and for some unexplained reason his memory flashed back to when he was almost eleven years old and the Don sent him to pick up an envelope from Big Loupa, the owner of the truck repair shop across Dock 3.

Frank walked into the shop and walked slowly toward Big Loupa. "Big" was an understatement. His nearly seven-foot frame and pyramid-shaped head and body stood outside the small garage office. Big Loupa looked at Frank and at his shadow and stood straighter playing with his shadow's length.

"What do you want, boy?" he yelled at Frank. "Come on, boy, speak up!" he barked, knowing his tone was scaring Frank. He liked to scare.

"Don Cabineri sent me to pick up the envelope," whispered Frank.

"Speak louder, you little fuck, what's a matter, you left your balls at home this morning?" He spit at the ground and continued. "Stupid little shit. *Don Cabineeeeeri sent me!*" he repeated, imitating a high-pitched girl. He opened the left drawer and took out a large brown envelope and held it out to Frank.

"Well what are you waiting for, ass wipe? What a fucking dork! Take it and get out of my sight, you little shit!" screamed the giant.

Frank reached for the envelope, his eyes looking at the floor. Eye contact with Big Loupa was always dangerous, especially today with the mood he had. Big Loupa grabbed his arm and pulled him so hard that Frank's small body fell forward, both knees hitting the cement floor, which tore up his kneecaps.

Squeezing his hands together, without a word, Frank stood and looked Big Loupa in the eyes. Big Loupa looked back and, giant hands by his sides, he yelled with delight.

"Madonna, look at those eyes! Look at that, Don Cabineri's little man has the eyes! The eyes that will make him one day command and kill men! *Gli occhi dell'onore inflessibile*, the eyes of unyielding honor. Bravo little man! What's your name?" asked Big Loupa, with almost a tone of respect.

Frank looked up at him and said assuredly, "My name is Frank. Frank Morris."

"Mr. Morris, I need to turn your pillows." Nurse Lanfee's voice returned him to his reality of pain and darkness. He squeezed her hand and knew that whatever his new face looked like, his eyes would always be the eyes of unyielding honor.

CHAPTER 15

1962, NEW YORK CITY

"**G**ood morning, Mr. Morris, today's the big day! Doctor Jennings is going to remove your bandages and you will be able to see and eat normally," Nurse Lanfee almost yelled as she entered the room. Frank sat upright on his bed, and spoke through the bandages.

"Nothing happens to anybody which he is not able to bear, and believe me, sis, the world better be ready to bear my new face," he said mockingly.

She laughed while arranging things on the night table beside his bed.

"I have a surprise, Mr. Morris. I've brought you a transistor radio to make the long nights pass more pleasurably. I fall asleep all the time with the radio on," she added, the sounds of the radio's static reaching his ears. The static turned to twittering and finally music filled the room.

"This is Fred Bernard and you have been listening to the original cast album from the 1956 musical *Li'l Abner*."

"I love musicals," chimed Nurse Lanfee, and she slightly lowered the volume.

"Sorry to be a party pooper, but can you find something closer to the '60s? These tunes make me want a sedative," he replied and moved his head sideways away from the radio.

"Very funny, Mr. Morris, I will see what I can find," she answered, letting out a sigh, followed by static, as she searched to find another radio station. She found a signal and the speaker started singing . . .

"That was Elvis Presley and 'Return to Sender,' the number four song in the top 100 song playlist, and you are listening to KPGM. Up next we have number three, Telstar and the Tornados."

"Now that's better!" Frank perked up, while instrumental music filled the room. A few minutes passed, and the music stopped abruptly. The nurse moved toward the night table to fix what she thought was a bad radio connection, and just before her hand reached the radio dial a clear, troubled-sounding voice came from the transistor.

"We'll have to stand by here just a moment, there may be something . . . happening. Yes, there is. There's a bulletin just handed me from Dallas, Texas . . . an unknown sniper fired three shots at President Kennedy. This is, uh, in connection with President Kennedy, who is now touring Texas as you know. Uh . . . I'll tell you exactly how this reads. 'Dallas—an unknown sniper fired three shots at . . .' and then there's five letters: P-M-O-U-X, then a flash, Kennedy's name is

misspelled, flash again, and at the bottom of this head-line it says, 'Kennedy seriously wounded.'"

"My God, no!" Nurse Lanfee gasped, almost to God himself. Frank tensed, tried to concentrate and digest the news. He did not care much for politicians, but for some reason he always felt that Kennedy was different. Maybe it was that he was also of Irish descent, and Frank believed his father would want him to support the president, or maybe it was that Kennedy also had eyes of unyielding honor. After the flash was read and recapped, the music started but was interrupted several times. Then right after the first interruption, two radio station staff members conversing came through the set . . .

Staff member #1: . . . has been shot.

Staff member #2: Who?

Member #1: Kennedy.

Member #2: The president?

Member #1: Yeah.

This was immediately followed by a bulletin from the WLW newsroom, which read as follows:

"Here is a bulletin from the WLW Comex Newsroom: A late bulletin from Dallas, where three shots were fired at President Kennedy's motorcade today in downtown Dallas. No casualties were reported initially, however the latest flash indicates President Kennedy was seriously wounded, perhaps fatally, by an assassin's bullet. That's all the information we have. A bulletin. A sniper apparently seriously wounded President Kennedy in downtown Dallas today, perhaps fatally. We'll keep you posted as the news comes in to the WLW newsroom."

"My God, Frank, it can't be true," added Nurse Lanfee with a shaking, crying voice, calling him Frank for the first time.

"Let's wait to see what is true; remember the reporters always exaggerate, it's the way they sell news," he replied with a steady voice, trying to calm her.

His inability to see made the situation worse and he suddenly felt insecure and helpless. He needed to take his bandages off, as soon as possible.

"Call the fucking doctor and tell him to come as fast as possible, I need to take off these fucking bandages," said Frank, his tone elevated. "And tell him that if he delays there will be a problem, understood? And believe me he does not want to have a problem with me."

His demeanor shook the nurse back to reality. He had never spoken to her in this manner, so she immediately replied with a trembling, scared voice, "Yes, Mr. Morris, I will call him right away."

Nurse Lanfee hurried down the hallway. A few minutes later she returned, and coming close to him she said with a steady voice, "The doctor is on his way; he was in his office downtown and should be here in about an hour."

"OK, thank you, nurse," replied Frank, feeling bad that he spoke so brusquely before. They had spent almost five weeks together and she never gave him any reason to feel bad.

The radio continued repeating the news almost every five minutes, and roughly forty-five minutes after the first announcement, there was a deafening silence. No music, no voice, no static, and then . . .

"*Ladies and gentlemen, the president of the United States is dead. John F. Kennedy has died from the wounds he received during an assassination in Dallas, less than an hour ago. We repeat, it has just been announced that President Kennedy is dead.*"

After a few seconds of silence, the anchorman repeated the news. "*John Fitzgerald Kennedy, the thirty-fifth president of the United States, is dead at the age of forty-six. Shot by an assassin as he drove through the streets of Dallas, Texas, less than an hour ago. Repeating this, the president is dead, killed in Dallas, Texas, by a gunshot wound.*"

The first movement to Beethoven's "Pastoral Symphony" filled the room. Frank heard Nurse Lanfee crying and visualized the assassin's bullets tearing through Kennedy's body. He was sure that it must have been a head shot. Frank knew his trade well and assassins always aimed for the head. His thoughts were interrupted by the sad, trembling voice of the news anchor.

"*President John Kennedy is dead. The thirty-fifth president of the United States, he was forty-six years old. According to the Constitution, Vice President Lyndon Johnson will now succeed Mr. Kennedy in office. Mr. Johnson will become the thirty-sixth president of the United States, very probably within a few hours upon taking the oath of office.*"

After the news anchor announcement, his coanchor added, "*Well, as a matter of fact, Alan, Lyndon Johnson is now the president whether he takes the oath or not. He is the president.*"

The comment was followed by "The Star Spangled Banner." Frank listened to the words in darkness and flashes of Roy Easten lying dead in the Korean trench materialized in his mind.

His eyes and fists clenched and the pain he felt was cleansing. An image flashed on and off, mingling Roy Easten's face with that boy's face on Alcatraz. The dog tags shined into his blind eyes, and he wondered once again why he had lived, and they had died.

CHAPTER 16

1969, NEW YORK CITY, THE BRONX

Frank Morris softly pumped the gas pedal, listening to the sound of the 409-cubic-inch V8 engine growl like a lion satisfied after a meal. He was in love with his two-door 1962 dark blue Chevy Bel Air sedan, and would brag about it every chance he got, "*La mia Bel è la mia bellezza.* My Bel is my beauty."

He looked at the mirror and ran his fingers through his thick black hair. Even after seven years, he still could not get used to seeing his new face. He pressed the gas pedal once again and switched the ignition off. Pushing open the heavy car door he pulled his six-foot, heavily muscled body slowly out of the car. He closed the door and ran his hand caressingly across the cold sheet metal top of the squared-off car roof.

He looked up at the clear summer night sky of New York and at the majestic view of the full moon and remembered the previous evening's historic event. Frank had watched the moon landing on television and shared the exhilaration and disbelief with another half a billion people, hearing Neil Armstrong's voice coming all the way from the moon and proclaiming that it was a small step for a man but a giant leap for mankind. He was both proud and jealous of Armstrong's achievement; it made him think about his own life and the choices he had made.

For the last seven years, he had been the Cabineri family's infamous ghost hit man, taking out enemies and would-be threats. He had been especially busy after the recent unsuccessful assassination attempt on Don Cabineri, planned and executed by Johnny Tollodali and his eight-man crew. The Don had been saved at the last minute by Dino Laventi's bravery and self-sacrifice. Dino's expert eyes had rapidly recognized the incoming threat and shielded the Don with his body; his chest and face were riddled with bullets from multiple machine guns blazing from the windows of two cars speeding by.

The Don, Mama Cabineri, and their girls were devastated by the loss of their most trusted long-time bodyguard and friend. When Frank heard the news, he did not wait for the Don to give him instructions for revenge. He found and killed the first two of the Tollodali crew right outside their own house. Other hits followed in sequence over a period of a few weeks; the motherfuckers hid but Frank located and executed them one by one. Today was the last and most important hit on his list, and he especially enjoyed taking out the man who gave the command. Tollodali had had it coming for a long time.

After Tollodali had "made his bones" he had received a good living from the Cabineri family—a percentage of a West Side "book" and a union payroll slot. Frank found out after the assassination attempt that Johnny also had extra side activities that supplemented his income. Mainly stickups, strictly against the family rules. But Tollodali's gambling habit led to big debts, and the Don's enemies offered to get rid of his debts if he killed the Don.

Tollodali turned traitor and tried to take out the Don. Frank knew that this was a big mistake; you shouldn't bite the hand that feeds you.

Frank's ghost identity allowed him to move freely and untouched between the borders of crime and law. He meticulously planned and carried out, with speed and accuracy, the hits needed, and always cleaned up any remaining mess. The police or enemies could not trace someone that did not exist, and this strength gave him the upper hand in comparison to other hit men. Plus, the police would give up their homicide investigations quickly when they did not find any clues and the victim was nothing more than a low-life gangster.

Frank hoped that Johnny's bad gambling habit would not go away and that it was only a matter of time before he would surface looking for a loan. So, he visited a couple of known loan sharks and politely questioned and persuaded them for information or recent contacts with Johnny Tollodali.

After a couple of social calls, he uncovered the location of Johnny's hideout in the Bronx.

Frank preferred his executions to be public—it was always a strong message to would-be traitors, and frightened and warned everyone that the Cabineri family was powerful.

Frank began his attack plan and entered a small Greek restaurant right next to Johnny's building. He sat right next to the storefront window where he could see anyone that exited or entered. He ordered a Greek salad, pork shish kabob with extra tzatziki sauce, and a glass of red wine. He finished his meal and waited for Johnny's departure. Fifteen minutes later, Johnny Tollodali exited his building, lit a cigarette, and passed right in front of the restaurant. Frank smiled to himself—his planning and timing was always right on the money.

Frank left $50 on the table and quickly left the restaurant, following Tollodali down the street. He slowly gained on Johnny, closing the distance between them. When he reached him, he called out his name and, as he turned, Frank grabbed him tightly by his long hair with his right hand and pulled his face hard, down and low.

"Don Cabineri sends you his regards, motherfucker," Frank coolly said to him, simultaneously pulling his .45 out of his left pocket. He raised the gun and smashed Johnny across the face, breaking his nose and cheekbone.

Johnny screamed, and Frank swiftly shoved the gun deep into his mouth, breaking a couple of teeth. He looked deep into Johnny's wide-opened eyes and fired, blowing half the back of Johnny's head all over the street with fragments of skull bone and blood.

Frank darted between the shocked pedestrians yelling, "My God, they shot a guy, someone call the police!" He turned at the first corner and walked slowly around the block, back to his parked car, almost a half hour after the event. He could see that an ambulance had arrived and the police were asking witnesses for information.

It was amazing how the account of a crime varied from witness to witness . . . *I saw a tall, short, fat, no skinny man pulled a gun and killed the man who was running, walking, talking, etc.* This was another reason why Frank loved public hits.

Frank got into his Chevy and sped to White Plains Road, turned right toward the Cross Bronx Expressway, and headed downtown. He enjoyed the smooth ride and power of his car and felt relaxed and contented with the execution of Tollodali. Killing the main target always gave him a sense of achievement. Through the windshield, he could see the bright full moon and his thoughts once again returned to mankind's recent accomplishment.

CHAPTER 17

1978, NEW YORK CITY, NEW YORK PUBLIC LIBRARY

The silence in the main reading room of the New York Public Library was always curative for Frank Morris. His now-long, dyed hair protruded from under a black New York Yankees baseball cap. Not even his best friends from the old neighborhood would recognize him. Fifteen years had passed since his metamorphosis, and aging only added to the plastic surgeon's handicraft, bequeathing his new face a unique authenticity. He was fifty-two years old but looked closer to sixty.

His forehead and eyebrow area had pronounced horizontal creases and wrinkles, and he had vertical creases between his eyebrows, which had sagged closer to his eyelids. His blue eyes were now light green with the help of colored contact lenses, but their stare was something that had not, and would never be, altered.

Looking older was a valuable weapon against his enemies, who underrated his physical capabilities.

Frank visited the library at least twice a week, but never on the same days. He had no regular, daily routine for anything he did, randomizing his schedule for everything—shopping, eating out, walks, visits, and so forth. He viewed habitual living as a weakness and knew it could also be a detriment. As a matter of fact, the first information that he would gather on one of his targets was always their routine and habits.

He called the library his "safe office," and this was more than true. Where else can you find silence, privacy, and access to information more so than in the giant main reading room of a public library?

Anonymity and safety are greatly enhanced in public places, but especially in a place where people are so involved in pursuits such as quiet reading, research, and other activities. Anyone who is interested in studying a particular person sticks out like a fly in a bowl full of milk. In this environment, Frank focused and planned every detail of his missions. For security reasons, he never checked any books out, avoiding giving his home address. Instead, he would read and fill notebooks by copying what he found interesting.

He was a seeker of knowledge, and with his enhanced memory, fifteen years of regular book digestion had provided a tremendous amount of information that helped in his line of work. One could say that he was the most educated assassin in the history of organized crime.

Don Cabineri had made sure when he was growing up to introduce him to the power of Marcus Aurelius, and Frank drank from his wisdom every day. He would relentlessly study *The Meditations of Marcus Aurelius*, memorizing his quotes and analyzing their meaning and application.

The Don was right when he had said so long ago in the tenement, "*Nothing happens to anybody which he is not fitted by nature to bear.*" His whole life was living proof of this, and it was his ultimate strength. His parents' deaths, Korea, the family, Alcatraz, escape, re-birth, and now life in the shadows.

Over fifteen years Frank had transformed into the *pugnale d'onore segreto*, the dagger of honor, and had served the Don's commands bringing justice and honor to the Cabineri family. He looked at the giant clock hanging at the end of the library reading room. It was half past twelve, and he silently packed up his things and put them in a brown briefcase that sat at his feet.

Four hours had passed since he arrived that morning, and he instinctively scanned the giant room one more time and headed for the main entrance. Frank walked out of the library on 5th Avenue, turned left for East 42nd Street, then right on East 42nd, heading toward Grand Central Station. The world-famous landmark in midtown Manhattan was not only a major transportation hub, but also a shopping, dining, and cultural destination.

Grand Central Station was to Frank what the jungle was to Tarzan, it was his territory. It gave him the invisibility he needed, and he knew the complexity of its forty-eight acres like the back of his hand. He used its huge footprint and belowground platform, stretching forty-four feet below the street, to move in safety. For Frank, the Grand Central Station's labyrinth was a safe haven for him and his contacts.

He smiled, remembering that only last week he had gone to the movies to see the newly released Superman, and saw that Lex Luther's secret lair was in a hidden, forgotten tunnel underneath Grand Central. Frank loved movies, and watching films was the only time his mind escaped from reality. Movie theaters, much like the library, gave him the desirable combination of solitary and public safety.

Frank rented a private locker in the basement of the station and would randomly check it for messages from Don Cabineri or Antonio. Since his metamorphosis he had zero physical or telephone contact with them, or anyone else from the family. Only the Don and Antonio knew that he existed. His new name was Bruce Mollo, a lower east side registered plumber and owner of Apollo Inc., a plumbing company that existed only on paper; the Don had set up everything to appear legit. For the rest of the world, Frank Morris had drowned in the cold waters off San Francisco Bay almost fifteen years ago.

The locker's contents were always a wax-sealed brown paper envelope. The Don loved the dramatics of old-time secret delivery, and the wax sealing was his way of pronouncing the tone of secrecy between them: a broken seal meant a broken secret and danger. Their contact rules had been discussed in detail and all three knew them by heart. An added security measure was the small dot of red ink under the hot wax. One had to scrape the wax away to find it, ensuring the message was authentic.

Frank would pick up an envelope and immediately go to the public washrooms on the first floor of the station, enter an empty stall, lower his pants, and pretend he was taking a dump. Following the opening, verification, and reading of the message, he would tear the paper into bits and flush them down the toilet. The details had to be memorized, never written.

Frank always smiled when he destroyed the messages, and sometimes he would even whisper to himself . . . *Good morning, Mr. Hunt. Your mission, should you choose to accept it . . . should any member of your team be caught or killed, the Secretary will disavow all knowledge of your actions . . . This message will self-destruct in five seconds.* Late-night reruns of the *Mission Impossible* series was one of the few TV shows he watched.

He crossed the street and passed the familiar, colorful, hot dog cart covered by a giant umbrella on the corner. The steam rising from the cart filled the belly of the umbrella and slowly found its way skyward. Its contact with the chilling December wind turned it into thick white clouds that rose, danced, and disintegrated in all directions.

Immediately after the hot dog stand, there was a Newsstand kiosk, a convenient daily stop for New Yorkers looking for newspapers, glossy magazines, and maybe some candy, soda, or a pack of cigarettes. Frank checked his pocket for his Marlboros and found an empty pack. He usually finished a pack every two days. He stopped and stood in line behind a couple of customers. Between their moving heads and shoulders he tried to read the headlines on the *New York Times*. He had not picked up the paper yet, and wondered what the latest news was.

The woman in front of him was wearing a large hat, obstructing his line of sight. Finally, she moved closer to the kiosk and he was able to see the top of a newspaper stack. He focused on the large, bold, typeset letters of the headline and froze.

CABINERI ASSASSINATED: NEW YORK CRIME BOSS DEAD

Frank pushed forcefully through the line of patrons and grabbed the newspaper, and quickly moved aside.

"Take it easy, buddy!" yelled the man accompanying the lady in the hat.

Frank glanced at him without speaking, and returned his focus to the article.

"Joseph Cabineri, 78, was a Sicilian American mobster, notable for being boss of the Cabineri NY crime family for nearly four decades until his assassination yesterday in his midtown office. Reportedly a key witness under federal protection will testify that the assassination was ordered by Paolo Daballia, the Don's second in command. The key witness broke the mafia's code of silence when he realized he was also a target and that only the police could keep him alive."

Frank reread the paragraph at least four times, feeling his pulse rise and his temples tighten. He needed to find his composure quickly. Training and survival instinct immediately took command of his actions, and he calmed himself while looking around for any suspicious movements. The article replayed in his mind continuously. He had to find a way to contact Antonio as soon as possible.

Certain he was not being watched or followed, he turned back toward Grand Central Station and swiftly made his way to the basement, continuously scanning the area and the faces of the passing commuters.

Frank reached his locker and opened it using the key that hung around his neck, hidden beneath his shirt. He opened the door anxiously, hoping for a message, but the locker was empty. Emptiness filled him as well.

Cabineri Assassinated, New York Crime Boss Dead.

At that moment the news became grim reality, and he felt the pain of losing a father for the second time in his life. Don Cabineri had been a father to him from the first day he made him part of his family, and the pain and loss was the same as any son would feel.

He slowly closed and locked the locker, unable to hold back the tears from rolling down his face. His deepest emotions flowed through his veins for the man that had protected and raised him, the man that had taught him what honor meant. Honor gave meaning to life, and a life without honor was empty and meaningless.

Destiny had once again taken the only person that meant something to him. But he knew in that moment that he would follow destiny's path, and rip from the cowards and traitors everything they held dear, especially their own precious lives. He would honor and avenge his father or die!

As he exited the station, the evening air was crispy and sharp. A cold wind passed between the buildings, filling every empty void. He walked back toward the library, focusing on the information he had. *The assassination was ordered by Paolo Daballia, the Don's second in command.*

Daballia, he thought. *Why would Daballia commit this damnable act? And if he did then Antonio was also a target. Daballia knew how loyal Antonio was to the Don. He would never allow him to live.*

Frank inhaled the cold air, trying to clear his head, and continued walking and scanning the area.

"If Daballia is the traitor, he must have planned this well. He would know that if the attempt on the Don's life failed he would be a dead man the next day. Therefore, Daballia would plan to take out all the men loyal to the Don at the same time or at least as soon as possible. Antonio would be one of his top targets, and if Antonio is alive he knows he is on the top of the list," he mumbled to himself.

He gathered his thoughts some more. Based on limited information, he had started to put things into perspective. "If Antonio had died with the Don, the newspaper would have reported it. If Antonio is alive, he is in hiding and probably trying to contact him. Antonio could only hide in one safe location, the location only known to the Don, Antonio, and himself. The old safe house across from the church!"

He looked across Madison Avenue and hailed an oncoming cab. The cab stopped abruptly, and Frank slid into the backseat while delivering the address. "Alright, 345 Hicks Street in Brooklyn Heights, and step on it," said Frank with assertion.

CHAPTER 18

1978, NEW YORK CITY, GREENWICH VILLAGE

H igh above the city, thousands of microscopic cloud droplets began to freeze together, randomly forming unique hexagonal snow crystals. When their individual mass reached maturity, gravity summoned them to begin their short life's destiny; to fall through the atmosphere colliding with their other newly born brothers while swirling toward the earth.

Thousands of feet below, the screeching sound of the taxi brakes combined with the slipping tires on the frozen street broke the late evening silence of Grove Street in Greenwich Village.

A few moments later, the cab door creaked open and Grace Patton gracefully stepped out, grasping closed the top of her coat against the bite of the December wind.

She had not missed these cold New York winters, and it felt even colder after having tasted the mildness of California weather for the past year. Hearing the cab's departure, she turned her gaze toward the dark sky and took a deep, cold breath. Yellowed light poured from an iced-over metal streetlamp, illuminating her white skin and the perfectly symmetrical details of her face.

Almond-shaped light blue eyes sparkled in the light, and beneath them a beautifully-formed nose exhaled a soft cloud of condensation, as warm breath met freezing air. Despite the discomfort, she smiled, and her naturally red, full lips ever so slightly revealed the whiteness and straight line of near-perfect teeth.

The toughest judge would admit that Grace's face and faultless body transcended the boundaries of beauty, especially when combined with her naturally blond, long wavy hair, which gently mixed with the wind and snowflakes.

She looked at the snowflakes that suddenly emerged from behind the darkness of the lamppost, wavering toward her, and felt a tingle of excitement, thinking that Christmas would be white this year.

Closing her eyes, she anticipated the feeling of snowflakes melting on her face. Her cheeks felt like they were on fire from both the chilling wind and her anxiousness to see him. Since yesterday's phone call her anticipation had continuously grown. Scott was very precious to her, and she had greatly missed him this past year.

The diffused reflections of the spectrums of surrounding light twinkled off the surface of the flakes just before they contacted the living tissue and warmth of her skin, transforming them into small droplets that hungrily embraced and dripped down toward her neck.

After what seemed an eternity she opened her eyes and turned, facing the Brooklyn Heights-style apartment buildings and focusing on number 63, she slowly crossed the empty street toward the snow-covered wooden staircase.

The sound of an approaching car coming from the street below snapped him back to reality. He was preparing the next affidavit, and dropping his pen he ran and opened the curtains in time to see a yellow taxi coming to a stop. Scott saw the back of her head and long blond hair escaping the cab. She looked heavenward just at that moment when snow began to fall.

"A full year!" he whispered to himself with excitement. Not waiting to see her turn toward the house, he closed the curtain. The doorbell buzzed, and he waited to hear the elevator reaching his floor. Finally, he heard footsteps approaching and he opened the door.

Their gazes embraced, sending a river of happy memory waves through their bodies. He fought back the sentimentality and opened his arms.

She looked at him, a white glow painted on her exposed, long white neck, creeping up her face to her blond hairline. They hugged and then backed away to look at each other from head to toe.

Grace looked toward the depth of the living room, simultaneously entering with measured steps.

"Is this your house, Sir Easten?" she asked with an aristocratic English accent.

"Yes, it's my castle, Countess," he answered with the same tone. "Please, have a seat."

"Does the house offer a drink?" she asked with theatric flair, settling onto a dark brown leather sofa.

They played this game in college, pretending that they were actors in a very important scene. He picked up her cue and fell into character.

"Please," he answered, showing her a small table lined with a variety of liquor.

"Want one?" she quickly asked, following with, "Still whiskey?" A double question was always a good indication of nervousness and insecurity.

"Yes, always whiskey," he answered unemotionally; legal books were stacked everywhere and yellow notepads lined the couch and tables.

"But one thing has changed, my lord, you have been knighted by the queen and I am the distressed widow of the late Earl of Wessex," she retorted. She tried to stay in character, but her expression broke into a laugh that she tried to hide by turning her face away quickly.

"Yes, some things have changed, Countess," Scott answered with full composure.

"I wasn't sure about coming tonight," she replied.

"I lit a fire in the bedroom upstairs," he responded. "My plan was simple. We drink and then we go upstairs and sleep together . . . But on my way to opening the door, I changed my mind. So, let's just have one drink, and you can tell me how happy you are now that your husband is dead."

Scott's last phrase was just too perfect and they both broke down laughing with all their hearts. They finally stopped and looked at each other with smiling eyes.

"You changed your mind?" she asked with a frowning, sweet expression.

Scott smiled and answered, "Yes I did, Countess!"

They both laughed again, and she ran into his arms, and they embraced as best friends do.

"I really missed you, Scotty," she whispered.

"Me too, Grace, I can't believe a year has passed since I left San Francisco," he replied.

"Yes, a full year, my God! I can't believe a full year has passed since your mother's funeral," she said soberly and continued trying to change the mood. "I always admired your mother, Scott, she was a real warrior, a true Amazon. Remember when we got arrested at the demonstration at Berkeley and she came up from San Francisco to bail us out. I will never forget her voice screaming at the officer in charge, calling him a fascist and showing him your father's war medals. She looked great in her uniform and he shit in his pants not knowing how to handle her."

"Yes, she was the greatest. I miss her a lot," he replied, slightly lowering his eyes. She reached for his arm tenderly and changed the topic with her usual joyful tone.

"I saw your name on the front page of the *Times* . . . 'Assistant District Attorney Scott Easten, part of the team probing into New York organized crime,'" she spouted proudly, giving him a thumbs-up. "Congratulations, Scott, I always believed you would reach the top."

"Thank you, Gracie," he responded with the embarrassed look he always got when someone praised him. "It's been a hell of a ride, and this case is a real opportunity. Something that does not happen, better than I ever imagined. If everything goes well, we may make a real dent in the darkness!"

His tone had turned serious, and she knew how important it was to him.

"Dent in the darkness," she repeated. "I remember you always saying that when we were at Berkeley. And I'm sure you'll make more than a dent, Scott."

"I hope you're right, Gracie," he replied, and he walked toward the bar.

"Enough about me! Tell me your news," he said, pouring Scotch into two glasses.

"I'm doing great," Grace began. "As I told you on the phone, the new job in Sacramento is really exciting and, you know me, providing legal services to those who are unable to afford them is what I always wanted to do."

"But that's why we used to call you Miss Pro Bono 1972," he replied and they both laughed.

He looked at his watch, and realizing it was 10 p.m. he crossed the room and switched on the TV.

"Sorry, Gracie, need to see what's on the news about today's events," he apologized to her and turned the dial to Channel 5.

"Welcome to WABC, The 10 O' Clock News with Steve Bravel. Good evening! I am Steve Bravel!"

Grace sat down next to him and they both focused on the anchorman.

"In what law enforcement officials described as one of the highest-ranking desertions in the American Mafia's

history, one of the top captains of the Cabineri crime family has defected and is expected to be a government witness against top members of the Cabineri organization.

"The Cabineri confidant, Giorgio Mantia, who was indicted just last year as a co-defendant with Mr. Joseph Cabineri on murder and racketeering charges, has entered the Federal Witness Protection Program and was secretly transferred last week from a federal jail in Manhattan where he had been held without bail with Mr. Paolo Daballia, the family underboss of the deceased Joseph Cabineri.

"Mr. Joseph Cabineri, head of the Cabineri family, was gunned down in his midtown office last week. The authorities claim they have evidence the execution was ordered by Paolo Daballia.

"Furthermore, authorities believe that, due to close ties between Mantia and Daballia, Mantia's testimony could provide a crushing blow to not only the Cabineri organization, but also to the other affiliated crime families.

And now on to other local news, the postal strike was averted . . ."

Scott lowered the TV volume to a whisper.

"Now that's what I call a storm," said Grace, with a wall-to-wall smile.

"Yeah, it's a storm alright, and I'm right in the storm's eye, as they say. And as you know, in the eye everything is dead silent while on the outside all hell is breaking loose," replied Scott, taking a swallow of Scotch.

"Great analogy, Scott," said Grace, laughing with excitement. "The witness protection program is the eye. Seemingly safe, but surrounded by howling winds and destruction—love it!"

Scott laughed with her, but his eyes had a serious and troubled look.

"What's wrong, Scotty, worried about the witness?" she asked.

The phone rang loudly, and Grace's eyes jumped, startled. Scott picked up the black handset.

"Hello," Scott answered.

"OK, John, I'll be there in an hour depending on the traffic. That's fine. OK. 'How's Santa doing?' Right, OK, see you soon!" Scott spoke quickly but with an even tone.

He hung up and turned to Grace.

"Sorry, I can't talk about it, Grace, you know how it is," Scott began. "Listen, I need to head out but you make yourself at home and don't wait up. I don't know what time I'm going to be back, OK, Miss Pro Bono?"

Putting on his coat, he leaned over to kiss her forehead before he turned to leave.

"Be careful, counselor, and remember, the law always *Fiat justitia ruat cælum*—Let justice be done though the heavens fall," she called after him playfully.

"That's exactly right, and as professor Smithson would say, 'Justice must be realized, regardless of consequence,'" returned Scott with an exaggerated British accent. "Lock up, Gracie! Oh, I have a surprise in the freezer! Enjoy the New York cheesecake!"

CHAPTER 19

1978, NEW YORK CITY, BROOKLYN HEIGHTS

T he taxi headed southwest through the city and turned right onto Franklin D. Roosevelt Drive, toward the Brooklyn Bridge. Despite the extreme cold, thick snow began to fall, turning the bridge's limestone and granite towers into giant shadows.

As the cab turned off Exit 2, Frank looked up at the distinctive web-like pattern of the bridge's cables.

Growing up in Brooklyn, he had crossed the bridge's pedestrian walkway hundreds of times with friends. The almost thirty-minute crossing would give them plenty of time to horse around and discuss the day's events. Sometimes, Frank and Antonio would take the walk late at night stopping midway to look at the city lights and the river below. They would share their teenage dreams and talk about the girls they liked.

Antonio's father was a captain in the Cabineri family and lived very close to the Don's house. Mrs. Cabineri and Antonio's mother spent a great deal of time together, caring for the children and occasionally preparing large feasts. The Don would often invite important family members, their wives, and kids for Sunday brunches, and all the children would fill the one-acre yard with the sounds of havoc and joy.

Swiftly traversing the bridge's two-mile span, the driver continued straight onto Brooklyn Bridge Boulevard, as the snow left a soft white blanket on the sidewalks and frozen streets.

Traffic had slowed due to icing, and pedestrians edging their way home hid their faces inside of coats or behind scarves. Finally, the cabbie turned right on Kane, and headed for the first corner, Hicks Street.

"Stop before the curb," ordered Frank, and the driver nodded. Frank handed him a twenty and told him to keep the change.

Now on foot, he turned right on Hicks, and headed the direction of the safe house; halfway up, and on the opposite side of the block. From this direction, Frank had a clear view of the third-floor apartment windows and exterior. Almost two years had passed since he last used the hideout, for a job he had planned and executed, but he remembered this being the safest way to approach. Snow crunched underfoot as he scanned the street in both directions for pedestrians. It was empty, almost deserted, as the snow had picked up intensity.

The apartment windows were dark, and his anxiousness grew, thinking Antonio had not made it to safety. He crossed the street, once again checking for signs of activity, and started up the exterior wooden stairs to the landing. Finding his key, he inserted it but noticed the door was already unlocked. Immediately, he reached inside his pocket, pulling out a Colt M1911 semi-automatic.

Frank nervously opened the door, holding his breath, and squinted into the darkness of the main corridor. Allowing his eyes to adjust, he silently shut the door behind him, then crept a few steps into the foyer.

Peering up the main staircase, a lifeless body came into focus halfway up. His entire body tightened, and adrenaline took control of his reflexes. He turned his body sideways, back to the wall, bending slightly to check the staircase for any movement.

As he approached the body, he saw that the man's face—what was left—had been blown into the back of his head. Only a shotgun with a short barrel and large spread could do this type of damage. He reenacted the shooting in his mind and visualized the body flying backward, landing and sliding down the steps with gravity's pull. There were no muscle spasms; the man had died instantly, no time to even see his life flash before his eyes.

Frank reached the next landing and stopped short, spotting a second victim. The man's white shirt was dyed red, and the left side of his neck was torn open. His eyes still showed the surprise he felt when the shotgun blast hit him directly in the chest. The blue hallway carpet had swallowed his blood, creating an abstract dark purple stain, the dead man's last creation of this life.

Frank carefully stepped over the body and turned left onto the first step of the staircase. At the top of the staircase, a man was crouched low, aiming his Smith & Wesson Model 19 down the second-floor hallway. Back to the wall, Frank leveled his gun and proceeded up the stairs, ready to fire.

He stopped midway, as the gunman instinctively half-turned, and Frank shot him in the base of the spine. He collapsed like a sack of potatoes and slid toward Frank, his head bouncing off the treads on the way down. Glassy eyes spoke of the man's demise, but he opened his lips, and his last breath echoed into emptiness and darkness.

The landing above gave Frank his first look at the apartment door, which was open. He advanced and pushed against it, ever so slightly, to see inside. The growling sound of pain reached him, and he swung the door open, hammer cocked and ready.

Before him was Antonio, covered in blood and sitting on the couch directly in front of the door, a shotgun leveled in Frank's direction. Antonio took aim, his finger tightening around the trigger.

"Antonio, it's me, *paisan*, it's Frank! Frank Morris, buddy!!" Frank yelled out to him. They had not seen each other in almost ten years. Antonio's eyes opened with surprise and another jab of pain. "*Andiamo e ritorniamo paisan*. Let's go and let's return, brother," whispered Frank, and Antonio looked into his eyes, recognizing his brother and their favorite saying.

"Frankie, Frankie. They got me, brother, mother-fuckers killed the Don and . . . " Antonio gasped and coughed more blood onto his shirt, unable to complete the sentence.

Frank took the shotgun from his hands and ran to the bathroom for towels. He folded one into a square pad and put in on Antonio's pulsating bullet wound. Frank saw the bullet had entered his chest, slightly above his heart, and the blood flow was indication of mortal wounding.

"Here we go, buddy, hold this for me and put pressure on it, everything will be ok," he whispered to Antonio. After a few moments of quiet, he asked, "What happened, Antonio? The papers are saying Daballia is behind the hit on the Don."

Antonio's glazing eyes closed a couple of times and he nodded, grunting once again with pain. "Yes, Daballia, he is behind everything, those motherfuck-ers in the hall are Garvenoti's men, and you know . . ." Antonio coughed up blood once again.

"Take it easy, buddy, let's get you well and you will tell me everything," Frank lied to him, knowing that only a few minutes of life remained.

"Don't bullshit a bullshitter, Frankie," replied An-tonio, smiling with pain. "Listen brother, they don't know about you, Frankie, nobody knows, you have the family now. You have to honor us, but—" More deep coughing followed, and a few seconds of silence before Antonio breathed enough air to continue.

"Listen, the feds have Mantia. He's afraid Daballia is going to take him out. He's ready to spill his guts and take everyone down. You have to stop him but you also have to—"

He coughed uncontrollably, his lungs filling with his own blood. Their eyes met, and both knew the end had come. Antonio's last gasp for air opened his eyes and his gaze froze, looking beyond this life.

Frank closed his eyes and held the only true friend he had ever had. Weeping, he buried his face in Antonio's lap and sobbed, unable to constrain himself. Destiny had taken his father, brother, and any remaining humanity he may have had. With their deaths, nobody on earth knew he existed. He was truly a ghost. A ghost that would avenge his family and seek justice and honor for them. He would be unyielding!

Wailing police sirens grew louder and Frank emptied what was left of the liquor cabinet on anything that would burn. At the door, he looked back at Antonio's body for the last time and took a match to an old rolled-up newspaper. He threw it in the middle of the living room, and in seconds, flames began to engulf the place.

He ran past the bodies on the way down, and exited into the freezing snowstorm, disappearing quickly down the street. Skidding tires announced the arrival of the first patrol car, and he turned left on Joralemon Street, ran to the next corner, and swiftly took a right on Garden Place, disappearing into the empty street.

CHAPTER 20

1978, NEW JERSEY, BAYONNE

The TV set made a series of low whistling and crackling sounds that would fluctuate in volume continuously.

"This fucking TV is driving me nuts!" yelled Giorgio. "What do I need to do to get a fucking TV that works? Well? I mean it looks like you boys don't give a fuck so what am I supposed to do?"

Giorgio continued his bitching and the two FBI agents Davis and Gazalti just continued playing their card game as if he had said nothing. Being cooped up in an apartment for almost two months with this guy was driving everyone crazy.

"That's right, assholes, don't pay attention to me," continued the mobster. "Well let me tell you mother-fuckers something about Giorgio Mantia! Every guy who did not pay attention to me ended up with his face looking like his ass."

"Take it easy, Giorgio," said Scott, calm but authoritative.

"Oh, excuse me Mr. Big Attorney, I did not mean to rattle your balls. I'm so sorry, Mr. Assistant DA, please accept my apologies," cracked Giorgio with a dramatic tone, while offering a flicking motion, hand to chin, toward Scott.

"I've told them about the TV set and they are bringing a new one tomorrow," replied Scott, unfazed.

"You said the same shit a week ago," grumbled Giorgio with a full mouth of pizza.

"Good evening and welcome to the NYBS evening news. We begin our news tonight with the latest issuings of subpoenas in connection to the assassination of Joseph Cabineri, head of New York City's crime family. Reporter John Roberts spoke with Marc Kington, head of the organized crime task force, this morning outside the Brooklyn district attorney's office."

"Mr. Kington, what is the official position of the district attorney's office after the latest events?"

Giorgio Mantia's eyes focused on the TV, a half-empty pizza box and empty bottles of Coke strewn in front of him on the coffee table. His third Coke was half empty, and he had just surgically pulled another piece of pepperoni from the top of his next slice.

The reporter repeated his previous question at a higher volume, pushing his microphone between the other extended hands and mics in Mr. Kington's face. Kington stepped back and addressed the crowd.

"The district attorney's position is unchanging, Mr. Roberts. We must reclaim our streets and stop this plague of extortion, bribery, hijacking, loan sharking, and insurance fraud," he said. "The Task Force's main goal is to put an end to violence. There is absolutely no reason why an innocent eight-year-old boy should be caught in a hail of bullets while playing with his friends in the park. The district attorney's office will continue making arrests; this is only the beginning of our cleanup."

Scott watched how Kington enjoyed the attention and limelight. He had learned quickly that working for the DA's office was 50% public relations and 50% political lobbying. He walked over and turned the volume up a few notches.

"Earlier this morning, Mr. Roberts, FBI agents surrounded the office of Paolo Daballia, underboss of the Cabineri crime family, and placed him under arrest. They also served him a warrant demanding his appearance in federal court."

Marc Kington turned toward the camera and said with determination, "We will reclaim our streets, Mr. Roberts, and the wonderful people of Brooklyn will feel safe in their neighborhoods."

"That's bullshit; the DA can't do shit, and you know why, Scotty my boy? Because in order to bring order you need strength and the right people to manage the situation," announced Giorgio while swallowing another piece of pizza.

Scott knew he was wrong. In this case all that the DA needed was Giorgio's testimony. With it, the Cabineri family was going down hard and other crime families would get caught in the tidal wave of damning evidence. His testimony would be bigger than Joseph Valachi's.

That's why arrests were taking place all over the city. It had been planned meticulously, and Scott played a vital role, down to the time and day the arrests should take place. Daballia got taken in late today, a Friday, with the hope that he wouldn't post bail, and be stuck in jail the entire weekend. For these types of criminals, even a single full day in jail could cause them trouble.

"Well, Giorgio, in this case we don't need muscle and strength, because we have you, my friend," answered Scott with a knowing smile.

Giorgio's eyes filled with anger. He would never have ratted out the family, but that piece of shit Daballia killing his own Don, and then wanting to clip half of the families' captains, gave him no choice. The motherfucker had to go down, and Giorgio knew that the DA would fuck the great and mighty Paolo Daballia really bad with the help of his testimony. He had the facts, the knowledge, the history to make sure he would rot in jail for the rest of his life.

"Yes, you do, Scotty my boy. Yes, you do. Unless that fucking new TV set is not here tomorrow, and I tell your DA boss to go fuck himself," replied Giorgio with a heavy Brooklyn Italian accent.

He finished another piece of pizza and played with his large, crooked nose. He would hold it and push it toward the side that it leaned until it touched his cheek, then he would let it flex back to normal. Scott had watched him do that a hundred times since they brought him to the safe house.

"How'd you get that broken nose, Giorgio?" he asked.

"It's a long story, Scotty," Giorgio replied.

"It's OK, we have all the time in the world, Giorgio, and I love long stories. I'm sure the guys would love to hear about it also. Right, boys?" Scott asked the agents, still playing cards.

"Well you'll enjoy it because it has to do with the first time I got arrested by assholes like yourselves," replied Giorgio, followed by laughter and a loud burp.

"I had been driving around in a friend's car and the cops stopped me and found a couple of guns in the trunk. So help me, God, I did not know the guns were there," Giorgio said, making his cross as testimony that he was not lying.

They all laughed, and Giorgio continued after downing the half bottle of Coke.

"They took me to the station and drilled the shit out of me for two hours but I said nothing. The motherfuckers started working me over—kicked, punched, and kneed my head, and finally they threw me on the floor. I'm sure you boys know the drill," he said, looking toward the two agents. "Then they pulled me up and pushed me on the chair; I was pretty banged up. One of them asked me again where I found the guns, and I just said, 'What guns?' The motherfucker took out his gun and pointed it straight between my eyes."

Giorgio made a gun with his hand and put his index finger between his eyes and continued.

"'Are you going to talk?' he asked me over and over, each time louder until he was screaming. I was so fucking tired I started yelling back at the guy. 'Go ahead, shoot me motherfucker!'"

Giorgio stopped and looked at them proudly, then burped again and continued.

"He slammed the fucking gun barrel on the bridge of my nose. I can still hear the bone cracking. I got really pissed off and hit the motherfucking prick on the right side of his jaw. I felt it break and that's all I can remember until I woke up in my cell the next day." Giorgio laughed and sat back belching once again.

"That's a hell of a story, Giorgio. What happened after? Did you do time?" asked Scott.

Giorgio smiled and whispered, "Cabineri fixed everything and I was out the next day. The family had power everywhere back then. Joe was the best of all the bosses; he was always taking care of us. Just like a father takes care of his family."

Giorgio's voice sounded bitter and sad, his face darkened, and he looked at the TV set in silence. The news was still on, the weatherman talking about an upcoming snowstorm.

CHAPTER 21

1978, NEW YORK CITY, BROOKLYN HEIGHTS

F rank hustled down Kane Street and turned left off Henry, where luckily a cab was passing, and he hailed it. The streets were empty, which gave him a sense of safety because he could easily tell if he was being followed.

"Corner of Essex and Delancey, Lower East Side. And I'm not in a hurry, so don't try to break the world record," he told the cab driver with a tone that left no room for disagreement.

The image of Antonio's dead eyes flashed before him. He needed to get to safety as fast as possible. Logic had to prevail if he wanted to survive, so he sat back and tried to collect himself. He replayed Antonio's last words for any hints.

"Listen, the feds have Mantia. He's afraid that Daballia is going to take him out. He's ready to spill his guts

and take everyone down. You must stop him, but you also have to . . ."

What did Antonio want to tell him? He asked himself over and over as the cab headed toward the Brooklyn Bridge. I need to get to the cave, Frank thought, knowing that his haven always gave him focus and strength.

Outside, the snowstorm was getting worse and it looked like New York was in for a good old-fashioned December blizzard. Thirty minutes later, the cab reached its destination. He paid the driver without speaking, looking up and down Delancey Street. The only signs of life were an old couple crossing the street, and a couple of kids having a snowball fight farther down.

The gods were providing the best weather for him; the snowstorm had saved his life, he thought. He was sure more of Daballia's hit men were outside the safe house. A hit like that was always secured with plenty of backup. He looked once again over his shoulder and turned onto Orchard Street, stopping with his back in the doorway of the corner building.

From that position he could clearly see 97 Orchard—five stories tall, windows dark, front door nailed shut and covered with boards.

His tenement had been condemned in 1934, just four years after Don Cabineri had taken him away. Ever since Frank reached the age where he could walk the streets alone, he had returned to his family home. He recalled his first return, seeing the building empty of life.

The tenement's hollowness matched his own emptiness and drove deeper his sense of loss. He spoke to no one about his visits, and finally one night, when he was about sixteen, he found a way into the desolate building and returned to his family's apartment.

Their apartment was ravaged. The kitchen table was intact, but the chairs were broken as if there had been a bar brawl, and the bed dismantled, its pieces scattered across the floor.

He went to the corner next to the window and sat looking at the damaged interior and the unmoving shadows. Only the streetlamp light entered the room, casting web-like shadows on the floor and walls. He followed the shadows for hours trying to bring back to life his childhood memories, sounds, and life.

Needing to hide from the outside world, he returned many times. This apartment was his secret, his world, his cave. He never told anyone about it and after his return from Alcatraz and his new life it became his lair—a wild animal's well-hidden resting place.

Little by little, he had cleaned up the small apartment and slowly transformed it into his headquarters, equipping it with a security system and tools of his trade, medical supplies, weapons, etc. He painted the inside of the front window black, allowing only a corner of glass so he could monitor the street below. He found a way to get electric power from the building next door and had food and water to sustain him, in the event he needed to hide for a long duration.

Briskly across and onto Delancey once again, he then turned down the first parallel street, Allen, and a minute later reached the back of his tenement. The back door was nailed shut, but Frank had created an entry point between the boards, and rigged them to appear fixed in place. If he could escape Alcatraz, he was more than capable of designing a way to enter and exit an abandoned building.

Making sure there was no one around to witness his clever entrance, he pushed on the lowest nailed board and it turned, giving motion to the middle board simultaneously. Like the hands of a clock, one board rotated down and the other moved up, providing enough space for his body to pass. Bending his body ninety degrees, he pushed the door open and disappeared inside, while behind him the boards returned to their original position.

His eyes and nose began to adjust to the darkness and pungent odors of the decaying building, mixed with the smells of the city that infiltrated its interior through broken windows and crumbling brick.

The wooden staircase he climbed had been the very reason for the tenement's condemning in 1934. A building act ordered all tenements to install steel staircases and flushable, sewer-connected toilets— one for every two families. Despite fierce opposition from landlords, who feared decreased profits, many improvements were enforced, but some were not. Frank figured that the owner of this tenement did not have the funds for such a renovation.

Frank had explored all of the other apartments as well. Many had remained untouched for decades, time capsules of sorts. It was as though people had just picked up and left, home goods and furniture scattered everywhere.

Once on the second floor, he unlocked his old door, inspected the two freezing rooms, started a small electric heater, and sat at the kitchen table. He switched on a small desk lamp for light.

"Listen, the feds have Mantia, he's afraid that Daballia is going to take him out. He's ready to spill his guts, taking down everyone. You must stop him, but you also have to . . ." Antonio's eyes and words continued to repeat in his mind. You must stop him, but you also have to what? Have to what? he asked himself, desperately searching for the answer. He closed his eyes and concentrated on the silence.

He started to break down the information. *First we have the issue with Mantia,* he thought. Frank had known Mantia for years, and knew he was a few years younger than him. He recalled him hanging around the pool hall a lot. He was a stand-up guy, never caused trouble, and the Don trusted him. One thing that was sure: Mantia was loyal to the Don. Therefore, Antonio was right. The only reason Mantia would rat on the family was if he was 100% certain that Daballia wanted him dead, and no one could protect him better than the cops.

Frank never liked Daballia, but the Don needed to balance the family interests, and Daballia controlled the garment district and the Amalgamated Clothing Workers, plus other unions. The labor racket was big, bringing millions of dollars to the family, so the Don made him second in command and kept the family strong. The Cabineri family was leading the pack and Don Cabineri's ability to balance power was his biggest strength.

Daballia was originally a drug dealer, operating out of 102 Mott Street, but was arrested in 1958 for selling narcotics, and spent nineteen months in the penitentiary. He also had a loan shark business, and after he got out the Don wanted to expand the family's interests, so he gave Daballia permission to enter the prostitution racket.

Frank had wondered why the Don increased Daballia's power and on one occasion had respectfully asked Don Cabineri for an explanation. The Don had looked at him with frozen eyes, answering, *"Daballia's loyalty to the family had to be achieved by feeding his hunger. His contribution has kept the peace and brought a definitive end to the last conflict. Remember when the garment district came close to having major strikes? Daballia stepped in, and his men got involved in the street battles. Daballia came to me with the information that the other families were secretly supporting the strikes to weaken our family."*

The Don explained in this way, justifying his decision with the details and depth of his strategy, and also taking the opportunity to mentor and teach Frank the inner workings of the family business.

"With my support to Daballia, and his promotion to second in command, war was avoided, and I have the fox in my den, and under control," the Don went on. "You see, Francesco, strategy is stronger than muscle. Muscle should be used always strategically, never driven by emotion. Anger blinds and leads to fatal mistakes."

Frank had always tried to use the Don's advice, and now more than ever he knew that his next moves must be calculated and not emotional. So why did

Daballia hit the Don? Did the other families support him? Frank knew that his questions needed answers quickly if he was to survive.

His anonymity was not yet compromised, and it was his strength, but with Antonio and the Don gone he would have to surface to some of the still-loyal Cabineri family members. He needed their help to fight and win, especially if the other families supported Daballia.

He poured himself a Scotch and started writing names on a large white sketchbook laying on the kitchen table. This was his method for detailing and visualizing his strategy.

He wrote two names in large block letters on the top of the white paper, allowing a big space between the names *Mantia* and *Daballia.*

A vertical line drawn down the center of the paper separated equally the space between the two names. He took a sip of Scotch, lit a Lucky Strike, and stared at the names.

Below each name he jotted all the possible friends and foes on both sides. After a couple of minutes of reflection, he picked up a red pen and circled the Cabineri family members that would be the safest to approach for help: Salvatore Ducalia and Charlie Lubollini.

Salvatore Ducalia was a trusted and loyal captain in the family; Frank had done a couple of jobs with him before his arrest in the early '60s. Charlie Lubollini was a trusted soldier, and Salvatore's best muscle.

Frank continued his deductions and stopped to pour another half glass of Scotch in combination with a new Lucky Strike.

He contemplated his options for a while, and concluded that his contact would have to be with a very limited number of people. If his anonymity was lost, everything would be lost.

The best and safest would be Salvatore. But the hard part was to find a way to contact Salvatore in total secret. Plus, the fact that Salvatore had never seen his new face would make it a difficult task to get close and convince him of his true identity.

Furthermore, finding him in the first place would be difficult, since Salvatore would also be running or in hiding after the Don's assassination.

Frank sat back, took a drag, and exhaled straight up to the ceiling, watching white streams of smoke slowly dissolve. He closed his eyes, trying to remember anything that would give him a clue as to where Salvatore could be hiding. His photographic memory searched as if going through a photo album, and suddenly he remembered that Salvatore had bought a country cabin near Upper Nyack, on the banks of the Hudson, north of New York City. There, he would practice his shooting skills while hunting. Salvatore called it business with pleasure.

If he took Interstate 87 and crossed the Mario Cuomo Bridge it would take him a little more than an hour to get to the area, and he estimated another hour to search and find Salvatore's cabin. This was now his number one priority; he would then decide his next moves regarding Mantia and Daballia.

Frank hurriedly packed a small bag and put on a warmer coat and gloves. Finishing his Scotch with one swallow, he switched off the table light and heater and left the tenement the same way he had entered.

Once outside he started the twenty-minute walk to the parking garage on East 4th Street. He used four parking garages spread over the city; every time he used his van he would park in a different garage. The van was registered to Apollo Inc.

At the parking garage he took the elevator to the eighth floor, where he located his van, cranked up the engine, and started down the winding ramp to the street below. He turned the radio on to keep tabs on the news and began navigating toward the interstate.

Frank needed answers, and hoped Salvatore could provide some of them, but he knew that finding Daballia's hit men would be difficult because usually hits were ordered from the top down, through lieutenants, to gunmen who knew neither their employers nor their intended victims. This way it was far more burdensome for the law to link the family to a murder. Regardless of the method, he needed proof that Daballia had ordered the hit, and once he had that proof, he would do what honor demanded.

CHAPTER 22

1978, NEW JERSEY, BAYONNE

Scott entered the safe house unbuttoning his coat, his face red from the cold. December nights in New York often brought bitter winds that felt like razors crossing your face. It had been five years since he moved to New York from San Francisco, but he knew he would never adjust to the weather.

"Holy smokes it's freezing out there, guys," he greeted the agents, while looking around for Giorgio.

"Where's Santa?" he asked.

"Taking a crap, man. With all the shit he eats and drinks I hope he doesn't explode before he goes to court," said Davis, the younger of the two FBI agents.

"I heard that, asshole," yelled Giorgio, as he entered the living room wearing a stained white t-shirt that stretched over his broad shoulders and large wobbling beer pot. He was in his early fifties but you could tell that he had not stepped into a gym in the last twenty years.

"OK, guys, let's cut the crap. Giorgio, we need to go over your testimony in detail," interrupted Scott with authority.

"You know something, counselor, you're really breaking my balls," Giorgio reacted, grabbing his nether regions for effect.

"C'mon, Giorgio, you know this is for your own good. The better your testimony, the deeper the hole you're digging for all of them," responded Scott.

Giorgio looked at the draped window as if it was open, then turned to Scott and gestured toward the living room table they used to have their talks.

"Let's go, counselor, let's begin," Giorgio said, reaching for the chair and sitting with wide open legs on it. Scott took a seat right across from him and opened a brand-new yellow legal notepad.

"OK, Giorgio, it is important that we make the jury believe in you and what you say. But for this to happen they need to know who you are. We need to build your character and beliefs for them to understand who Giorgio Mantia is," Scott explained, while glancing at his previous notes.

Giorgio lit a cigarette and blew smoke toward the overhanging table light. The smoke swirled upward and surrounded the lightbulb as it moved around it like a snake.

"Giorgio, please tell the jury what it was like growing up in your neighborhood." Scott asked the question with the same tone he always used in court.

"Yes, sir," replied Giorgio. "Well, sir, it was a hellhole. We only had two swimming pools and six bedrooms, but the worst was that we only had one bathroom," he answered in a laughter that came out half screaming and half coughing.

"Come on, Giorgio! Stop fucking around!" Scott screamed at him, hitting his hand on the wooden table, making the glasses jump in the air.

"OK, OK, take it easy, Scott, just trying to relax. This shit gets me really nervous. All this bullshit—remember this, say that, make the jury do this, do that. Fuck the jury, fuck you all!" Giorgio screamed back at Scott.

Scott had not seen him like this and he understood that being locked up for two weeks and having all the preparation and pressure had taken a toll on Giorgio and himself. He tried to bring some calm to the room.

"Look, Giorgio, I know this is not easy. But I also know that you are doing what you believe is right. That's what counts. These guys must go down, and you're the one that can topple their castle like a house of cards," Scott said encouragingly, looking Giorgio straight in the eyes. "I know you can do this, but we need to work together and play the game right. The jury must believe you. Then everything will happen just as we have talked about. Daballia will regret the things he has done, and believe me, he will not get out of jail in this lifetime."

Scott noticed that the mention of Daballia made Giorgio's eyes widen like a lion's before it attacks.

"OK, Scott, sorry for my bullshit. You're right, let's do this, *paisan*."

Giorgio had never called him *paisan* before, and he felt a strange bond building between them. Scott took a breath and repeated his initial question.

"OK, Giorgio, please tell the jury what it was like growing up in your neighborhood."

Giorgio lit another cigarette and with a confident voice continued, "Growing up in the crowded and dark tenements of Little Italy was not easy. The neighborhood was sprawling with mob guys, looking for recruits in the youths that hung out at the pool halls and luncheonettes. Just like a Sicilian village, the mob's power loomed over everyone, and they were only mentioned by the common people in whispers."

"That's great, Giorgio, you're doing great. Please continue," offered Scott.

Giorgio took a long drag off his cigarette and once again exhaled the smoke forcefully toward the lightbulb.

"I was born in Little Italy and have one older sister," Giorgio went on. "I had a brother who died before I was born. My mother's name was Maria. She was born in Sicily and arrived in America when she was five years old. My father, Gavino Mantia, jumped from a freighter when he landed in New York and was an illegal alien up 'til a few years ago when he earned his citizenship. My mother worked for a Jewish dress manufacturer in Manhattan's garment center as a skilled seamstress. My father worked as a short-order cook for a small restaurant in Little Italy, Jovanni's."

"OK, Giorgio, now please tell the jury how you became involved with organized crime," asked Scott, as if they were in court.

"Every Sunday, I would go with my father to mass and we would pass the corner pool hall. There was always a group of men lined up in front, all smartly dressed in tailored suits and expensive Italian knit shirts. Most of them wore large diamond rings," Giorgio said nostalgically. "My father would always make us stay on the opposite side of the street and some of the men would see us passing, and wave toward us yelling, 'How you doing Gavino?!'"

"My father would nervously wave back and pick up his step, leading me by the hand," recalled Giorgio. "One day I asked him if he knew those men and he nervously whispered in my ear, 'Yes, I know some of them, but I want you to stay away from them. They believe that honest work is stupid and that riches should be grabbed and not earned. They are very powerful men, Giorgio, but we always should stay away from them. We should never know anything they do, and we never ask questions about their concerns. Do you understand? That's why we always walk on the other side of the street.'

"I was nine years old, but I understood that my father was scared of these men, scared of their power," he continued. "I did not like that he was scared. I felt embarrassed by his weakness. I wanted to be feared rather than fear these men. You could say that I admired their power and strength.

"A few years later when I turned fifteen, I started hanging around the pool hall almost every day. Gradually, some of those guys noticed me and began to send me on errands, giving me a couple of bucks each time. I was doing bad in school, hated the drill, and spent a lot of time in Al's Gym lifting weights and learning to box, so I had a pretty hefty build for my age.

"One day, I was hanging around the hall and saw a few boys from another neighborhood trying to steal a bike from across the street. I started yelling at them to leave the bike alone, and they came all together after me, sure they would teach me a lesson. Well, I kicked the shit out of the first two and the other one ran like hell. The guys saw the whole thing from the pool hall and came out yelling smart talk, 'Giorgio, nice left kid!' 'Hits like a hammer!' 'Giorgio the hammer!'

"That was it. They all laughed and from that moment, I was Giorgio *Martello*, 'the hammer' in Italian," he said with a look of pride. After another drag, he continued.

"You see, the mob uses nicknames for each other to avoid identification by the feds," Giorgio explained. "Don Cabineri, whose nickname was Joe lo Squalo, Joe the Shark, insisted his real name was never to be spoken aloud. Also, we used hand gestures, like Don Cabineri's men were told instead of saying his name to rub their thumb across their chin."

"So, Giorgio, when did you officially become part of the Cabineri crime family?" Scott inquired.

"One day I was helping my mother and sister in the dress factory. I was about seventeen, and in the warehouse with Mr. Jovani the foreman, a nice guy who always showed a lot of respect to my family," said Giorgio, looking tense. "Two huge guys walked in. They looked Irish to me. They walked up to Mr. Jovani, pushing garments off tables and onto the floor. They started to push him around and one of them told him that all of his workers must belong to the union if he wanted the place to continue to operate. They said he needed to give them monthly union dues for every worker.

"I was so mad I wanted to jump on them, but Mr. Jovani looked at me and I understood that I would just make things worse. The taller of the two pushed Mr. Jovani and said to him that he should 'take care of this' or the result would be bad. 'Someone will get hurt,' he threatened.

"My hands tightened into fists, and the tall Irish guy looked at me with menacing eyes. 'What the fuck you looking at, kid?'" Giorgio was trying to imitate an Irish accent but doing a comically bad job. "'Go home and suck on your mother's fucking tit, before I kick your WAP face in,'" he yelled while walking, exiting backward and pointing an index finger at both Mr. Jovani and me."

Pretending he was speaking to the jury, Giorgio continued.

"'*See you soon, Mr. Wop!*' the Irish fucker yelled, walking out of the shop."

Giorgio stopped his narration and looked to Scott for comments.

"You're doing great, Giorgio, keep the jury focused on your life and struggles," Scott instructed. "This way we will build their empathy. They see you as a criminal, but you had no choice. Society did not help you, society made you what you are. And if they accept that society is to blame, then Giorgio, we have them. Because *they* are society and they feel bad, responsible even. And this leads to guilt. Guilt, my friend Giorgio, is our freedom ticket. Their guilt will weigh on their conscience, and the only way to clear their conscience is by helping you."

Giorgio was silent, but his face showed that Scott was making an impression.

"You have a way with words, counselor; you would have made a great fucking salesman," he responded, chuckling.

"Thank you, Giorgio, and by the way, you'll have to cut out the profanity when you tell the story. The judge is not going to sit by and listen to 'fuck this' and 'fuck that.' OK, *paisan*?" Scott felt that he had gained Giorgio's trust, and his tone was friendly but also authoritative.

Giorgio lit another cigarette and began his stand-up comedy routine with a makeshift high-pitched voice.

"Dear members of the jury, Judge, and everyone else in the room. I am a victim. A victim of society. I was born innocent and society made me guilty. Yes! Ladies and gentlemen, society put a gun in my hand and had its finger on the trigger. Dear Honorable Judge, please believe me, you motherfucking son of a bitch or I'll break your neck!"

His theatrics had even the FBI crew cracking up laughing. Scott laughed, too, but quickly composed himself, looking at his watch.

"OK, let's get serious again and finish up on your story. Remember if you want to finish Daballia for good, the jury is your gun," Scott said, refocusing

Giorgio on his task. Giorgio swallowed a half-full can of beer and continued with another large belch.

"OK, so after this story with Mr. Jovani, I went to the pool hall and met up with Daballia. He was a made guy and he had sent me on a couple of deliveries for the family. I told him what happened, and he immediately recognized the tall Irish fuck. 'That fucking O'Brien has been fucking around in our territory for the past few months. If the Irish pricks from Queens think they can move in on our turf, those Belle Harbor cunts have another thing coming. The Don knows, and has told me to resolve the issue.'

"Daballia had a way with words, mixing a 'fuck' here with a 'resolve' there, trying to sound educated. The guys would make fun of his best quotes like: 'And I responded to the Judge, your honor I really appreciate your fucking wooden mallet!'" Giorgio laughed once again, not restraining his need to joke around.

"Stop fucking around, Giorgio! I have an appointment and need to leave soon," commanded Scott with anger.

"OK, boss take it easy, I'm just telling it as it is, that's all," Giorgio answered, then shifted his body around in the armchair and continued. "Anyways, this whole Irish story led me to my first button, eh, my first hit; I would finally make my bones. Daballia asked me to meet up with him late the next day, and we took his car up to Queens. He had gotten information on where O'Brien's girlfriend lived, and knew he would be there that evening. We got to the house and waited in the car for a couple of hours.

Finally, a little after midnight, O'Brien came out and headed straight for his car."

At this, Giorgio lit another cigarette and took on a more serious tone.

"We got out of the car and followed him. When O'Brien got into his car, Daballia drew his gun, approaching the driver's side. O'Brien lowered the car window and as he put his keys in the ignition, he saw Daballia's incoming shadow. But it was too late. Daballia fired and the bullet hit O'Brien in the face, turning it into a mask of blood.

"Daballia yanked the car door open and handed me his gun. '*Put another two into the fuck!*' he ordered me. I took the gun, thought about Mr. Jovanni and fired two shots into the top of O'Brien's head. Blood sprayed our faces and coats, and Daballia took the gun from my hand and threw a pouch of drugs on the floor of O'Brien's car. He slammed the door shut and pulled me by the arm toward our car.

"'Good job, kid, the boss will be happy,' he whispered, looking at all sides of the quiet street for witnesses. Some of the apartment window lights had come on after the gunshots but, in this neighborhood, nobody would dare stick their head out.

"We got into Daballia's car and drove off. '*Why didn't you drop the gun?*' I asked, knowing the usual drill after a hit; get rid of the unregistered gun as soon as possible.

"'*If they find a gun, the cops will think it's a gang or family hit. But with the bag of drugs, fucking O'Brien becomes just another Irish drug dealer that got clipped.*'

"After that, I was in the family for good."

Giorgio stopped and took another swallow of beer while looking at Scott for his reaction. Scott wrote down some notes:

Character build-up information for jury: Giorgio Mantia's first arrest was at eighteen and he was sentenced to eight months at the New Hampton farms reformatory.

(Jury Note: This was about a year after the O'Brien hit.)

His probation report declared that Giorgio already had a "Definite criminal pattern of conduct" by this age.

(Jury Note: Society had already given up on Giorgio Mantia.)

His first probation officer wrote: "Giorgio Mantia's admitted philosophy as told to me is the following: 'I never was a joe, and if I have to be a joe I'd rather be dead.' When I asked Mr. Mantia to define what a joe is to him he explained 'that a joe is a person who works and saves and puts his money aside and does not indulge in no extravagance.' He further stipulated, 'My old man is a joe and I will never be like my old man.'"

(Note to Jury: We have other witness accounts that when Giorgio Mantia came out of prison his criminal associates acclaimed him as a stand-up guy, because he had taken the punishment like a man and had not squealed.)

Scott closed his notebook and said, "OK, Giorgio, that's great stuff. We need to trim the edges but it's really good stuff. Let's take a break for today."

Scott got up from his seat and looked once again at his watch. He wanted to get home to Grace; they had lots of catching up to do.

"OK, counselor, good timing because I need to take a shit," replied Giorgio.

"Thank you for sharing! See you tomorrow, guys," added Scott, waving to the agents while closing the door.

CHAPTER 23

1978, NEW YORK, UPPER NYACK

F rank continued down I-87 and stopped for gas just after crossing the Mario Cuomo Bridge. He needed to communicate with Salvatore before he arrived; this would have been impossible if it was not for the Don's ability to anticipate and prepare for the future.

He remembered reading the Don's instructions after his plastic surgery and felt a mix of admiration and sadness.

Francesco, you must always prepare for the unexpected by asking yourself questions related to possible scenarios that may transpire. One question is this: 'What happens if you need to contact someone in the family that thinks you are dead?' After your escape, the world thinks you are dead and so does the rest of the family except for me and Antonio. Therefore, what would happen if I and Antonio die? How will you introduce yourself to the remaining family members? The face of Frank Morris is no more, they have no knowledge of your existence.

Frank remembered every word as though Don Cabineri was next to him, whispering these thoughts in his ear. He sat in his car smelling the gasoline as it ran from the gas pump, looking into the passing headlights, and continued to recall the Don's instructions.

Francesco, I have thought about these questions and believe that I have found a solution. I will instruct every current and new family member that one day in the future they may receive a phone call from a stranger that gives them this very special message: 'Death smiles at us all, but all a man can do is smile back. -Marcus Aurelius.' They are commanded to follow this stranger's instruction as if they were my very own. In turn figlio mio, my son, you will need to make sure that they remember and obey my instructions. So I will instruct them to answer, 'Ave Caesar.' This Roman salutation will be their testament of allegiance to you, Francesco, because if that day ever comes, you, my son, you will be the new father of our family, you will be Don Francesco Cabineri.

Fifteen years ago, Frank thought the Don's fascination with the Roman Empire had him imagining events that would never transpire. But out of respect, he accepted the instruction without question or reservation. *Now,* he thought, the Don once again had been a true prophet of his own demise, and a protector of Frank's life.

Frank snapped out of his trance when the gas attendant knocked on the car window to signal the tank was full. After paying, he parked the car in a side parking lot and headed for the glowing phone booth on the side of the building.

Wind and snow rushed in, colliding with the booth's walls and sending a small tornado of snowflakes into the low ceiling. Frank took out a small black telephone book and searched for Salvatore's telephone number at the cabin. Antonio had given him all the important family telephone numbers as the Don had requested. Frank dialed the number and a low voice answered hesitantly, "Hello?"

Frank recognized Salvatore's voice; after a few seconds of silence Salvatore repeated the "Hello" but this time with a dab of anger and a smear of fear. Frank took a deep breath of cold air and said calmly, "Death smiles at us all, but all a man can do is smile back. Marcus Aurelius." The message had surprised Salvatore, and the only response was silence and heavy breathing on the line.

Finally came the sound of Salvatore clearing his throat and the almost inaudible response, "Ave Caesar."

Frank felt a shiver run through his body, and closed his eyes, trying to compose his next words.

"Salvatore, listen carefully. I am very close to the cabin. I will arrive soon and explain what is going on. Understood?" Frank asked, waiting for confirmation. Almost half a minute passed before Salvatore answered, "Yes," and without a second word, he ended the call.

Frank knew Salvatore had been shocked and frightened by his call. He would need to be extremely careful. There was no way to predict how someone would react to a stranger telling him that he's a man from his past, long thought dead, but actually alive and with a new face. This might be too much for any man, even more so considering the events of the last few days.

Once in his van, Frank proceeded north several miles. He turned onto a snowy country road, and eventually came to a long, even snowier drive that led up to the cabin. Smoke billowed from the chimney, and the lights were on. *This is a good sign*, he thought. If Salvatore was truly worried, he would have turned out all the lights in preparation for a fight. The lot and surroundings were, however, in total darkness, and Frank had no flashlight. He parked about three hundred feet from the front door and exited, trying to get used to the darkness. Fresh snow obscured the path, as did the moonless and overcast night.

All around was even darker forest, and the wind rebounded through the trees, rustling the weak branches, whipping each other and the empty air. The temperature was well below zero and the ground was fully frozen beneath Frank's heavy boots. He was wearing enough clothes so he didn't feel cold, even with the wind hitting from all directions.

At the cabin door he felt his heart rate rise, a reaction to the adrenaline and anticipation flowing through his body. He knocked and heard heavy steps approaching the door, which opened slowly.

At six feet even, Salvatore Ducalia was tall for a first-generation Italian American, and his curly jet-black hair made him look even taller. His face was that of an unfinished marble statue, full of chiseled features. He was built like a bull, and it was common knowledge that with his giant hands he could quickly snap a man's neck.

Frank entered the cabin and saw that Salvatore had a .45 pushed into his belt on the side of his waist. It was natural that he would be suspicious of a stranger, even if the Don had asked him to obey. They looked into each other's eyes and observed each other's facial features for several seconds, the fire sending yellow shades across their foreheads and cheeks. Frank spoke first.

"Salvatore, I need you to listen very closely. Nobody alive knows what I am about to tell you."

Salvatore's eyes shined and widened expectantly, and Frank continued while outstretching both hands in a pleading manner.

"You need to look only at my eyes. Don't look at my face but only into my eyes . . . I am Frank Morris."

Frank searched for a response, trying to read Salvatore's expression, which was one of complete confusion.

"After my escape from Alcatraz I was brought in by Antonio and Vinnie," Frank went on. "They took me to a safe house that no one knew about. The Don arranged for me to have plastic surgery and this is the result. I've been hiding and working for the family ever since."

Salvatore sat near the lit fireplace and suddenly looked much older than his age.

"What the fuck are you telling me, man?! Frank has been dead almost fifteen years now," he objected. "You're fucking with me; you think I believe that fucked-up story, asshole?!"

His reaction was spontaneous, his tone angry. Frank had anticipated this possibility, and immediately tried to balance the situation.

"Listen, I understand how crazy this story sounds, so I'll tell you what," Frank offered. "Why don't you ask me anything that you believe only Frank Morris would or could remember. Go ahead, test me."

Frank's reply was received with a look he had seen before—a pissed-off reaction that comes when confusion blurs reason.

Salvatore put his hand on his gun and yelled angrily, "Listen, fuck face, stop telling me what to do or I'll shove this gun so far up your ass your eyes will pop out."

Frank kept his body completely still and his hands open to show he had no weapon.

"Death smiles at us all, but all a man can do is smile back. Marcus Aurelius." Frank spoke the words slowly, with a tone of total control.

Salvatore froze. He removed his hand from his weapon, and the aggressive expression mellowed into one of calm contemplation. It was as though Aurelius' words altered his state of mind. It seemed they had the power to influence both his conscious and subconscious reasoning, as if he had been hypnotized to acknowledge certain trigger words.

Frank knew the Don's commands had holding power on family members, especially those closest to him. The fundamental strength of Cabineri family loyalty was based on unquestionable power and dedication to the Don. His words and commands were everything. Salvatore looked at him as if he was seeing him for the first time, his eyes peering deep into Frank's.

"Frankie, is that really you?" Salvatore said with brotherly emotion.

"Yes, *paisan*, it's me, or at least behind the skin," replied Frank. "Salvatore, I know how difficult it is to believe, and I need you to believe me one hundred percent, so listen. Remember the day we hit Ricki's warehouse and we were speeding in Tom's '57 Chevy toward the Meadowbrook Parkway on the other side of Jones Beach, remember what happened right after we left the tollgate?"

Salvatore's eyes lit up, as he remembered and realized that only Frank could know this story. "I remember," he replied, waiting for Frank to continue.

"Well we took off, wheels spinning, and a passing bird slammed into our windshield, bouncing over the Chevy and straight into the tollhouse window, scaring the living shit out of the toll guy!" recounted Frank. "We called it the Donald Duck, and whenever we said it nobody knew what the hell we were talking about, remember?"

Salvatore's eyes filled with tears and he lunged toward Frank with open arms, taking him by surprise. They hugged and patted each other on the back and started to laugh like a couple of kids. Than Salvatore pulled back, his hands still on Frank's shoulders, and looking straight into his eyes he said with a trembling voice, "Ave Caesar!"

Frank put his hand behind Salvatore's neck and, forehead to forehead, whispered to his old friend, "It's good to see you again, brother."

"My God, Frankie, I can't believe it," Salvatore blurted. "Fuck me, it's unbelievable! So many years! Where have you been? What happened? Why did you hide?"

"OK, Salvatore, I'll explain everything soon enough, but now we have serious business, my friend," Frank replied. "We need to move fast and hit back, and I need to know everything you know about the Don's hit. Everything is important, trust me."

Salvatore nodded in agreement.

"You're right, Frank. Let me get us a drink and I will tell you everything I know. What do you want? Beer? Whiskey?" Salvatore asked as he walked toward the open kitchen.

"Beer sounds good," answered Frank.

Salvatore returned with a couple of beers, handed one to Frank, and sat next to the fireplace.

"What happened, Salvatore?" asked Frank with a tone of curiosity and controlled anger.

"I was in the front office, Frankie, and just after lunch, five guys arrived flashing IRS badges. I don't know if you knew, but the Don had been having trouble with his tax records, and that fuck Daballia knew it." Salvatore was sweating as he retold the events, even though the cabin was freezing, blazing fireplace notwithstanding.

"I know how hard this is, but I need you to concentrate and tell me every tiny detail. We're going to get these motherfuckers, that's a promise!" Frank told him and lit up a Lucky.

Salvatore nodded and continued.

"I know, Frankie, but I was there, and I fucked up, brother. I could have saved him," he confessed, his voice breaking with despair and anger.

"Don't blame anyone but Daballia, he's the motherfucking traitor that gave the order. Tell me everything," Frank responded, pushing his friend to continue.

"Yes, and the prick passed the information to the IRS. The Don knew about the audit from his sources in the IRS, and was expecting them, so he told Johnny and me to be unarmed," explained Salvatore.

He took a swallow of beer from his half-empty glass and continued.

"That was a bad mistake, leaving our guns home. When the IRS guys came in, they took us all in the Don's office and made us line up, faces to the wall," Salvatore went on. "The Don protested, but they pulled out guns and pushed him into the accountant's office. You know, the one next to his. I heard them saying they wanted to see the books, and I knew something was wrong. I tried to turn around and the last thing I remember is seeing a leather sap coming toward my skull."

Salvatore stopped and wiped his face with a paper towel. The sweat was running down his forehead into his eyes, but he continued.

"I was out for a long time and when I finally came to, I found Johnny with his throat cut lying next to me. I ran into the accountant's office and found the Don," he said shakily. "Brother, they butchered him. He had at least eight stab wounds plus a couple of shots to the heart and one in the face. His face, Frankie!"

Salvatore broke down and started to cry, his face in his hands. Frank held back his own emotions and rested a hand on the big man's back while he let him grieve.

"What did you do immediately after that? It's important. Who did you talk to?" pressed Frank gently. Salvatore raised his head and continued.

"It was no more than a few minutes after I found his body that I picked up the phone and called the Don's house. It was Mantia's turn to oversee home protection that day, and it rang for a long time before he answered."

Salvatore went on to describe the call.

"'Giorgio, this is Salvatore. Listen, Giorgio!'" I said, "'In a minute I'm going to tell you very bad news. Now prepare yourself because when I tell you I want you to act very casual. I don't want anyone else in the house to find out, especially Mama Cabineri. You got that?'

"'OK,' said Giorgio, a confused note to his response.

"'Good. First things first. Tell Mrs. Cabineri that the Don has decided to move her, for her safety, to another house in the west end. You got that? In an hour, a couple of my men are going to come to take her away with them. You take off right after the pick-up and head to the warehouse and wait for instructions. Tell them when they come that I want them to call me before they leave. Just tell them that. OK?'

"'Yeah, yeah, I got it,' Giorgio said." His voice was excited, the tension in Salvatore's voice finally alerting him that this was going to be important.

"'They killed Don Cabineri. It's true. Don't say anything. Tomorrow morning I will tell her. You got that?'" cautioned Salvatore. "'Now listen close. Daballia gave the order, you understand? Daballia will be coming after us, you hear me?'

"A hoarse, whispered 'Yes' was all Giorgio could muster. He was shaky and finished with, 'Sure, Salvatore, sure, I understand.'"

"'Thank you, Giorgio. I will see you soon and keep your head low.'"

"That was the last thing I told him," Salvatore said, finishing that part of the story. "Then I made a call to Johnny Kalibradi, and told him to come to the office right away. You remember Johnny? The Don had him on guard duty at the house a couple of years now, and he also run errands for Mama Cabineri and the girls."

"When Kalibradi came to the office we called the cops, reporting that we heard gunfire, then went straight to the warehouse and waited for Mantia. He never showed up. We went looking but couldn't find him anywhere. Finally, the next day, we heard he had gone to the feds."

Salvatore was breathless but had more details to include.

"Remember Sally? Johnnie's girlfriend? Well she works in the district attorney's office as a secretary, and she tipped us off that Mantia was being moved to a safe house."

Salvatore took a quick swallow of beer and lit a cigarette.

"That's great news! Could she find out where they are keeping him?" asked Frank.

"I already asked her to keep her eyes and ears open. If she hears anything she's going to call me," replied Salvatore.

"Excellent, we need to find Mantia and take him out. He will burn the whole family if he testifies," added Frank, and Salvatore nodded in agreement.

"Now listen closely, Daballia also needs to get rid of Mantia, and this we will use to our advantage. Mantia is our bait, so we first need to find out where he is, then leak the information to Daballia. When he moves to hit Mantia, we'll be waiting for him. If we can get them both to be in the same place, we will kill two birds with one stone," explained Frank.

"Sounds like a fucking Donald Duck Slam Dunk!" Salvatore replied with a smile and wink.

Frank smiled back and continued his instructions.

"I'm sorry I have to keep you here, Salvatore. I need to have you ready and it's just too dangerous for you on the streets right now," cautioned Frank.

"I will bring you everything we need for the job tomorrow," Salvatore replied. "I don't mind at all, Frankie."

"Good," Frank said, lighting another cigarette. "Just stay by the phone and I'll call you when I'm ready for you. I need to scout the area before we plan our strategy, OK?"

"Sure thing, Frankie," Salvatore replied.

"Listen, you know that Don Cabineri was a man of honor, and helped all of us survive. He took me in when my parents died and raised me like a son. He taught me to always take your revenge on the most powerful as long as you keep your eyes open, with knowledge," Frank went on.

"Knowledge is the most powerful weapon, so with the right knowledge your strategy and decisions cannot be wrong. We need to know everything there is to know about Daballia's situation and plans. This is our priority."

Frank sat down in a large leather armchair. He looked directly into the fireplace, focusing on the twirling, dancing yellow flames as if they would reveal the answers he was searching for. He then started to think out loud, and directed his thoughts to Salvatore.

"Daballia betrayed the Don and the whole family. He ordered an act of abomination. But why? We need to understand the reason he did this, his motivation."

Salvatore nodded in agreement and Frank continued.

"Daballia was second in command in the Cabineri family structure. Don Cabineri made him a millionaire, and he had one of the most powerful posts in the organization. What could Daballia gain by betraying his own family, betraying the man that gave him respect and power?" Frank asked out loud. "He's rich, so it was not the money."

"Maybe he wanted more power . . . but more power to do what? His family is one of the most powerful crime families in the country, and he was its operational king. Did he want revenge for some imaginary insult? If this was true it was something between the Don and Daballia and unknown to everyone else, something very personal."

Frank looked at Salvatore searching for any clue. Had he ever heard any insult directed to Daballia from the Don? Salvatore understood his questioning gaze and responded immediately.

"Nothing, Frank, the Don always spoke with respect to Daballia and to everyone else about him. I never heard anything," Salvatore answered.

"So, the reason was not more money, power, or revenge," Frank summarized his logic, and lit another cigarette. For a few minutes he sat in silence, his eyes lost in the jumping flames and shadows. He suddenly cleared his throat and continued.

"What reasons remain for Daballia to kill his Don? Contempt? Jealousy?" Frank's voice punctuated each word like a whip hitting its target.

"Jealousy? Everyone has been jealous of somebody in their lives, someone is always better looking, stronger, taller, smarter, richer, the list goes on," Frank philosophized. "Jealousy is also linked to a feeling of protectiveness regarding our own advantages or attachments. We are filled with jealousy when someone looks at our wife or girlfriend. We want to protect ourselves from losing something dear to us."

Salvatore listened to Frank and realized that this was not the man he used to know. Frank's words revealed a new man with a high level of education. A man who had studied and learned and understood, a man of knowledge. Frank continued his thoughts, speaking slower and softer.

"But jealousy has a brother, a brother that is more evil and more dangerous. And that brother's name is *envy*!" Frank said the word slightly louder than the rest and waited for the cabin's silence to return before he continued speaking.

"Envy is a craving to have a quality, possession, or something belonging to someone else. But if you cannot have it, you don't want them to have it either," Frank said, moving his thought process along. "So, you struggle to obtain it, and if you cannot, you try to destroy the one that has it."

At this, Frank stood up and walked closer to the fireplace. He stood there for a few minutes and turned toward Salvatore.

"The wicked envy and hate; it is their way of admiring," continued Frank. "Victor Hugo said that a long time ago. That is our conclusion, Salvatore! Daballia's motivation was envy. He envied Don Cabineri's character, leadership, and strength. His envy turned into a hunger that needed to be satisfied and fed. He killed Don Cabineri because he knew that he could never possess his qualities."

Frank sat down once again in the armchair.

"I don't understand what this gives us, Frank," puzzled Salvatore, frustrated. "So Daballia was envious of the Don. So fucking what?"

"It gives us everything," declared Frank. "This means that Daballia did not have the support of the other families. He acted on his own, with no logical reason to get rid of the Don. So Daballia is on his own, and they will not support his consolidation of power within the Cabineri family. They will wait for him to gain control by himself. They must be very angry with Daballia's decision to kill the Don; it drove Mantia to become an informer, and that could damage all the families. This is on Daballia's head; remember the families don't like publicity and trouble with the government."

Salvatore made a violent gesture, and exploded, "When the fucking action comes I will be ready! Daballia knows that, and that's one reason he wants to take me out. I made my bones when I was nineteen, and I've been there every time the family had a war. I was always a big help to the old man. Daballia will go down, and I will personally fuck his envy with my big dick!"

Frank understood Salvatore's explosion; he had loved the Don as much as anyone and all this talk snapped his nerves. He was a soldier, and wanted action rather than words. Patience was a strength he did not possess. Frank knew this, and needed to hold him back. They needed to take their time for any plan to work.

"Patience, my friend, we will take our revenge, but the time must be right," Frank replied with confidence.

"Daballia is a dead man. I don't care if we fight all the families in New York. I say we hit him now!" Salvatore continued standing and pacing like a caged tiger in front of the fireplace.

Frank walked up to his long-lost friend, and locked eyes with him.

"And I say NO!" he shouted.

Frank knew Salvatore was not used to taking orders from anyone except the Don, but now was the time to truly take command.

"Remember what 'Ave Caesar' means. If you say it, you must obey by it. And I need to know right now that you will." Frank spoke with strength and determination, with his voice and his eyes.

Salvatore looked at Frank and realized more than ever that the Don was dead. He had always followed the Don's commands without doubt, and as he looked into Frank's determined eyes he knew that he must do the same for his friend. He took Frank's hand and with respect kissed it, whispering his pledge of obedience, "Ave Caesar!"

From that moment, Frank knew Salvatore would be his to command.

"Revenge, brother, tastes better when you eat it cold," Frank said, sealing the moment, as he put on his coat. "I'm heading back to the city, and like we agreed, you stay put and wait for my call."

"What happens if I have news first, especially from our girl in the DA's office?" Salvatore asked.

"I will be calling you every two hours," responded Frank immediately, and he turned to open the door.

"Wait up, Frank, I have something for you," Salvatore yelled out while running into the small cabin's bedroom. Rushing back to Frank, he handed him a folder. "This is everything Sally put together regarding the district attorney's information on Mantia and the Cabineri family."

Frank took the brown folder and shook Salvatore's hand tightly.

"Thank you, Salvatore, thank you for everything, brother," Frank said, and he opened the cabin door, letting the howling wind and snow invade the heat and light. He closed the door behind him and Salvatore watched him disappear into the darkness. After a while he saw the van's lights illuminate the flying flakes and make a rapid one-eighty turn. Then the red taillights faded to black.

Frank felt strange that after so many years of solitude he had contacted someone from the past. Memories flooded his mind and he remembered going with Salvatore, Antonio, and Vinnie to Sally's ill-famed house. It was known that Salvatore was generously endowed by nature and that most of the girls at Sally's avoided sharing their bed with him as best they could. He paid double the going rate for services by Sally's most experienced and fearless ladies of the night, and would always ask for a loan before they got to the place. Vinnie would bitch that every time Salvatore wanted to fuck, he needed to rob a bank. Frank's smile faded as he reflected once again on what had happened to the Don and Antonio. He concentrated on the road and headed back to the city.

CHAPTER 24

1978, NEW YORK CITY, GREENWICH VILLAGE

S cott opened his apartment door and found Grace curled up on the living room couch. She was very beautiful, but for some reason from the moment they met at Berkeley they both felt a connection that only a brother and sister could feel. They immediately surrendered to it, and never risked ruining it in any way. They were both from single-parent households and neither had siblings. Grace had lost her father in a car accident when she was six. This common loneliness had built a relationship that would make most brothers and sisters jealous.

"Hi, sis!" Scott said. He always called her that, another instinctive decision that she had accepted as natural. "Hope you enjoyed the cheesecake!"

"It was amazing, and my taste buds will sue the baker for torturing them with pleasure!"

Her giggles and his laughter filled the small bachelor apartment.

"How was your day, Mr. Assistant District Attorney?" she asked with a smile. Scott took off his coat and sat next to her.

"It's not over yet, I have a meeting with the DA later. I'll tell you about my day after he finishes with me," he explained. Grace could see the tiredness landscaping his face.

"Scott, I know how important this job is to you, but, you have to take care of yourself," Grace said in a loving and caring manner.

"I know, sis, but I can't do that before the trial. This is the big one, believe me," he replied, noticing that she had her arms crossed and shoulders hunched. He realized the apartment was cold and fetched a blanket, draping it around her shoulders and over her legs. She shivered and hugged it tight around herself.

"Thanks," she said softly. "You're going to make someone very happy one day, Scotty, you know that?"

"Well I don't know about that, but I am sure that when that day comes you will be the first to know," Scott replied.

"I should hope so!" she said with mock demand, then reached over and began to read the overleaf of a book from the coffee table.

"*The Gangs of New York: An Informal History of the Underworld* is an American nonfiction book by Herbert Asbury, first published in 1927," she recited, then flipped through the pages and continued.

"The political geniuses of the Tammany Hall, quick to see the practical value of the gangsters, and to realize the advisability of providing them with meeting and hiding places, that their favor might be curried, and their peculiar talents employed on election day to assure government of, by, and for Tammany."

She turned the book's pages quickly and said with an eye roll, "Interesting, relaxing reading."

"That's how it was back in the 1830s, and 150 years later it's pretty much the same shit," Scott stated. "We need to stop it, extinguish it. It's a cancer and the law is the only medicine that can cure it."

Scott's facial expressions and seriousness took her by surprise. He had always been very serious about justice and protecting the innocent, but she had never seen this look before.

"What's wrong, Scotty? I know you can't talk about it, but I've never seen you so wired up," she inquired with a bit of trepidation.

"This case comes once in a lifetime, a real chance to make a difference, really change things," Scott replied solemnly.

Grace studied him. *His eyes had changed*, she thought. They had a darkness that comes from seeing and hearing about wicked deeds. She looked away and put back the book on the coffee table.

Scott stood up and said, "Let me read you something I think will make you understand better."

Scott walked to his desk and picked up a large brown folder. He took out a yellow legal notepad and some papers, then selected one and started to read.

Senate Hearings
COMMITTEE – United States Senate. Permanent Investigations Subcommittee.
HELD HEARINGS – Sept. 25-Oct. 16, 1963 on organized crime. September 25, 27, October 1, 2, 8 and 9 1963.

"Only fifteen years ago. Now listen to this," noted Scott for effect.

"Joseph Valachi, a convicted murderer and, according to his testimony, a former member of an underworld crime syndicate he called 'Cosa Nostra,' was the star witness at a widely publicized 1963 Senate investigation of organized crime.

"Remember the Valachi papers? We had a study session at Berkeley. It's considered as a major legal precedent. One bad guy comes forth against the whole Mafia and lives to talk about it. It made the witness protection program what it is today!" Scott continued while Grace pushed her body farther into the soft pillows of the couch.

"In September and October, the Senate Government Operations Permanent Investigations Subcommittee heard Valachi unfold a complex story of murder, terror, crime, and vice as he described the organization and named alleged members. The 1963 investigation was prompted by information given federal authorities by Valachi, 58, who was serving a life sentence in the federal penitentiary at Atlanta, Ga. Because he informed on the secret activities of the nationwide syndicate which allegedly dominated the underworld, Valachi said, he had been marked for execution by his former colleagues. Before his Committee appearance federal authorities, to protect Valachi's life, moved him about the country in secret under a heavy guard."

"Giorgio Mantia, my dear sis, is even bigger than Valachi. He is a key witness in my case and will do real damage to them. He has also been marked for execution by his former colleagues, and federal authorities are moving him around in secret to protect him," he whispered, as if someone was outside the apartment door listening. Grace instinctively looked at the door and then back to Scott.

"According to Federal Bureau of Investigation Director J. Edgar Hoover, 'The Valachi case represents the biggest intelligence breakthrough yet in combating organized crime and racketeering in the United States.'"

"Mantia is the biggest intelligence breakthrough in combating organized crime since Valachi," Scott said excitedly. "Now, do you understand why?"

Grace came closer and gave him a kiss on the forehead.

"Yes, Scotty, I do understand, and it scares me. These men are capable of anything," she nervously replied.

"Yes they are, but they must be stopped once and for all," Scott responded, then pulling out another document, he continued to read.

"Attorney General Robert F. Kennedy told the Subcommittee that the Federal Government was dealing with 'a private government of organized crime, a government with an annual income of billions, resting on a base of human suffering and moral corrosion.' He said it was particularly difficult to expose these operations because witnesses were intimidated, and corrupt public officials protected the rackets' leaders."

"Attorney General Robert F. Kennedy, for Christ's sake! They killed him, they killed his brother, they must be stopped, and I need to do anything in my power to help stop them!"

His tone sent shivers of fear down her spine, and she realized that he would not stop until the job was finished. All she could do was support and encourage him.

"I know you will stop them, Scotty, and I am here to help in any way I can," Grace said, suppressing her fear, her voice somehow calm and strong. She moved closer and they held each other in silence.

Breaking their embrace, Scott stood up and got ready to leave.

"Got to head out. I'm sorry for leaving you alone again. I was planning to take you out for dinner tonight," Scott said while grabbing his briefcase.

"It's OK, don't worry about me. I will relax and read about the gangs of New York," Grace replied happily.

Scott winked and opened the door, then he turned and said, "Thank you, sis, thank you for everything!"

CHAPTER 25

1978, NEW YORK CITY, LOWER EAST SIDE

F rank drove back to New York the same way he came. The roads were still empty and again he thought of the coincidence of the storm's timing. He could not ask for better cover. His contact with Salvatore had accomplished his first objective, and now he had to plan the next steps. He would need all the knowledge he had accumulated all these years as a professional criminal.

Distracting himself, he watched the rare sets of passing headlights and emptied his mind of all thoughts. He would need his mental strength, and the car ride back was a chance to refill his batteries. But hate was proving a powerful adversary, and flashes of Daballia's face kept him from this goal.

He loved the Don like a father, and Daballia took him away, killing him like an animal. Salvatore's detailed description of the Don's killing replayed in his mind, and the only desire he had was to grab Daballia's throat and press the balls of his thumbs down on his windpipe, watching his tongue come out of his mouth and his eyes roll up into the waiting hands of death.

As he passed Pier 88 and West 48th Street, the moored ships in the Hudson River brought back memories of the smoke rising above the three funnels of the Normandy.

Recalling his first assignment was like a lighthouse providing a sense of purpose and a revelation of destiny. He burned the ship and his adoptive father was pleased. The purpose of his act was not clear, but he knew it was important for the family, and that was all that mattered.

Back at 97 Orchard Street, Frank entered his lair, and made sure the street below and the square block of roofs were clear. He poured a Scotch and sat at the kitchen table, then stretched his legs and felt the pain of his old war wounds run from his knees to his ankles. The cold weather served as a reminder of the origins of the pain.

He opened Salvatore's brown folder and removed all the documents, setting them on his lap. On the top of the pile was a cutout news article clipped from the New York Times. He held the clipping and started to read:

"NEW YORK (*Reuters*)–The Manhattan district attorney unveiled indictments on Tuesday of four reputed Mafia gangsters, saying that after the assassination of Joseph

Cabineri, the head of the New York Cabineri crime family, a critical witness has come forward and is under protective custody.

Heading the investigation is the newly appointed assistant district attorney, Scott Easten—"

Frank froze. The name Scott Easten jogged his memory, activating a chain reaction of images from Korea and Alcatraz that flashed before his eyes. He reread the name a couple of times, verifying its spelling. The more he repeated the name the more stimulation he exerted on his memory recall. He continued to speed-read the article for more clues.

"Heading the investigation is newly appointed assistant district attorney, Scott Easten, who attests that the notorious Cabineri crime family had been engaged in extortion, loan sharking, and gambling around the New York City region, but also engaged in new ventures such as trading in prescription drugs.

"While in the last few decades we have seen a decline, organized crime is by no means extinct," Easten told reporters at a news conference.

The four reputed members of the Cabineri crime family include a Teamsters Union president, who is charged with enterprise corruption, the state version of the federal crime of racketeering. According to the indictment, the election of alleged Cabineri associate Jonathan Bernvalle to president of

Teamsters 917 on Long Island "was explicitly supported" by his fellow mobsters.

He then "used his position in Local 917 to benefit himself and a crew from the Cabineri organized crime family," the indictment said. "The union, which represents about 1,900 workers in liquor, automotive, parking and other industries, became a hub for gambling and loan sharking," Easten said.

"Whatever name you call it, the Mafia, Cosa Nostra, the mob, the 258-page indictment demonstrates that organized crime is still operating in New York City and it still has its hooks in the labor movement," he said. All but one of the defendants was arrested on Tuesday.

Investigators used court-ordered wiretaps and search warrants in their probe."

Frank stopped reading and frantically shuffled through the other documents on his lap, searching for any other reference related to Scott Easten. Some of the papers fell on the floor, and reaching for them he dropped the remaining ones. He kicked the kitchen table leg and the table almost turned over, sending the scotch flying and smashing the glass on the hardwood floor.

Frank stopped moving, grabbed the side of his head with both of his hands and focused on regaining control. Taking deep breaths, he slowly calmed himself, looked down at the documents, and started to collect everything. He then pulled the table back to its original position and cleaned up the broken glass, poured himself another drink, and slowly sat at the table again. He started to look at each document one by one, starting from the top of the pile and scanning quickly for the name Scott Easten. The second to last document revealed what he was looking for:

"New York City Manhattan District Attorney (Public Affairs Profile–Released to Media 23-JUNE-1978)

Assistant District Attorney Scott Easten

Assistant District Attorney Scott R. Easten of Queens County was born and raised in San Francisco, California. He graduated from California University Berkeley School of Law in 1970 and was admitted to the Bar by the State Bar of California in November 1971. Easten joined the San Francisco district attorney's office as an assistant district attorney, where he supervised grand jury investigations and prosecuted cases involving murder, organized crime, career criminals, political corruption, international art fraud, and white-collar crime.

In 1977, he moved to New York City because, according to Easten, he "wanted to fight organized crime at its very source."

Easten joined the New York district attorney's office as an assistant district attorney, where he is currently supervising grand jury investigations and prosecuting cases involving murder, organized crime, and career criminals.

Easten was admitted to the Bar in New York State, Washington State, and Washington,

D.C., and to practice before the United States Supreme Court, the U.S. District Courts for the Southern District of New York and Western and Eastern Districts of Washington, and the U.S. Second and Ninth Circuit Courts of Appeals.

Frank read it twice and put down the paper. Scott R. Easten: R for Roy, *this cannot be happening*, he thought. Scott Easten, the assistant district attorney, is the boy he met at Alcatraz almost sixteen years ago; the boy who wore Roy's dog tags; Roy Easten's son. He wiped the sweat from his brow. In the last few minutes he had become drenched with a cold sweat that sent shivers down his body.

The humidity of the deserted apartment compounded the cold, and his hands and feet were frozen, but his face felt like it was on fire. He looked at his watch and saw it was 5:00 a.m. In an hour he would have been awake for twenty-four hours straight, and his body was sending messages of major fatigue and stress.

Once again, Roy Easten, the man who saved his life, had discovered him. Frank breathed deeply the pain and guilt of Roy Easten's sacrifice. He found himself back in his dark Alcatraz prison cell questioning the reason he had survived and Roy had died. This question would haunt him for the rest of his life, or at least until the gods revealed the answer.

Yet again, Roy Easten reaches out, finds him, and sends his son. Why? Frank felt drained; his adrenaline had been pumping full throttle ever since he first saw Scott's name. He moved to the cot and laid down. He needed sleep, rest and time, time that he did not have. The day's tiredness overcame his body and mind, and he surrendered, sleep once again saving him from the realities of life.

Frank woke to the sound and vibration of a snowplow passing on the street below. His head was pounding, his vision fogged. It was 11:00 a.m., and he realized that he needed to call Salvatore. *Fuck!* He had missed the first "every two hour" callback they had agreed to. He sat up and held his head for a couple of minutes, allowing the dizziness to subside. *First food*, then he would call Salvatore. He washed his face and changed his shirt and pants, which he had slept in, giving him the appearance of one of the homeless guys down the street.

He exited the building, checking in all directions. The storm had passed but the streets were still pretty empty. He walked to a small pizza parlor on a side street just a few blocks away. The lunch hour was just beginning, and those stuck at home due to the snow were hungry for takeout. The telephone rang continuously, and the counterman was shouting orders into the kitchen in broken English, with a heavy unrecognizable accent. Frank pointed to the leftover slices in the hot storage window, and raised his two fingers. The counterman took his wooden shovel and scooped two cold slices into the huge brick oven.

After a few minutes he looked at Frank, and raising three fingers, pulled out the tray and put the slices in a small paper box. *Silent hand communication always worked best when there was a language barrier,* thought Frank.

Handing over four dollars, Frank waved a back-hand signal for him to keep the change, then exited the parlor as the next customer said, "Gimme a slice," and the counterman answered once again something that required a United Nations translator. Frank laughed a little to himself and walked across the street to a corner telephone booth.

He dialed Salvatore's number, heard a "hello" and replied, "It's me, any news?"

"What's up, Frankie, where the fuck have you been, man?! You said every two hours and it's been like six hours, man!" Salvatore complained with a worried voice. "I was scared something happened to you; everything ok?"

"I'm sorry, brother, everything is good. I'm ok, and it won't happen again—sorry!" replied Frank sincerely.

"OK, Frank, never mind. So do you have any news?" Salvatore closed the issue and asked.

"No, but I'm going through the documents you gave me. How about you? Any news from Sally?" Frank asked.

"Yes, she called this morning. Says it's possible she will get more information on the location tonight. The guy heading the investigation, Scott Easten or something like that, has a meeting at the district attorney's office tonight."

Salvatore knew that this was great news, but played it cool to gauge Frank's reaction.

"The guy's name is Scott Easten, and that's fucking great news, brother! If he is there, we can put a tail on him and he will lead us to Mantia," Frank replied with excitement.

"Yes, brother! That sounds like a plan!" replied Salvatore.

"OK, listen up, I got some things to do. It's 12:30, and I will call you at 2:30 and we'll plan the stakeout at the DA's office, OK?" asked Frank.

"Yes, sir, talk at 2:30, brother!" replied Salvatore and he hung up.

Frank rushed back to the tenement thinking about the latest news. He entered his apartment and started to put things into perspective.

If Sally's information was correct, they could follow Scott after his meeting and he could lead them to Mantia's hideout. They could not lose him no matter what, and that meant they would need a third follow man. If one lost Scott, the other would follow and so forth. Salvatore would have to find another trustworthy guy for the job.

I'll ask him next time I call, Frank thought.

Frank finished going through the documents, making sure he didn't miss any important information. He put them back into the folder and sat back listening to the silence. He needed to plan carefully; every step had to be perfectly executed if he was to get both Mantia and Daballia with one stroke. Swallowing his drink in several gulps, he closed his eyes and felt the loss of the Don more than ever.

What would the Don do? he asked himself. In the silence of the small apartment he heard the Don's voice as if he was sitting next to him.

"Francesco, I know that you are upset but there's a lot I can't tell you, not because of lack of trust but because it's not the right time for you to know. Learning to act exactly at the right time wins every war. That, my son, needs patience, and patience is the mightiest weapon a man can have. Impatience, on the other hand, has destroyed many great men, Francesco. But, the art of patience is something that can only be learned with time. Patience exists only if time exists, do you understand?"

Frank remembered the Don's words, and that they had saved his life; he would not have survived Korea, Alcatraz, and his ghost life if he did not have patience.

Frank kept his eyes closed and continued to listen.

"Francesco, listen, my son. All the people around me are loyal because I give them what they need. The day I stop giving I will lose their loyalty. That is basic human nature, but, being a true family means that loyalty is not dependent on what you receive but on the blood that flows in your veins."

Frank opened his eyes and looked at his watch. It was time to call Salvatore.

CHAPTER 26

1978, NEW YORK CITY, COLUMBUS PARK

"Hello," Salvatore's voice came through.

"Listen up, we need to meet at the district attorney's office. It's next to Columbus Park, you know the place?" Frank asked.

"Yes, I know it," answered Salvatore.

"OK, we need one more guy with us, and we need separate cars. We'll stake out the place and when Easten leaves we all tail him separately, and if one of us loses him the other will not. Is that clear, brother?" Frank instructed.

"It's clear, and I know the right guy for the job. Remember Sonny Bats?" Salvatore asked.

"Sonny Bats, yes, I remember him from the job we did uptown," Frank agreed. "OK so, we need to be there at 8:30. We can meet at the small park in front of the building and give Sonny the newspaper shot of Easten, so he can recognize him. Bring walkie-talkies with you and pass one to me when you get there."

"OK, boss, let's do this!" Salvatore said deferentially.

Salvatore did not fear any man, and he did not fear the gods. He had chosen to fear and love Don Cabineri, and now he chose to do the same with Frank.

Frank understood the tone and replied accordingly, "Excellent, *Caporegime*!" reminding Salvatore that he remained a ranking member of the family.

"Ave Caesar!" replied Salvatore, about to hang up.

"Wait, Salvatore! I have another job for you," Frank said, his tone more grave. "I need to send Daballia a written message. Can you get it to him?"

Salvatore waited a few moments to answer.

"Yea, I can have Falucci take it to Lemensa. Lemensa is Daballia's fucking head watchdog. Falucci can leave it at Lemensa's bar in the Bronx tonight and he will find it tomorrow morning addressed to Daballia," Salvatore answered, feeling good to contribute another piece of the plan.

"Alright, do you have a typewriter? We need it typed, not written," Frank stated hopefully.

"Yea, I can get Susan to write it up right away," Salvatore replied.

"OK, get a pen and write down exactly what I will tell you," Frank instructed, then waited for Salvatore to locate his ballpoint.

"OK, got it. Go ahead, Frankie," he said.

Frank lit a cigarette, concentrated, and started to talk.

"'Death smiles at us all, but all a man can do is smile back,' Marcus Aurelius. The Don wants a meeting tomorrow. He wants to hear you say 'Ave Caesar!' If you don't come, Mantia will live! If you don't come, the kiss of death will find you!—*Il bacio della morte ti troverà*."

"Did you get that, Salvatore?" Frank asked.

"Now that's what I call a fucking message, Frank. I would give anything to see Daballia's fucking face when he reads it!" replied Salvatore, sounding like a kid with a new bike.

"For this to work we need to find where Mantia is being kept—tonight! I'm hoping Easten will lead us to the safe house. After that, Daballia has no choice if he wants to win. He needs Mantia out of the way, and after this message he needs to find out who Don Cabineri has named Caesar because he needs to kill him too. He cannot take control of the family if he has the Don's heir running around," Frank said, revealing the rest of his plan to Salvatore.

"When Daballia comes to the meeting we will be waiting," Frank added.

"Fucking right, Frank! Payback time for both those motherfucking traitors!" replied Salvatore.

Frank could hear Salvatore grinning.

"I've got at least twenty men ready to hit the street in less than twenty-four hours. Daballia shows one hair of his asshole and he's dead!" Salvatore added enthusiastically.

"No button men!" Frank cautioned. "It has to be only us, and we can't have anyone else knowing our plans. Daballia has ears everywhere."

"But he's going to bring an army with him, Frankie," Salvatore replied.

"I've got a plan that will force him to come alone," Frank hinted. "But for now we got to get ready. I will explain everything later tonight, OK, Salvatore?"

"OK, Boss, see you at Columbus Park," Salvatore said and hung up.

Frank ran up to the first tenement building on Orchard Street and climbed the stairs to the roof. He traveled over a few rooftops and reached his own ruinous residence, descending the steps of the fire escape to the backyard and finally slipping into the building.

Finally Frank Morris was prepared to go into battle. He opened his closet and grabbed a black shirt, pants, and a jacket, then laid them on the cot and brushed them carefully. He always wore black. It was the best camouflage for dark corridors and alleyways.

Before his jacket, came his shoulder holster, which he adjusted for maximum freedom of motion. From the suitcase next to the cot he removed a new .38 Police Special, untraceable. He disassembled and oiled it, checked the hammer, then reassembled it, after which he aimed at the window, arm outstretched, and clicked the trigger. After loading the cylinders, Frank slid his new piece into its holster and secured the leather safety strap. He made sure he had not forgotten anything, then looked at his watch, closed the apartment, and headed for the parking lot.

The New York County district attorney's office was only ten minutes away. He went through Chinatown and turned left on Mulberry Street right after the original Chinatown Ice Cream Factory. Up to Worth Street with Columbus Park on his right, he turned right and slowly pulled to a stop right at the five points, on the corner of Worth and Baxter Streets. He turned off the engine and noted the time. He was early.

From this position, if he continued on Baxter, he would pass right in front of the DA's office. Baxter Street ran along the periphery of the park, and he decided to wait there until Salvatore arrived. Frank lit a cigarette and slightly rolled down his window, blowing smoke into the cold air. A tree, heavy with snow, moved its branches in unison with the wind.

A few minutes later, Salvatore's dark blue Buick slowly passed and stopped about twenty car lengths ahead. He saw Salvatore get out and walk toward him holding a brown paper bag. Frank opened the passenger-side window, through which Salvatore tossed the bag, without breaking stride. He passed the van and, after a minute, casually returned to his own car. Frank took the walkie-talkie out of the bag and turned it on, playing with the volume and hearing a hissing sound. Suddenly Salvatore's voice came through.

"One, two, three, Frank, can you hear me?" he said.

"Yes, loud and clear! Over!" Frank answered.

"OK great, over!" replied Salvatore.

"Is Bats here? Over," Frank asked.

"Yea, he's on the other corner of the building. Over," came the answer.

Frank checked his military timepiece. It was 20:45. *Scott would be arriving soon*, he thought. He looked up and down the street scanning for cars.

Suddenly, the lights of a car turned onto Baxter and slowly approached him. He rotated his body to hide from view, and called on the walkie-talkie.

"Heads up, Salvatore, it may be him, over," he whispered, then waited for the car to pass, and returned to his upright position. The passing car stopped directly in front of the building. The driver's door opened, and a tall blond man stepped out. The man looked up and down the street, then stepped quickly up the large staircase and into the entrance.

Frank observed, and instinctively compared his features, as much as he could remember, with Roy Easten's. Even after so many years his memory recognized the similarities, sending small waves of shivers down his spine. Frank did not need a DNA test to confirm that Scott looked and moved like his dead father. Scott was Roy Easten's son, he was sure of it.

Salvatore's voice crackled over the walkie-talkie, "That's the guy, that's Easten," he said with excitement, forgetting the "over" command.

There was no reply. Silence filled the van and Frank was filled with a confusing feeling of guilt. He could not stop his mind from the recurring flashes of Korea and the last few moments of Roy Easten's life. He saw his body explode under the hand grenade, shielding Frank from death, and then his dead eyes staring back when they turned his body. Frank was sweating again and his hands were tightened painfully around the steering wheel.

"Frank! Can you hear me, over!" Salvatore's hissing shocked him back to reality. He shook his head and wiped the sweat from his forehead as he picked up the walkie-talkie.

"It's him, maybe. He fits the newspaper picture, although I couldn't see his face because of the distance, over," he replied, a bit erratically. He fought to gain back control and continued.

"Now we wait. Be ready to move fast; we don't know how long he will be inside, OK? Over."

"OK, Bats also confirmed seeing him. He's parked on the other corner but can see the entrance of the building, over," Salvatore replied. He had heard the strangeness in Frank's voice and pressed, "Frank! Everything OK, boss?"

It took Frank a few seconds, but he responded with confidence.

"Yes, everything is good, keep your eyes sharp!" Silence followed as they waited for Easten to return to his car. Minutes passed like hours until finally Frank saw Scott coming out of the building, heading straight for his car.

"OK, Salvatore, here we go," called Frank. "You go first, I'll follow. Tell Bats to follow me, OK? Over."

Scott got into his car, and a minute later he drove off. Salvatore gave him a few moments' lead and kept about a half block between the moving cars. Frank followed Salvatore closely, eyeing Scott's car ahead. They slowly headed for West Street and then the Holland Tunnel, moving under the Hudson River. Then they turned on Interstate 78 for the New Jersey Turnpike.

At the tolls the three vehicles split up, taking separate toll lanes but keeping Scott in their scope, their convoy a safe distance behind, but never losing sight of their target. As they turned off toward Bayview Avenue and drove into Greenville, Frank was convinced that Scott was taking them to Mantia's safe house.

Passing Greenville and heading for Constable Hook, Scott continued down 440 and suddenly turned right off a ramp that led directly into a neighborhood. Salvatore got taken by surprise, and did not make the turn. Frank took up the lead position, keeping Scott in his sights.

Scott turned on 19th Street, then left on Broadway and right on 16th Street. It was clear he was trying to shake off anyone that could be following.

"Hello, Frank, I lost him, do you have him? Over." Salvatore's voice came over the walkie-talkie with tension.

"Yes, I have him," returned Frank. "We're on 16th heading west, over."

Scott turned again on JFK Boulevard and right on 12th Street, left at the first corner and left again at the next corner. Frank stopped, realizing Scott was taking him around the block again, made a U-turn, and headed back to the first corner street. Gambling that he was right, he waited to see Scott's car pass by. A minute later Scott's Buick went past, and Frank smiled.

He whispered to himself, "You're smart, kid, but I'm smarter."

Following again, he kept approximately a half block between their cars. Finally, Scott turned right on 8th Street and continued to the end, overlooking Newark Bay. Frank slowed down and stopped the car almost at the same time Scott parked outside a two-story run-down house. He watched as the young man got out, ran up to the door, and rang the bell. A minute passed and he entered.

Frank was sure that this was the safe house. He looked up and down the street and it was vacant. He picked up the walkie-talkie.

"Salvatore, we got him, the house is on 8th Street, last house before the bay, over," called Frank.

"OK, Frankie, that's great, what now? Over."

"Head back to the cabin and wait there for instructions, and I will call you when I get back," Frank instructed. "And make sure everything went OK with Daballia's message, he needs to get it tomorrow morning, OK? Over."

"Got it, Frankie. Will do, talk later, over."

The radio's hissing stopped, and Frank looked at the house and the lights coming through the first- and second-floor windows. He inspected the area carefully and identified everything they should know when they hit the place.

He lit a cigarette, looked at the house one last time, started the van's engine, and drove on, feeling more drained and exhausted with every minute that passed. Back on the interstate, he emptied his mind again. He had to subdue Scott's effect on him. It would put everything in jeopardy and he had to control himself.

Frank knew it was destiny that had brought them together and destiny would command their future. He focused straight ahead and entered the Holland Tunnel, heading back to his lair.

CHAPTER 27

1978, NEW JERSEY, NORTH JERSEY

D aballia's naked, sixty-year-old athletic body stood over the bed, ogling the two young women embracing, touching, and kissing each other. Daballia's jet-black, thick hair was combed back and held in place with a special nongreasy French hairstyling cream. The door knocked softly, and his relaxed face immediately turned angry at the interruption. He continued to watch the intertwined lovers and called out.

"This better be good! Entra!" He directed his comment to whoever was behind the door while wrapping a large white towel around his waist.

Lemensa entered, his eyes looking away from the bed.

"Don Daballia, I found this envelope addressed to you at the bar this morning," Lemensa whispered, not wanting to interrupt the activity on the bed.

Daballia took a deep breath and extended his arm, waiting for Lemensa to put the letter in his hand. He took the envelope and looked at both sides, then carefully tore it and with two fingers slid the letter out. Snapping it open in the air, he started to read.

"'Death smiles at us all, but all a man can do is smile back,' Marcus Aurelius. Don Cabineri says hello! The Don wants a meeting tomorrow. He wants to hear you say, 'Ave Caesar!' He will send you the address tomorrow morning! If you don't come, Mantia will live! If you don't come, the kiss of death will find you!—*Il bacio della morte ti troverà*."

Daballia's breathing became quicker and he pushed air into his lungs forcefully through his nostrils, like an angry bull. His facial muscles involuntarily contracted and twitched into a mask of violent rage. The young women stopped, watching the blood rush through his face, turning it completely red.

"Get the fuck out!" Lemensa yelled to them, waving his hand repeatedly toward the door. They did not stop to think. Fear and intuition directed them to pick up their clothes and run naked out the bedroom door. Lemensa closed the door after them and turned toward Daballia, waiting for orders.

Lemensa was a man that many had tried to kill, but his strongest weapon was that he did not fear anything, not even death. His only fear was Don Daballia.

"*Figlio di puttana*—son of a whore!" Daballia screamed, clearing glasses and bottles off the nearby coffee table, sending them crashing on the Italian marble floor. Although adrenaline was pumping through his body, making his hands tremble, he turned to Lemensa and said with a controlled voice, "Cabineri's whores think they can scare me? I want you to find out who is behind this!" barked Daballia. "Everyone involved will die. Everyone and everything around them will die!"

He fumed and strode to the small bar next to the Jacuzzi. Picking up a bottle of whiskey he filled a glass and poured it down his throat, some spilling onto his chest. He turned toward Lemensa, moving his finger up and down, and continued.

"Did you find out anything about Mantia?" he asked.

Lemensa nodded his enormous head and replied, "We don't know where they are keeping him, but we found out that they are moving him to another place this morning, but just for one day. The fuckers moved up the trial to tomorrow."

Lemensa always spoke one word at a time; his voice had a deep sandpaper grinding tone, and his Italian-American accent was hard to understand if you did not listen carefully.

"Motherfuckers, they think they can fuck around with me! That fucking cunt, Easten. Young prick thinks he's got it made because he has Mantia," Daballia raged. "We must send a message to everyone, and this time I will get that message even to the motherfucking whore the district attorney. I want

Mantia dead before he gets to the court, but Lemensa you also get Easten."

Daballia spoke to Lemensa but was looking at his reflection in the giant mirror behind the circular bed. Lemensa's face could not hide his surprise. He had been ordered to kill many men, but never an assistant district attorney. Daballia saw his expression and displayed a wicked grin.

"Tomorrow, my friend, we will send a message to the whole fucking world," said the Don.

He emptied his glass and continued while pouring another.

"Tomorrow they will understand that there is a new *capo di tutti i capi*, boss of all bosses, and even the fucking district attorney will understand that nobody fucks with Daballia," announced the Don. "*Capisci, mio angelo della morte*? Do you understand, my angel of death?"

Lemensa respectfully bowed his head and replied, "*Come comanda, don Daballia,* as you command, Don Daballia!"

"Tell the girls to come back," Daballia instructed, downing his drink.

Lemensa left the room, and after a few minutes the two young women entered wearing white silk robes that pronounced the shape of their breasts and nipples. He cocked his head toward the bed and they slowly dropped their robes and climbed on, lying next to each other, looking back at him with teasing eyes.

He untied his towel and climbed on the bed on all fours, positioning himself directly above their bodies, then began to touch them gently. Daballia sensed they were both scared and this excited him even more. Slowly their flesh was electrified by his touch and kisses; their anticipation grew into growls and caresses of passion that they all shared with each other.

They both whispered, "Fuck us!" The art of sexual pleasure was their profession, and they knew how to make a man crazy with desire.

Daballia took turns satisfying them while asking if they liked it.

"Oh, yes, we do! Yes, we do!" they answered repeatedly until his passion grew into a powerful climax, followed with a thundering sound in his throat, filled with satisfaction.

Both women laughed and continued making love to each other, while Daballia fell back, gasping for breath, and thinking about the next day.

The mud surrounded him, pushing down on his body, the weight compressing the air out of his lungs. The weight turned into pain, and with every breath he felt like he was being squashed into the earth. He reached for Roy's hand, but he just stood there looking at him with tearful, angry eyes. He tried to speak but the mud filled his mouth and only growling sounds reached his ears. Slowly, the pain reached its zenith and he wished for death to make it stop. He pushed against the mud's weight, gasping for air, when suddenly his instinct for survival woke him, tearing the nightmare into small pieces of reality.

Frank's eyes opened, and he clutched for air as his hands pushed away the imaginary mud. He was covered in perspiration and his eyes frantically searched the apartment for images that would bring him back to the real world.

He yanked the blanket and sheet off his body and sat upright on the side of the cot, legs hanging over the side and feet touching the freezing floor. It took several moments for his heart and breathing to slow, and he inhaled as deeply as he could, feeling the sweat running down his body. Looking at the bed he saw large wet spots, left by his upper body and head on the pillow and sheet.

He checked the time. It was a few minutes after 10 a.m., and he quickly dressed and headed for the telephone booth. He needed to know if Salvatore had any response to his message to Daballia. Moving with quick strides, he felt a lot better having the cold wind clear his head. He dialed and waited for Salvatore to pick up.

"Hello?!" his friend answered breathlessly.

"It's me, what's up?" Frank asked.

Salvatore hesitated, and Frank sensed something was wrong.

"Salvatore, what's going on?" Frank pushed for a response.

"Boss, Sandy called me about an hour ago, the motherfuckers moved Mantia this morning," Salvatore rattled off. "They moved the trial up! It's scheduled for tomorrow at ten in the morning at the U.S. Federal District Court."

Salvatore stopped and waited, his breathing even heavier than before. Frank tightened his fingers around the telephone and tried to contain his anger.

"Motherfucking sons of bitches," he whispered, his mind speeding through alternative scenarios.

"If we know, we must assume that Daballia knows, which means he will plan to hit Mantia at the court," deduced Frank. He stopped to weigh the odds and added, "OK, listen up, try to find out who will get the orders to hit Mantia. It's very unlikely that he will use family guys. This is a contract job, so you need to put our ears on the street as soon as possible."

"OK, boss, it's going to be tough but we have no choice. I need to do this myself, so I'll leave for the city right away," Salvatore answered with urgency.

"Yes, but keep your eyes open; don't forget that Daballia is also looking for you, brother," Frank replied, and slowly described his logic. "Tomorrow we need to be at the court; maybe we will recognize Daballia's boys, take them out before they can get to Mantia. We need to keep Mantia alive. If we have Mantia we have Daballia."

"OK, Frank, it's a good plan," said Salvatore. "But how are we going to communicate? I'm going to be on the move all day; what if I need to tell you something?"

"Go to Benny's pool room in the Bronx at 6 p.m. sharp. I'm going to call and ask for you. OK?" Frank answered.

"OK, Frank, talk later."

Frank could hear Salvatore's tense voice and he gave a final order. "Salvatore, remember what the Don used to say when things got tough," Frank recalled. "'*We must do what needs to be done because we are more honorable than the men we kill.*'"

"I remember," responded Salvatore, and he hung up.

Frank headed for the van. He needed to do some reconnaissance at the U.S. Federal District Court. He always felt more secure when he could look at the battlefield before the battle.

1978, NEW YORK CITY, U.S. FEDERAL DISTRICT COURT

Reporters and curious New Yorkers gathered very early in front of the U.S. Federal District Court. It wasn't every day they could see a top mafia man testify against his own family.

The large marble staircase had been outfitted with two corridors of metal rails, and a heavy police presence prevented the unauthorized from entering. Both sides of the rails were slowly filling with people waiting to see the key witness and prosecution team pass. It was the first day of the trial, and judge and jury were present for opening deliberations. Also, the court would describe to the jury the federal rules of criminal procedure that would govern the upcoming proceedings.

The N.Y.P.D. and FBI were out in force, officers and agents with machine guns patrolling all sides of the court building. A barracks-like structure had been set up on the corner of the large federal building as an operational headquarters. They were not taking chances in protecting their witness.

Frank blended into the crowd, scanning faces and the positions of every cop in the vicinity. He sensed Daballia's men were already in the area, and scoured the peripheral rooftops and apartment windows for telltale signs, but could only identify a couple of police snipers.

Five black, similar-model Buick sedans arrived. Immediately, FBI agents poured from the vehicles and surrounded the perimeter. Frank saw Scott exit the third SUV, followed by Mantia and another agent. Mantia was grinning as he looked at the flashes of the cameras and the reporters yelling questions at him. Publicity was new to him, and he liked it.

Scott and the agent held Mantia by the arms, and side-by-side began climbing the long staircase. Police held back reporters and onlookers as the group of men passed.

Frank was on high alert, knowing that if Daballia was planning something this would be the time to do it. Scott and Mantia were halfway up the stairs when a slow-moving tanker truck turned onto Tillary Street, just after the Cadman Plaza park. It was full of liquefied petroleum gas, and could not be seen from the staircase.

Frank barely heard the distant sound of the truck's brakes as it came to a stop in front of the police barricade that prevented traffic from reaching Brooklyn Bridge Boulevard, the street directly in front of the federal building.

Policemen approached the vehicle from both sides and, just as they neared the doors, an explosion and giant flame engulfed everything in the surrounding area, sending a blast wave so powerful that all the windows on both sides of the street shattered. Flames shot high in the air, immediately followed by a thick cloud of black smoke.

The explosion was far enough away not to reach the masses around the entrance, but the shock wave reached the few people that were passing the street corner and some onlookers standing on the periphery of the crowd.

The panic was instant, and everyone instinctively ducked to protect themselves. Frank saw Mantia's head turn toward the explosion and at the same time half his face exploded into pieces. The sound of the gunshot reached him a second later, and he looked frantically at the top-floor windows of the building across the street. He looked back toward Mantia and saw Scott bending over his body, trying to protect him. Frank knew that Mantia did not need protection—he was dead.

A second shot rang out and one of the FBI agents that had escorted Mantia was hit in the chest with such power he flew back, taking a guard with him to the ground.

Another bullet hit the ground, and another a running spectator. Frank realized the shooter was targeting Scott, and without a second thought, ran toward the direction of Mantia's fallen body. He pushed against panicked people running the opposite direction, knocking a couple of them to the ground.

Finally he got close and saw Scott still covering and protecting Mantia's body. He approached him from the back and started yelling toward him.

"Easten, get the fuck out of there, they are targeting you!"

His voice wasn't reaching Scott, so he got closer and continued to yell at the top of his lungs. Suddenly a bullet hit one of the photographers, who was taking what he thought would be the best picture of his career, Mantia's exploded face. But the assassin's bullet ended his career, making that picture the last one he would ever take.

Frank continued to yell and push, getting slowly closer to Scott. Suddenly he saw a pregnant woman who had fallen on the staircase and was moving toward Scott. She was in his path and only a few feet away. Frank helped her get up, and guided her away from Scott, toward the left side of the staircase. As he turned, another bullet hit a policeman kneeling right next to Scott's bending body.

He heard return fire and the sound of a breaking window from across the street, and quickly turned his gaze in time to see a man fall from the tenth floor. Mercifully, the sound of the impact was muffled by the cries of the crowd. *They got the fucker*, he thought, and turned once again toward Scott, who was now standing, looking at the fallen assassin, and then back down at Mantia's dead body.

Frank was standing right next to Scott and felt a strange sensation. He wanted to grab him like a father would a son. This was Roy's son, and he felt compelled to tell him everything: how his father had saved his life, how they had met at Alcatraz, and that he lived every day with the guilt of his father's sacrifice. Scott looked into his eyes as if he recognized him, then suddenly launched toward Frank, pushing him out of the way and yelling, "Gun, gun!"

The sound of a Colt M1911 semi-automatic pistol pierced Frank's ears as he fell backward. He landed on his back and heard the shot just before his head struck marble, bringing him close to blacking out. For a few seconds he lost his orientation, but was pulled back to reality by rapid return fire rattling the body of the assailant. The assassin was thrown backward, blood spraying from his chest in all directions.

Daballia had planted a second assassin in the crowd, he realized, and stood up to thank Scott for sparing him. Two police officers bent over a body, and Frank quickly scanned for Scott but could not locate him. One of the officers stood up, yelling for an ambulance as he ran down the stairs. As he passed Frank he revealed Scott's fallen body, blood flowing from a hole just below his Adam's apple.

Frank looked at Scott's open eyes and recognized death. His legs gave way, and he fell on his knees, staring at another fallen Easten man. All surrounding movements and sounds became a slow-motion film clip. He felt the wind created by passersby and the muffled sound of the ambulances coming and going, but could not move his own limbs. His hearing was congested, his field of vision reduced to half. He knew these symptoms would soon lead to his fainting.

A paramedic arrived and quickly tore open Scott's blood-soaked shirt. The sun's rays reflected off the shiny metal dog tags on Scott's chest, sending flashes of light into Frank's eyes. The paramedic aimed a small flashlight into Scott's eyes, but stopped after a few seconds. He turned toward one of the police officers, head shaking. It was too late.

Suddenly, Salvatore's strong arms were grabbing under Frank's arms and picking him up. He wiped blood from the back of Frank's head and turned his face toward him, looking straight into his eyes.

"You're hurt, Frank, we got to get out of here now!" Salvatore whispered in his ear, pulling toward the bottom of the staircase.

"Scott, I need to help Scott," replied Frank, turning his head back toward Scott's fallen body.

"He's gone, boss, dead. We need to leave now!" commanded Salvatore, confused with Frank's strange reaction.

Salvatore tightened his grip on Frank and crossed Tillary Street toward the Korean War Veterans Plaza. As they stepped into the plaza they passed a large granite plaque with an inscription. Frank's vision was slightly clearer and his eyes focused on the inscription as they passed.

VETERANS PLAZA
In memory of those heroes
who made the supreme sacrifice
during the Korean War
June 26, 1950 to July 27, 1953.
They will remain in our hearts and minds forever.
Korean War Veterans Chapter #171
Brooklyn, NY

"Roy, I'm so sorry," Frank's voice barely exited his throat.

Salvatore heard him and picked up their pace while making sure they were not being followed. *All these years in New York,* Frank thought, *and today was the first time he had passed this place.*

They crossed the plaza and Salvatore headed for his parked Buick, opening first the passenger door and sliding Frank inside.

"Just lie back, Frankie, I'll take care of you," he said comfortingly. "Close your eyes and I'll take us home."

Frank did as he was told, and rested his head against the window, eyes closed. Scott's empty eyes looked back at him and slowly the vibration and soft rocking of the car let the sleep embrace him.

They arrived at the cabin a little after midnight and Salvatore helped Frank out of the car, taking him directly to the small visitor's bedroom next to the kitchen. Frank knew that his pounding head and blurred vision indicated a slight concussion from his fall.

Frank sat on the side of the bed and whispered to Salvatore, "I want you to reach Daballia. Tell him that I want to meet tomorrow night at his compound. Assure him that there will be no reprisals. Tell him I want to give him what he wants. Don't answer any questions, just repeat my message." Frank groaned with pain, waiting for a response.

"OK, Frank, but don't you think tomorrow is too early. I mean, you're a mess," Salvatore said.

Frank raised his hand, telling him to stop.

"It has to be tomorrow, we have no choice," Frank responded. "Daballia knows that we have had no time to regroup and will believe that we want to negotiate rather than fight. The minute they let us in the compound we come out fighting."

CHAPTER 29

1978, NEW JERSEY, NORTH JERSEY

Frank stopped at the imposing steel gates of Daballia's estate.

Daballia always aspired to be the most notorious mobster of the United States—hell, even the world. His obsession led him to purchase the North Jersey estate of the infamous Albert Anastasia, who was the head of Murder Incorporated.

In the 1930s and '40s, Murder, Inc. were organized crime groups that acted as the enforcement arm of the Italian-American Mafia, Jewish mob, and connected organized crime groups in New York and elsewhere.

He was willing to live with a few ghosts and bought the old Anastasia estate in an auction for the price of $5.5 million. The seven-bedroom, 13,500-square-foot home was "just a little bigger than my first apartment in Little Italy," he would yell to his visitors while welcoming them to one of his extravagant parties.

Frank looked at the group of bodyguards with machine guns that surrounded the van, inspecting under the vehicle with mirrors. They opened the doors and looked carefully inside, guns pointing at Frank's face.

"Get out," ordered one of the guards gruffly. "We will park the van and take you up to the villa."

Frank did not respond but followed the instruction without hesitation.

Outside the van another guard searched him with rough swipes of his hands, up and down his body, legs, crotch, and waist.

They pushed him toward the mansion, four of them flanking, their guns pointed and their distance safe. Frank looked around and saw a couple more men hastily leaving from a small lodge house. Frank estimated about twelve men outside the mansion. It appeared Salvatore had anticipated correctly that Daballia would have about twenty men inside and around the compound.

The previous week's heavy snow had broken many branches of the trees on the sides and front of the mansion. The gardener had gathered them in a large pile that would make for a great bonfire. The rest of the estate had many private roads that had been plowed clean.

The mansion was large and intimidating. The façade was covered with natural gray stone, and there were two long, slim, rectangular windows on each side of the door. The front staircase reached a large balcony patio that lined the front of the estate. They climbed the staircase to a large and heavy oak double front door, and one of the escorts nodded to an armed guard stationed right outside, who opened it.

They entered a large circular hall, its height reaching the mansion's roof. The floor was covered with mirror-like polished Italian marble. Exactly opposite the main door a large marble spiral staircase led to the private rooms on the second floor.

The hall served as the main avenue of traffic to all adjacent first-floor rooms. Frank counted four side room doors on the periphery of the hall.

One of the guards grabbed Frank by the arm and pulled him toward the first set of double doors to his left. They entered, and there was Daballia, sitting rigidly on the sofa, smoking a cigar and watching its rising thick, white smoke. On the coffee table in front of Daballia was a glass of whiskey, and on the other side of the sofa stood Lemensa, his face expressionless. He was perspiring and the cigar in his hand was wet with his saliva. There was no one else in the room and the two guards who had entered with Frank stood a few feet behind him.

Daballia looked at Frank, furrowing his eyebrows, and began speaking in Sicilian.

"*I don't know who you are, but I can tell you that you got big balls,*" Daballia said, smiling, while moving his cigar potently toward Frank. He brought it to his lips and inhaled noisily.

"Before we begin I need to know who the fuck you are," he said in English, his tone faintly agitated.

Frank smiled, and nodding back, explained, "I am Frank Morris, the man that Don Cabineri raised from the dead. Do you remember me, Don Daballia?"

Frank's controlled tone and revelation caught Daballia and Lemensa by surprise. They quickly looked at each other and then both turned back to Frank.

"Frank Morris died a long time ago at Alcatraz, so what black lies are these?" Daballia replied, this time his anger in clear display.

"Don Daballia, with all respect, how could I come before you with this lie if I did not have evidence to prove who I am?" Frank responded, giving Daballia another surprise he did not expect. Daballia pushed back on the sofa and waved a hand toward himself, indicating silently for Frank to continue.

"I will tell you something that only Frank Morris and you could know."

He waited, letting time and silence become his allies. He checked the clock on the wall right behind Daballia and saw he had a couple of minutes before Salvatore would launch his attack.

"Before I continue, is it possible to sit down? I got a concussion at the court building and I get dizzy spells."

Daballia pointed to one of the dining room chairs and looked at one of the guards behind Frank, who brought the chair to Frank. Frank sat and nodded to the guard. He unbuttoned his jacket and leaned toward Daballia.

"Don Daballia, what I am about to tell you is a secret between yourself, Don Cabineri, and Frank Morris. It transpired in the Don's old Bronx office." Frank spoke slowly and focused on Daballia's eyes for any movement that would betray his emotions.

Frank then told of an event that had taken place before Alcatraz, when Daballia was rising in the hierarchy of the Cabineri family.

Frank and Don Cabineri had returned to the Bronx office late one night and walked in on Daballia and Lukanalie's wife. Lukanalie was a captain in the Cabineri family. The Don was fuming at Daballia, as he had broken one of the family commandments, "*Never look at the wives of friends.*" Friends, of course, meant a man who had taken the oath of silence, a "*made man*" with the family.

Daballia knew this could ruin him if made public; he swore and pleaded to the Don that it was a moment of weakness and that it would never happen again. If it was anyone else, the Don would have taken the necessary actions, but he conceded to Daballia's pleading because of the more urgent family issues at that time. The Don had made Frank swear in front of Daballia that he would never say anything to anyone.

"Should I continue?" Frank asked at this point, and waited.

Daballia's eyes opened just enough to betray his recollection of the secret event. Daballia swallowed his remaining whiskey and, pushing his chest out, replied in a soft tone, "You don't need to continue, Frank. It is amazing that it is you; your new face is perfectly natural. The Don must have paid a lot of money for a job like that."

Daballia's inference was intentional, emphasizing that Frank, without the Don, was nothing. Frank nodded in agreement, side-stepping the insult.

"I had a great respect for Don Cabineri and would do anything to change what has happened. But you, Frank, must understand that it was strictly a business matter," Daballia continued.

Frank knew that the time for his command was approaching, and his head filled with the pressure of pounding blood. He took a deep breath and smiled at Daballia, feeling his hands perspire. He prepared his body for action and, looking into Daballia's eyes, said coolly, "Death smiles at us all, but all a man can do is smile back."

With both his hands underneath the coffee table in front of Daballia, he overturned it violently, taking his host completely by surprise. The guard standing on his right side pointed his weapon and fired, hitting the other guard squarely above his right eye, the bullet exiting the man's skull followed by blood and bone fragments. Frank was on his knees, both hands reaching for the gun that the guard had dropped when he got hit. The other guard received two bullets from Lemensa in the chest before he could shoot back.

Frank finally grabbed the fallen gun and rolled, shooting Lemensa twice, in the neck and chest, knocking him off his feet. He fired two more rounds in the direction of Daballia's fleeing form, the bullets hitting the floor and walls, rebounding across the room.

From the corner of his eye, he saw another of Daballia's men coming through the door in his direction. This time he took aim, and the bullet hit the man right between the eyes, bashing him backward and through the door.

Frank swung his body in the direction Daballia had taken, down a long corridor leading to the kitchen. Frank put his back to the wall and moved sideways toward the opening of the door, looking through the crack for any movement.

He kicked the door open, his body turned sideways, making it a smaller target. Frank fired at the interior steadily from left to right. He stopped midway into the large kitchen, facing the left corner of the room. Next to a large, double-door refrigerator stood Daballia, holding a young woman in front of him, hand tightly around her waist. His other hand was aiming a gun directly at her temple, almost touching it.

She was frozen with fright, large black-olive eyes wide open and unblinking.

"Don't come any closer, Frank," Daballia said coldly, clenching his teeth with pain. Frank saw drops of blood falling to the white tile floor. *He must have hit him,* he thought.

He pointed his gun directly into Daballia's face, which was half-hidden behind the girl's head.

"Take it easy, Paolo, no need for anyone else to get hurt," Frank whispered, letting the silence of the room carry his voice.

"I said, don't come any closer," Daballia replied, pushing the muzzle of his gun into the temple of the girl. She cried out in pain and Daballia tightened his grip around her waist, pulling her closer to his body.

"Get the fuck back or I'll shoot her!" Daballia shouted, his voice bouncing off the walls.

Daballia tightened his grip around the girl's waist, making her face squint with pain. "Look at her face, Frank, you don't recognize her, do you?" asked Daballia.

"This is your niece, Julianna, Serafina's daughter." Daballia smiled, evil painted on his face.

"Lemensa picked her up yesterday; he missed your sister but don't worry, we will clean up the rest of the Cabineri family right after I finish with you," Daballia continued calmly, hoping his words would deteriorate Frank's reflexes.

"I always have a hidden ace, Frank, don't you know that? That's why your fucking Don is dead, and you will soon join him," continued Daballia.

Frank looked at the girl and recognized the likeness with his sister's uniquely shaped black-olive eyes, nose, and lips. He tightened his grip and he sensed more adrenaline flowing through his body. He inhaled deeply through his nose and responded with a commanding tone of voice. "OK, Paolo, so what do we do now? You know that this must end, and it will end here and now. *Questo deve finire,* Paolo—This must end, Paolo; *il tuo destino finisce ora,* your destiny ends now," Frank continued in Italian.

This was a message. The Sicilian communication codes, whether written, unwritten, spoken, or unspoken, had a significance that dominated and overpowered everyone that had sworn the oath of silence.

Daballia understood that Frank was giving him his last rights. His eyes slightly opened and then blinked rapidly.

Frank breathed out silently, waiting for Daballia's next blink, and fired his gun at the left eye peering from behind the girl's ear. The bullet grazed Julianna's ear, shattering Daballia's eye and entering his brain. His body shot backward, still holding the girl. He was dead before he hit the ground.

Julianna pushed open Daballia's frozen grip and rolled up next to his fallen body, crying in shock. Frank moved closer with his arm still stretched and gun pointing at his target.

He heard panting and running, and the voice of Salvatore coming from down the hall.

"Frank, Frank!" Salvatore flew into the room with searching eyes, checking to be sure his friend was OK. Then he saw Daballia's body.

"Shitting fucking cocksucker! *Figlio di puttana*—son of a whore!" He directed his words toward Daballia as if he was able to hear him, then he spat into his bloodied face.

Frank's face was cold and without expression.

He turned to his niece and gently turned her head, attentively looking at her wounded ear and said, "Everything is OK, Julianna, it's just a small graze; it's all over, sweetie. One of my men will take you home now, and please don't say anything to your mother and father." His fatherly tone and expression reminded her of her grandfather and she knew that this stranger was by some means part of her family. She stood up and Salvatore helped her toward the two men who had just entered the kitchen, guns drawn, waiting for instructions. Salvatore cocked his head upward, silently asking if everything was all right.

They nodded and one of them said, "The place is clear, Sonny Bats is dead, and we found two more of these fucks down in the basement. The bastards were hiding, fucking cowards!"

Salvatore raised a hand for him to stop talking and handed him the girl.

"Take her straight to the Don's house, and her grandmother will take care of her," Salvatore said and turned to Frank. Frank only heard that Sonny was dead. Salvatore had managed to plant him as one of Daballia's guards. *If it wasn't for Sonny, the battle with Daballia would have been lost,* he thought but said nothing.

"The house is clean, Frank; what do you want to do with the bodies?" Salvatore asked.

"Burn everything," said Frank. "I don't want these scums to have a burial, I want everything to turn into ash. They have lost the right to rot in the ground."

Salvatore heard Frank's tone and knew he was hearing the new Don Cabineri.

"*Lu Signiuruzzu li cosi li fici dritti, vinni lu diavulu e li sturcìu.* God made things straight, the devil came and twisted them."

His mother's words came to him and he remembered what was, and what is no more.

Frank looked at Daballia one last time, then he turned to Salvatore and gave his order.

"Do it!"

Frank walked out of the house and drove away from the city that was his home. He knew he would never return, and that from that day he would never kill again. His debt to the family had been paid, his oath consumed by the fire that would incinerate Daballia's body.

He headed north for I-87 with images of Roy and Scott Easten flashing before his eyes. He tightened his grip on the wheel, tears rolling down his face, tears of pain and guilt. They sacrificed their life for his, but why? Now he knew that he would never get the answer in this life, but maybe in the next. He suddenly remembered words long ago read, and up until now forgotten.

"Whatever happens to you was predisposed for you since the time of times, and an impenetrable intertwinement of causes, starting from then, has bound your life to that particular event."

"Predisposed for you since the time of times, *for you since the time of times*," he repeated in a whisper, tightening even more his fingers around the cold steering wheel.

The van headed north, the sun bowed to the oncoming darkness of the night, Frank Morris followed the cries of his unyielding destiny.

NEW YORK TIMES, DECEMBER 9, 2008

"Heroes still exist: New York City man saved by Good Samaritan after falling onto tracks. When a man tumbled onto the tracks at a downtown New York subway station, one passenger leaped into action. Surveillance video shows Doctor Jonathan Calson walking close to the edge of the platform Wednesday and falling to the tracks. Alejandro Derabosa jumps down to Calson, helping him up.

Doctor Calson is a resident at Bellevue Hospital and had just come off his shift at the emergency ward after two days assisting with the flu epidemic plaguing the city. The *Times* reports that the thirty-year-old Derabosa is recovering from a minor leg injury. Calson's injuries are more serious. He suffered a shattered knee, broken ribs, and a spleen injury that could require surgery. Transit officials laud Derabosa's actions as courageous but warn against jumping on the tracks. They say witnesses should alert a cashier or police officer.

Derabosa says he's no hero and just let instincts kick in. "I just saw him down and jumped . . . just instincts," he told the *Times*. "I'm not a hero. I mean, I was at the right place at the right time," he said.

This reporter feels obligated to report that medical interns and residents commonly work eighty to a hundred hours a week, with residents occasionally logging 136 (out of 168) hours in a week."

Maria Derabosa lowered the newspaper, tears filling her eyes. Reading her son's name and heroic act filled her with overwhelming joy and pride. The phone had been ringing continuously all morning with relatives and friends calling her with congratulatory and joyful messages.

She looked at the graduation picture of her son, among numerous other family pictures lining the top of the large mahogany living room buffet. Her emotions once again giving way to tears, she looked at the next picture of her late husband and a bittersweet sensation brought back happy family memories. She missed him more than anything in this world and knew that he would be a very proud father on this day. The tears continued, and she wiped them, looking at her daughter who was watching her all this time with a smiling face. "Mama, what am I going to do with you? You've been crying nonstop since this morning," her daughter said with a sweet tone.

"It's OK, *mi amor,* they are tears of joy," returned Maria, and she received a loving kiss from her daughter.

"*Eres tan dulce mamá, te amo*—You are so sweet, Mama, I love you," she said.

"Isabella, can you please bring me a glass of water, *mi amor*?" Maria asked her, and she quickly rushed to the kitchen.

Maria looked again at the pictures, and her gaze fell on her husband and herself on the Coney Island boardwalk when she was pregnant with Alejandro. They were both luminous with happiness and love, their first baby on the way and their whole life in front of them.

Her eyes closed, and her memory transported her back to that terrible day at the marble steps of the district court. The screams, the panic, and a strange man's powerful hands changing her path, saving her life. She could still hear the bullets and see that young man falling dead. She remembered reading the next day about that young man, Scott Easten, the new assistant district attorney, his life ending and her life continuing.

She had not seen her savior's face and never had a chance to thank him, but every night she prayed for him to be well no matter where he was.

"*El destino no puede ser cambiado*—Destiny cannot be changed," she whispered, opening her eyes and looking at her beautiful daughter coming toward her, holding a glass of water.

"Carve as we will the mysterious block of which

our life is made, the black vein of destiny

constantly reappears in it."

– *Les Miserables,* Victor Hugo

ABOUT THE AUTHOR

SPIROS GRATSIAS was born and raised in Montreal, Canada. Spiros is an engineer, designer, artist, illustrator, screen and fiction writer. He was the screenwriter of the award-winning short film animation "Inverse" based on a story from his book *Rootless Roots*.

In his other life, he is a Research and Development executive with over forty years' experience in the aerospace and consumer goods industry. Spiros lives in Athens, Greece and devotes much of his time to painting, illustrating and writing.

CPSIA information can be obtained
at www.ICGtesting.com
Printed in the USA
BVHW082114060322
630778BV00002B/99